G000093284

ABANDONED HEARTS

Lisa Stanbridge

www.BOROUGHSPUBLISHINGGROUP.com

PUBLISHER'S NOTE: This is a work of fiction. Names, characters, places and incidents either are the product of the author's imagination or are used fictitiously. Any resemblance to actual events, locales, business establishments or persons, living or dead, is coincidental. Boroughs Publishing Group does not have any control over and does not assume responsibility for author or third-party websites, blogs or critiques or their content.

ABANDONED HEARTS
Copyright © 2020 Lisa Stanbridge

All rights reserved. Unless specifically noted, no part of this publication may be reproduced, scanned, stored in a retrieval system or transmitted in any form or by any means, electronic, mechanical, photocopying, recording, or otherwise, known or hereinafter invented, without the express written permission of Boroughs Publishing Group. The scanning, uploading and distribution of this book via the Internet or by any other means without the permission of Boroughs Publishing Group is illegal and punishable by law. Participation in the piracy of copyrighted materials violates the author's rights.

ISBN 978-1-951055-73-8

To Pete for being the most amazing and supportive husband.
And to Frances – not just a critique partner, but my friend.
I wouldn't be the writer I am today without her.

ACKNOWLEDGMENTS

First and foremost, special thanks goes to my husband, Pete. The one person who's had total faith in me, and my writing abilities, when I often felt unworthy. Even though he's not a romance reader, he still took the time to read my novel and provide unbiased feedback.

A massive thank you also goes to Frances, my critique partner and friend. We met as strangers through Romance Writers of Australia's critique program. We bared our writer's souls and swapped stories, offering honest, and sometimes harsh, feedback. Now, seven years later, we're still working together! This story wouldn't be what it is today without her.

To so many people from Romance Writers of Australia who have helped me along the way, offering me advice and encouragement. The contests and those who judged them, the feedback was always so beneficial. This story entered many of those contests, sometimes getting embarrassingly low scores. But I persevered, took on the feedback, and now, here it is for the world to read!

The conferences were a huge help. At the 2019 Romance Writers of Australia conference, I pitched to Michelle Klayman. I'll never forget her taking away my pitch notes. I'd spent so long perfecting them, but she took control of the conversation, asked questions, and encouraged me to see that I didn't need my notes because I knew my story. She requested my full manuscript and the rest is history. Now, here it is. So, to Michelle, my editor Sue, and everyone else at Boroughs Publishing Group who've worked behind the scenes...THANK YOU! We authors dream of being published and you've helped mine come true.

And last but not least, to all my friends, family, and colleagues who have been on this journey with me and encouraged me to keep going. Thank you.

ABANDONED HEARTS

Chapter 1

Claire Stone opened the back door of the car and stepped out on to the cracked cement driveway. A soft, cool breeze rustled through trees lining the road. Birds chirped, and waves crashed against the shoreline. There were no cars. No horns. No constant noise.

Such a far cry from the city, but I think I'll like it here.

Turning, she faced the back of a two-storey beach house. Compared to the neighbouring properties, which were solidly built and semi-modern with meticulous gardens, this was an eyesore. It stood firmly on stilts, the white paint on the wooden slats peeling, in desperate need of a recoat. The yard was covered in dirt and sand, not a single shrub or flower in sight.

"First time in Busselton?"

Startled, she whipped her head around to where the driver stood, holding Claire's brown case.

"Yes." She ran her hands along the denim of her jeans. "It seems…small."

He chuckled and handed her the case. "City girl, I presume?"

She took it from him. "You could say that. I think this place is what I need."

"Well"—he stepped back—"good luck then. Make sure you check out the jetty. It's the longest in the southern hemisphere."

She smiled and tucked loose strands of hair behind her ear. "I'll keep that in mind. Thanks." She turned back to the house and took a few tentative steps forward. Stopping at the base of six rickety stairs leading to the door, she stared up. The screen door hung off its hinges and spiders had created webs in the corners. The large window on the right, providing a view into the kitchen, was in desperate need of a clean.

The car sped off, the smell of petrol lingering in the air. Claire placed one foot on the bottom step and grabbed hold of the splintered handrail, spiky bits of wood pricking her hand. She navigated the steps with caution, each one creaking from the combined weight of a human and a thirty-kilo suitcase. When she reached the top, she knocked gently on the door and called out, "Hello?"

When no one answered, she grabbed the rusted handle and pulled the screen door open. As she stepped inside, it closed behind her, but the dodgy hinges stopped it from shutting completely. She took in her surrounds. The laundry was surprisingly modern with built-in cupboards on one wall, and a washing machine, dryer and trough lining the other.

Claire took a step towards the open door in front of her, her sneakers squeaking on the white tiles. Seconds later, an older woman walked through, dressed in a blue and white calf-length dress covered with a frilly apron. Startled, Claire shrieked and stumbled back.

The woman stared at her in fright, a chubby hand flying up to her heart. "Good lord, you scared the bejeezus out of me." She panted slightly and pushed stray wisps of salt and pepper hair away from her rosy face, tucking them back into her bun. "You must be the new nurse. Claire, right?"

"Yes." Claire held out her hand. "It's nice to meet you. I'm sorry to have barged in. I knocked, but no one heard me."

The woman smiled warmly but ignored her hand and embraced her instead. "I'm Von." She stepped back. "I'm the housekeeper. Michael said you'd be here about now."

She froze. "Michael?"

"Daphne's son."

Claire swallowed hard and nodded. Of course. The agency had told her the patient lived with her son, but it'd been such a whirlwind to get here, she hadn't let herself think about it. She silently willed the butterflies in her stomach to stop fluttering. *Relax.*

"Now, follow me," Von said. "I'll show you to your room."

The butterflies stopped, and Claire breathed a little easier as they entered a small hallway. In front of them was another room, the door closed.

"This is Daphne's room," Von said in a low voice. "She's sleeping. I don't expect she'll wake for another hour or two."

Leaving the hallway, they entered a large open-plan lounge, dining and kitchen area. A set of French doors on the far wall led outside to the front of the house. Another set of six stairs, looking in better condition, led directly onto the sand. A few metres beyond was the ocean. The sun began its descent towards the horizon, dusk not far away. Small waves crashed against the shore.

"What a beautiful view," Claire murmured.

Von stopped and stared out the doors. "It certainly is. We're on the outskirts of town, and the neighbours keep to themselves, so we're in a tranquil area." She walked over to the door and slid it open, the sound of waves filling the quiet house.

Turning back to Claire, Von said, "Everything you need should be down here. This is your home now, so help yourself to anything. Whatever you need to tend to Daphne, such as medical supplies, can be found in the cupboard over there." She pointed to a large cupboard against the wall of the laundry. "The doctor calls around twice a week, but he's on call any time if you need him."

Claire nodded. The agency had already given her the doctor's details. She glanced around, her brow furrowing in confusion. "How do we get up to the second level?" She couldn't see any stairs inside.

Von grinned, her round, plump face lighting up. Chuckling, she gestured for Claire to follow. They exited through the French doors, down the stairs, then around to the right side of the house, where a flight of stairs led up to the second floor. They stopped at the base.

Von turned to her. "Michael and I joke that the builder must've been drunk when he built this place. It's not the most efficient design, especially in bad weather."

Von began climbing the stairs, and Claire followed.

"It's a charming house." Claire ran her hand along the bare wooden slats, the paint eroded long ago from the salt off the ocean.

"You don't have to be polite, dear," Von said with a chuckle. "It's certainly an eyesore."

"Well," Claire laughed softly, "I can't deny it could do with some TLC."

Von stopped on the landing in front of the screen door and turned to face Claire. "Michael's been talking about renovating it for years, and adding a decent garden, but he's too busy." She turned to the door and opened it. "Your room's through here."

Von stepped inside, and Claire followed, the door clicking shut after her. She stared down a long hallway. The floorboards were varnished and at the far end was a large floor-to- ceiling linen cupboard. Directly on her left was a bathroom.

"This is your room." Von opened the door to the room on the right and stepped inside.

Claire entered and put her case down. A light brown four-poster, king-size bed with a pink and white floral duvet was tucked in a corner. A matching pine dresser and wardrobe filled the rest of the room. Another door led into what looked like an en-suite. The ocean beckoned to Claire through a set of French doors leading out to a balcony.

"Wow. What an amazing room."

Von chuckled. "Yes, it is. Daphne inherited this house many years ago from her mother. It was quite a shambles inside and out, but over time she and Michael fixed up the inside. The outside needs a lot of work, but it's turned into quite a sought-after home. Prime location and all that. They have salespeople offering to buy all the time."

"I can imagine."

"Michael will inherit it once his mother passes. I know he's attached to it, so I don't expect he'd ever sell." Von cleared her throat and looked away.

A gloomy silence fell over them. Claire knew this was only a short-term job to care for the patient in her final days. Now that she was here, reality hit Claire square in the chest. She'd only ever worked in hospitals before now. A live-in position would be trying, physically *and* emotionally.

"Oh, look at the time," Von broke the silence, "it's nearly six, and I haven't started dinner yet."

Claire turned to her. "You cook too?"

"It's not my job, but I like to help out."

"Can I do anything to help?"

"You're a dear, thank you, but I'll be fine. Daphne usually needs help eating so I'll let you know when dinner's ready. In the meantime, get yourself settled and relax for a while."

With a smile, Von walked out. Claire shut the door, left her case on the floor, and flopped on the bed. It was soft, like lying on a cloud. Her eyelids drooped, the exhaustion from travelling hours from Adelaide to Perth, followed by a bus journey to Busselton settling in. When they began to close of their own accord, she forced herself into a sitting position. Now wasn't the time to fall asleep. She had duties to attend to soon. She could sleep later.

Standing, she strode across the room and opened her door. After checking the hallway was clear, she stepped out to investigate the remaining rooms on the floor. Opening the last door on the left, she peered into a study. Bookcases jam-packed with books lined the entire right wall from floor to ceiling. A computer desk equipped with a desktop computer, phone and printer sat under the window opposite her. She inhaled deeply, the intoxicating smell of books willing her to pick one up and read it. It'd been too long since she'd enjoyed such simple pleasures. *If I get some spare time, at least I know where to find one.*

After leaving the room, she opened another door in the hallway and peeked in. It was another bedroom, almost identical to hers. It only took her a few seconds to realise she must be looking into Michael's room.

It was neat and masculine, the walls painted crème and brown, like hers, but the queen-size bed and matching furniture were a rich mahogany. Being in his personal space made her uncomfortable, so she stepped back. She spotted a photo of a little boy in a school uniform, no more than five years of age, on his bedside cupboard.

I shouldn't be in here. Claire took another step back.

"Who are you, and what are you doing in my room?"

Heart leaping into her throat, Claire gasped and spun around, the door closing with a loud slam. A broad male figure stood at the end of the hallway, in front of the screen door. He was tall, muscular, and carried an air of authority. His ebony hair was messy, his skin and clothes streaked with oil. His gaze bore into her as her pounding heart vibrated through her body. He had to be Michael.

In the days leading up to her move, she'd conjured up image after image in her mind of what she thought Michael looked like. Old and balding was her expectation. He *definitely* wasn't that. He was younger, for one, and much more handsome.

Being so close to him sent warning bells ringing in her ears. The prickling sensation at the back of her skull was the first warning of the impending panic attack. "Uh..." She clasped her clammy and trembling hands in front of her. "I'm the new nurse, Claire Stone." Now would be the time to extend her hand in greeting but she didn't want him seeing the impact he had on her.

When Michael stepped closer, she instinctively took a couple of steps back. He was at least six foot two, and if they were any closer, she thought, the top of her head would only reach to his shoulders.

Their gazes met, and she shivered. His hazel eyes, flecked with gold, shone with interest for a moment, and he held her gaze a few seconds longer than necessary. Fear skirted along her skin, making the warning bells sound louder. A level of mutual curiosity silenced them for a nanosecond. There was no missing the chemistry in her veins trying to break free.

The moment passed, and Michael blinked, a frown tugging on his lips. His eyes turned cold and emotionless.

She could feel the warmth radiating off him and fear bubbled forth, his closeness becoming too much. She turned cold and swallowed hard, focusing on the breathing techniques her therapist, Laura, had taught her.

"I'm Michael Karalis," he said evenly. "I'd appreciate it if you wouldn't poke around in my personal space."

Claire managed a weak nod as her chest tightened. "I'm sorry." She cleared her throat. "I was only looking around. I didn't realise it was your room. I left as soon as I did."

His stare was cold. Hard. He said nothing else, strode past her, and proceeded to his bedroom. She jumped when his door slammed shut, rattling the walls.

Claire drew in a sharp breath and rushed into her bedroom. She shut the door and leaned against it, gasping for air as panic overwhelmed her. Sliding down the door, tears free-falling down her cheeks, fear crippled her. *This isn't supposed to happen. I've spent eighteen months in recovery. I'm supposed to be ready for this.*

Needing fresh air, she pushed herself to her feet and rushed across the room, opening the French doors. She stepped out on to the balcony, the cool spring breeze whipping across her face and through her hair. The slow draw of calming breaths helped ease the panic.

Spotting a glass table with two wicker chairs to her left, Claire sat and stretched her legs out. For a long while, she stared out over the ocean as the sun lowered, dusk setting in. The sound of waves crashing on the shore soothed her like a balm, washing away the panic.

The sun dipped beneath the horizon, casting an orange hue over everything. Glancing at her watch, she noted it was six-thirty. The early springtime sunsets in Western Australia were going to take a lot of getting used to.

When the mouth-watering smells of cooking food wafted up from below, she stood and went back into her room to shower and change. Dinner probably wasn't far away.

Placing her case on the bed, she opened it and picked out a fresh set of clothes. Now relaxed, proud of herself for the quick recovery, she was ready to face her new job head-on. If she wanted to remain professional and keep emotions out of her work, she needed all her wits about her.

Chapter 2

Michael slammed the bedroom door shut the same moment his phone pinged from his jeans pocket. Muttering under his breath, he pulled it out. One glance at the screen and he cursed when he saw Addison's name. His ex-wife. This was her fifth message in the last half hour. She'd never been a patient person. Well, tonight she could wait. He had plans, so he'd reply when *he* was ready.

He threw his phone on the bed then kicked off his work boots and walked to his ensuite. He set the taps of the shower to the highest heat, then peeled his oil-covered clothes off and threw them into the wicker basket. After he'd shaved, Michael stepped into the shower and scrubbed away the grime of the day. It was one of those days where every car had a damned oil leak.

Twenty minutes later, he was clean and dressed in a cocktail suit, ready for the evening's gala. He glanced one last time at his reflection in the mirror, smoothing back his hair. After adjusting his tie, he pocketed his wallet, keys and phone then turned to leave. As he did so, his gaze landed on the framed photo on his bedside cupboard of his five-year-old son, Oscar.

Eyes misting over, Michael placed a kiss on his thumb and pressed it against the glass over Oscar's face. "See you in a couple of weeks, buddy."

Michael's heart constricted painfully when he left his bedroom. Seeing his son four times a year wasn't enough.

Dashing down the hallway, he descended the stairs then took a sharp left and entered the main house. Mum's lifetime friend and housekeeper, Von, was busy making dinner. She looked over at him when he came in and smiled broadly, giving him a brief once over.

"Why, look at you. Don't you look dapper?"

Michael stood tall and grinned. "Thanks. Is Mum awake?"

Von looked toward Mum's bedroom. "I'm not sure. Claire's checking on her now."

As if on cue, Mum's bedroom door opened, and Claire slipped out. Michael bristled and pulled his shoulders back. Their earlier encounter hadn't gone well. He should've been politer, but the surprise of seeing a strange woman in his bedroom had sent his emotions skyrocketing, blurring all common sense.

"She's still sleeping," Claire announced. She stopped short when her gaze landed on him, eyes widening.

He shuffled on the spot and looked at his feet. Then again, she didn't seem to be entirely comfortable in his company either.

"Why don't you have some dinner first?" Von said. "She might be awake by the time you're done. You must be starving after all that travelling."

"I am and thank you. That sounds great."

"Have you met Michael yet, Claire?"

Michael looked up at Claire who'd sat at the table. She looked across at him, her cheeks tinging pink, and nodded. "Yes, we've met." Their gazes met briefly before she looked away.

He winced and cleared his throat. "Well, I'll leave you two to have dinner. I want to see Mum quickly before the limo arrives."

He strode over to kiss Von's cheek then made his way to Mum's room. It was in semi-darkness when he entered, the curtains still drawn. She laid in bed on her back, the light sound of snoring filling the room. A bandana wrapped around her head above sunken eyes told the tragic story. Seeing her in such a state, reality crashed down around him like a roaring waterfall.

I won't have a mother for much longer.

A sharp pain pierced his chest. The last two weeks had been hell. How did anyone prepare when they find out their mother had terminal cancer?

His throat threatened to close, emotion overwhelming him.

I'm not ready to lose her.

The faint sound of a car horn jerked him out of his emotional trance, and he blinked a couple of times. For now, she *was* here, and he'd savour every moment.

Leaning down, he kissed her forehead gently. "I love you, Mum," he whispered, then turned and left.

***

A cool breeze rushed inside when the limousine door opened, and Michael's friends and their partners clambered into the vehicle. He slipped his phone inside his jacket pocket and greeted everyone as they found their seats. Loud greetings were exchanged, laughter bellowed, and Michael could finally relax. It was nice to have a break from his turmoils for a while.

"Hey, Micky," his best mate, Norman, greeted, slapping him on the back. "How ya doin', man? I haven't seen you since this arvo."

"Can't complain." Michael looked Norman up and down and burst into laughter. "You look like a penguin in that suit."

Norman ran a hand over his smooth head. He was only thirty-two, the same age as Michael, but he'd started losing his hair early and had shaved it ever since. Add to it a short and pudgy stature, and suits didn't work for him. Jeans and t-shirts were more his style.

Mates since school, they'd even worked at the same fire department in Bunbury for years. Michael loved firefighting, but he gave it up when Oscar was born, not wanting to put his life on the line when he had a young son. So, with a mechanics trade under his belt, he started up a business in Busselton. Norman joined him six months later after his wife gave birth to their daughter, Juanita. Neither of them looked back.

Norman raised his eyebrows as he gave Michael a once-over. "And you look like a stuck-up arsehole."

Feigning hurt, Michael held a hand over his heart. "That's below the belt, mate. I thought I scrubbed up pretty nice."

"Don't listen to him, Mick," said Joanna, Norman's wife, as she sat next to her husband. "You look lovely."

Michael was a little envious of Norman and Joanna's relationship. They were connected in a way most couples could only dream of. Joanna was the type of woman he trusted—open, honest and respectful. She'd never do wrong by anyone.

Michael smirked and jokingly stuck up his nose while he adjusted his tie.

"See?" Norman punched Michael's arm. "Stuck up."

They shared a laugh and Michael accepted a glass of champagne handed to him as the driver commenced a short coastal drive.

After a few minutes of small talk, Norman affectionately asked, "How's the old lady doing?"

"So-so." Michael sighed. "She has good days and bad days. The new live-in nurse arrived today."

Norman nodded. "That's good. Is the nurse a local girl?"

"No, she's from South Australia. Adelaide, actually."

Norman raised an inquisitive eyebrow. "Adelaide? And she moved all the way here?"

Michael shrugged and took a sip of his champagne. "I'm not complaining. I'm relieved Mum can be comfortable now."

"What's the nurse like?"

"She seems nice enough, I suppose. I only met her briefly when I got home."

"C'mon, man, surely you talked to her?"

"Not really, no."

Norman chuckled. "You're such a rude bastard sometimes."

"She's a woman, what do you expect?"

Bugger. The words spewed out before he could stop them, and Michael cringed. Addison's earlier messages were still playing on his mind and the bitterness he'd felt then had followed him. He hadn't read them yet, but he could only imagine what she wanted. Perhaps he should've made time to reply, but it was too late now.

The limousine fell silent, and Michael could feel the eyes of every woman there boring holes through him.

"Hey," Joanna spoke up, "I heard that."

Michael's cheeks heated and he smiled sheepishly. "No offence, Jo." He lifted his glass to the other women. "Or to any of you."

The other women didn't seem too offended and resumed chatting to one another. Joanna was the only one who kept her questioning eyes fixed on him. When she caught him looking, she grinned and shook her head good-naturedly.

She was a stunning woman—her dark brown hair was cut into a short bob, and her large brown eyes held a constant sparkle. To the outside world, she and Norman were an odd-looking pair, but knowing them so well, Michael saw how well they gelled. They were a match made in heaven.

"None taken," she said. "Although I don't understand why you dislike the female sex so much."

Michael narrowed his eyes. She *did* know, but she was trying to rile him up so that he'd confess in front of the others. He wouldn't rise to the bait.

"I don't dislike you or my mother." He thought for a moment then added, "Oh and Von of course." He downed the last of his champagne and placed his glass down.

Joanna laughed and, to his relief, dropped the topic. She turned to her neighbour and struck up a conversation. Michael and Norman returned to chatting generalities until they arrived at their destination. When the door opened, the party filed out one by one, Michael and Norman the last to exit.

Loud music reverberated from the town hall a few feet away. They stopped at the end of the line extending out the door.

"When do we see the little man again?" Norman asked, turning to him.

Michael smiled. "In a couple of weeks."

"Oh good, let's make a plan to get together when he's here. Juanita's excited to see him again."

"Sounds good."

"And the custody battle?" Norman's brow furrowed. "Any movement on that?"

Michael puffed out a breath and shook his head. "It's tough right now, mate. With Mum being sick and all. What sort of environment is it for a five-year-old? I'm sure the courts would have a field day over that."

Norman nodded. "Yes, of course, I get it." He hesitated before adding, "But, well, afterwards?"

There was a pang to Michael's heart. He hated thinking about life after Mum, but it was the sad reality. He wanted full custody of Oscar, but so did Addison. To fight and prove he was a capable father, he needed all his wits about him *and* a stable life. He had neither right now. Norman was right though. He had to have a plan for afterwards.

With a begrudging nod, he said, "Then afterwards I'm going in guns blazing."

Norman grinned and slapped him on the shoulder. "That's my man. Jo and I will be right by your side. You know that, don't you?"

Michael nodded, but before he could say any more, his mobile rang. He removed it and cursed. "I'll meet you in there."

"Addison?" Norman mouthed in sympathy.

Michael rolled his eyes and nodded. His ex's impatience had reached the next level. There was no avoiding her this time.

Chapter 3

Claire sat at the table while Von stood staring out the kitchen window. The sound of the limousine driving away drifted through the window, and Von turned back, a soft smile on her face. It was clear she cared a great deal for Michael.

Claire hadn't formed the greatest first impression of him. He came across abrasive and rude. Then again, she probably shouldn't judge someone she didn't know. If the picture in his bedroom was anything to go by, he had a history. Probably not a pretty one, either. Just because she was broken and untrusting, didn't mean she had the right to judge him based on a first impression that could be *way* off.

When Von placed two steaming plates of meat and vegetables on the table, Claire's stomach rumbled loudly. "Sorry," she said with a nervous giggle as Von sat next to her, "I'm hungrier than I realised."

Von smiled kindly and picked up her knife and fork. "No need to apologise, dear."

As they ate, apart from the clink of metal on plates, it was blissfully quiet.

Claire's mind went over everything that'd happened in the last few hours and curiosity got the better of her. "Where was Mr Karalis off to? When I met him, he was covered in oil, so seeing him so dressed up was a bit of a surprise."

Claire's heart involuntarily stuttered at the memory of walking out of Daphne's room and seeing Michael's tall, broad frame in the dining area. He'd been chatting to Von, a natural, kind smile on his face. Add his attire of a black Italian suit, and he was nothing like the disarrayed man she ran into upstairs. The suit fit him like a glove, and his short ebony hair was gelled back, emphasising his square jaw.

He was easy on the eye, no doubt about it—typically tall, dark and handsome—but she'd sworn off men for life.

Von chuckled. "Yes, I imagine so. There's some big gala shindig at the local town hall in honour of the firefighters. They do it every year."

The fork Claire was lifting towards her mouth stopped mid-air, and her jaw dropped. "He…he's a firefighter?"

How can someone who came across so emotionless be so brave? *Stop judging, Claire.* She cleared her throat and finally popped the food in her mouth.

"Ex." Von placed her cutlery on the side of the plate and took a sip of water from her glass. "He gave it up years ago when his son was born, but he's invited to the gala every year as an honoured guest. He's a mechanic now."

Claire nodded and continued eating, but she couldn't fully fathom this. She was trying not to judge him, but she'd seen two different versions in one evening. It was impossible to figure him out.

More curious than ever, she asked, "I'm assuming you've known Mr Karalis for a while then?"

Von gave Claire a curious look. "You keep calling him 'Mr Karalis'. Why?"

Claire hesitated while she contemplated her answer. *I can't use his first name because it's too personal and dangerous.*

Not wanting to say this, she settled for partial honesty, "I don't know him very well, that's all."

Von nodded and shrugged. "In answer to your question, I've known him since he was a wee lad." She paused and looked at Claire for a long moment. "Michael's a little rough around the edges, but you'll get used to him."

Claire looked at her plate and quietly said, "I confess I did notice he came across a little…" She trailed off, mulling over the word.

"Brash?" Von offered.

Claire shrugged and looked up with a sheepish smile. "Yes."

Von nodded. "Yes, many people say the same thing." She sighed. "I suppose it's easier for me to like him because I've known him for so long. He hasn't had a good run in recent years, and with his mother on her deathbed, I'm afraid the stress is getting to him." She patted Claire's hand then picked up her cutlery. "It's not my place to reveal his woes but don't be too hard on him. Give him time."

Claire digested Von's words, and they ate in silence for a few moments longer.

"What made you move all the way here?" Von finally asked. "If I recall, Michael said you were from Adelaide, right?"

Nodding, Claire took her time chewing, contemplating her answer. She didn't want to lie but needed to be diplomatic. The last thing she wanted to do was draw attention to what she'd been through.

Finishing her mouthful, Claire said, "I had nothing to keep me there anymore."

Von raised an inquisitive eyebrow. "Not even any family? A boyfriend or husband?"

Shaking her head, Claire pushed a piece of broccoli around her plate with her fork. "My parents died when I was eighteen, and I have no other family." She made sure to avoid the husband reference altogether.

"What a terrible shame." Von shook her head. "It can get lonely being alone, can't it?"

Claire nodded, remembering the countless nights she'd lay awake crying. Not from loneliness but from fear.

"That was part of the reason I decided to take this job. A live-in arrangement meant I wouldn't be alone anymore." She averted her gaze.

A warm hand rested on her own, and she looked up into a pair of caring eyes. Von had a way of being sympathetic without making Claire uncomfortable.

"Well, you'll have enough to keep you busy here." Von smiled.

They finished off their meals, Von saying nothing more on the husband topic, much to Claire's relief.

"What about you?" Claire asked as she helped Von tidy up. "Do you have any family?"

Von's face lit up. "Yes, I have two daughters close by and four grandchildren. My husband died many years ago."

"I'm sorry."

"Oh, it's okay." Von forced a laugh. "I miss him terribly, but he's better off. He had cancer, you see. It's a terrible disease."

Claire's heart ached for her new friend. "It must be difficult for you. Being around Mrs Karalis in her condition, I mean."

"It can be, but I can't give up on her now. She's been a wonderful employer and an even better friend. The least I can do is be here for her."

Claire took the stacked-up plates to the sink while Von set about filling a tray with Daphne's food, which had been keeping warm in the oven.

Turning to Von, Claire smiled. "That's so sweet, Von. She's fortunate to have you."

Von's eyes filled with tears. "Oh, you're too kind. Well, I should get these dishes washed then I'll be off."

"You don't stay here?" The moment she spoke the words Claire knew the answer. There wouldn't be enough room for her.

"Good heavens, no." Von laughed. "I have my own home in town. Now, why don't you check on Daphne? She should be awake now. I'll see you in the morning."

Claire suddenly missed her mother more than ever. Memories of her parents were vague, but something about Von reminded Claire of her mother. Having an overwhelming urge to embrace her, Claire did so.

"What was that for?" Von asked when they pulled apart, her light brown eyes sparkling.

Claire looked away and cleared her throat. "To say thanks. You've helped me feel settled already."

Von chuckled. "Well, you're welcome then."

Claire picked up the tray of food, smiled her goodbye to Von and made her way to the room. Reaching the door, she balanced the tray in one hand and opened the door with the other. The light was on, and Daphne sat up in bed. Her cheeks had colour, but the rest of her was skin and bone. Her nightclothes hung off her. A bandana was wrapped around her head, and her face was pale and drawn.

The room itself was more of a hospital room than a standard bedroom. Various machines surrounded the queen bed against the left wall. A wheelchair sat next to the bed, and a railing lined the wall leading to the ensuite.

Daphne turned her head towards the door and looked at her quizzically.

"Hello there, Mrs Karalis." Claire approached the bed. "My name's Claire Stone. I'm your new nurse."

She sat on the chair next to the bed and placed the tray next to Daphne, moving the food around for easy access and getting the cutlery ready. The whole time she could feel Daphne's eyes on her.

When she looked up, Daphne had a small smile on her lips. "You're a very pretty girl." Her voice was weak.

Claire blushed. "Thank you, Mrs Ka—"

Daphne's cold hand took Claire's and squeezed it. "Call me Daphne, please. I'm not over the hill yet." Her voice grew stronger the more she spoke. "I'm only fifty-six."

Claire smiled. "Well then, Daphne, let's get some food into you. I hope you're hungry."

Daphne sighed. "I never feel hungry nowadays, but I'm told I need to eat. Are they trying to fatten me up?"

"No, of course not, but you have to stay healthy. You lose a lot of fluids and nutrients when you undergo treatment. You must build it back up again." Picking up the fork, Claire put a small amount of food on it and moved it toward her patient's mouth.

Shaking her head, Daphne lifted a shaky hand and took the fork from Claire. "Let me do it."

Nodding, Claire watched while Daphne slowly lifted the fork to her mouth. It was so sad watching cancer weaken a person so much they could barely do their normal day-to-day tasks.

Placing the plate on Daphne's lap, Claire advanced to the dresser, removing the clipboard with Daphne's up-to-date medical information and latest checks. Everything appeared straightforward. The only difference being the pain medication which she only needed three times a day for now.

Claire jotted down some notes and put the clipboard away. As a live-in nurse, she'd be on duty twenty-four seven. No more rostered shifts, no more days off, only broken sleep, watching a cancer patient deteriorate day by day, and finally, watching them die. She'd been aware of this when she accepted the job, but it only sunk in now how draining it would be.

Anything is better than thoughts of Ryan.

She turned cold at the memory of his name. She turned back to Daphne, who had a trail of food down the front of her nightgown and a forlorn look on her face.

"Oh dear." Daphne picked at the bits of food. "I can't seem to control the shakes today."

"There's no harm done." Claire strode back to her. Placing the plate and fork on the tray, she put it aside. "I'll get you a fresh nighty in a moment. Would you like more to eat?"

Daphne shook her head. "No, I'm fine, dear. When you see Von next, tell her from me it was delicious."

"I will." Claire picked up a glass of water from the tray. "Now, let's get some fluids into you."

"I couldn't eat or drink another thing." Annoyance flashed across Daphne's face.

"I understand, but you must keep your fluids up. A couple of sips." She inched the glass closer.

"Claire, please I couldn't—"

Claire stared at her firmly. "Daphne, no arguments." She lifted the rim of the glass to her lips. "Come on now."

Daphne relented and took a reluctant sip.

Placing the glass back on the tray, Claire began fluffing up the pillows. "There, was that so bad?"

"Are you always this bossy?" Claire caught Daphne's exasperated tone, but her amused smile lightened the mood.

"Yes, it's in my job description."

Daphne chuckled. "Well, then, we shall get on well."

Claire took the tray of dirty dishes out to the kitchen. When she passed the clock, she noticed it was almost nine. Her eyes were already drooping from tiredness, and she couldn't wait to collapse into bed.

Entering Daphne's room again, Claire rummaged around in the dresser for a clean nightgown. When she found one, she turned back to Daphne only to find she'd already tried to change but had got herself stuck. In the process of pulling it over her head, her arms had got caught in the neck of it. Giggling to herself, Claire went over and helped her remove it.

Daphne smiled sheepishly. "Forgive me, dear. I'm not myself this evening." Her face fell, and she shook her head with a sigh. "Some days I can take on the world, others I can't even do the most menial tasks."

"It's okay." To lighten the mood, Claire added a light-hearted joke. "It's your way of getting people to do things for you, right?"

It worked. Daphne smiled again and played along. "Well you know how it is, when your children grow up, you have to do whatever you can to get attention from anyone."

Claire chuckled. "You reminded me of my mum." She helped Daphne change. "One day she was trying on clothes but was taking a long time in the change rooms. I asked if she was okay and she said she needed help. When I opened the curtain, I saw her stuck in a skin-tight dress two sizes too small. I tried to help her, but it'd stuck to her like superglue. We called for help, but no one could do anything. In the end, they had to cut it off her. She also had to pay for the dress."

Daphne laughed so hard Claire worried she'd pass out from lack of oxygen. A giddy happiness fixed a wide grin on Claire's face. It'd been so long since she'd remembered a happy moment with her mother.

"Oh, my dear girl." Daphne breathed in deeply to catch her breath. "I haven't laughed so hard in a long time. Your mother must be so proud of you."

Claire's smile wavered, and she turned away to hide the tears pooling in her eyes. She took the dirty nightgown to the clothes basket and threw it in. Stopping in front of it, her back still to Daphne, she rubbed her chest where an ache had formed. Oh, how she longed to see her mother again. She wanted one last chance to hear her voice. Let her soft, musical laugh wash over her. Smell her lavender scent. Everything about her was so vague now.

"She died," Claire said for the second time that day. "When I was eighteen." She composed herself, then turned back.

Daphne's eyes were full of genuine sympathy. "Oh, I'm sorry. How old are you now then?"

"Twenty-seven." She sat on the chair beside Daphne's bed. "It'll be ten years next year since they died."

"They?"

Claire nodded but didn't elaborate for fear of breaking down.

"You mean your father's dead too?"

Claire nodded again and took a deep breath. "They died at the same time. It was a car accident."

"I'm so very sorry, Claire."

"It's okay. You learn to move on, right?" Daphne nodded in agreement but said nothing. Claire stood and fixed up the bedcovers. "Would you like help to shower now or in the morning?"

"In the morning if it's not too much trouble."

"It's no trouble at all." She checked her watch and noticed it was now after nine. "It's time for your night-time medication. I'll be back in a moment."

She went out to the cupboard in the kitchen and removed the medication container. Whoever the previous nurse was had an efficient system going. They'd bought a seven-day pillbox with slots for morning, afternoon, and evening. Removing the Sunday evening ones, she made a mental note to fill the empty ones later.

Entering Daphne's room again, she found her sitting up in bed, head drooping forward, snoring lightly. Claire stopped at the bed and gently shook her shoulder.

Daphne's head shot up, her eyes wide but bloodshot. "Oh, I'm sorry. All I seem to be doing these days is sleeping."

"That's okay, I'll let you sleep, but before you do, take these." She handed them over, and Daphne took them with a mouthful of water. "Now open wide." Daphne narrowed her eyes, and Claire laughed. "I have to check you've taken them." Daphne chuckled and did as she was told. "You wouldn't believe how many people try to get out of taking their meds."

"I don't blame them. Living on medication is no one's idea of fun."

"No, but if it helps, it's necessary."

Daphne heaved a sigh. "But is it helping? I don't know what half of this does, Claire. They say I have to take them, but I lose track of *why*. I know I'm going to die, so why bother?"

Claire sat next to her and took her hand. "I'm going to be honest with you, Daphne. You and I both know there's nothing else they can do for the cancer. The medication is for pain. Without it, you'd be in excruciating agony. You don't want that, do you?"

"No, of course not, but in the meantime, I'm confined to my bed and I sleep all the time. How is that benefitting me? I don't even get to spend time with the people I care about."

Claire looked away to hide her tears. Cancer was such an unfair disease. When she'd composed herself, she looked back at Daphne. "It benefits you because those who love you get to spend longer with you. And when you have good days, you get more time with them."

Forcing a smile, Daphne patted Claire's hand. "You're a good girl, Claire. I'm so glad the agency found you. Don't let my son bully you, you hear? He can be a little hard to handle sometimes."

"I'm sure he's not that bad." Claire hoped she could get some information out of her so she could understand him better.

"He never used to be…"

Claire waited for her to continue, but she didn't. She wanted to ask questions but decided not to. It wasn't her place.

Finally, Daphne said, "Tell me about your love life, Claire."

Swallowing, she thought of the best way to respond. She should've known the question would come up. Daphne seemed like the nosey yet likeable type.

"Non-existent," Claire said diplomatically.

Daphne eyed her suspiciously. "You're divorced, aren't you?"

She looked away and cringed. Was it that obvious?

Daphne chuckled. "I'm sorry dear, you can tell me off for prying."

Claire turned back and forced a smile. "No, it's okay, but yes, you're right."

"May I ask what happened?"

Claire froze, images of Ryan's angry face playing in her mind like a movie reel. She shook her head. "I'd rather not talk about it. Now, you should get some sleep."

Daphne's eyes never left her, but she didn't push the topic. "In a moment. If you don't mind, I may need a hand using the bathroom."

Once Daphne was settled, Claire took a break. Even though she didn't need to do a medication run until morning, she wanted to check on her patient every four hours for peace of mind. It was her first night, and she wanted to be sure there were no problems.

Chapter 4

Loud music pounded around the semi-darkened room, multicoloured light shafts from the disco ball decorating the rattling walls. With dinner over, most tables and chairs were empty as people danced. Michael sat at one of the empty tables, legs outstretched, a bottle of beer in his hand.

He sighed and took a long swig from the bottle. So much for a night away from his turmoils. Addison's call had soured the evening good and proper.

The music changed to something slower. Some people went back to their seats while other couples joined and began dancing together. Michael grunted and finished off his beer in one swig. That did it. There were too many happy couples. Too much laughter. Too much noise.

"Hey, Micky." Norman plopped down beside him. "Having a good evening?"

Michael pulled his legs in and sat straighter. "No. I was thinking of going home."

Norman frowned and leaned forward in his chair, beads of sweat on his head shining in the shafts of light. "It's only gone nine, man."

"I'm done, sorry." Michael stood and managed an apologetic smile. "I'm not in the partying mood, I suppose."

Realisation crossed Norman's face, and he stood also. "Right, Addison's call, of course. What did she want?"

"Another hundred bucks. Oscar needs more clothes. Apparently, he's already outgrown the clothes I gave her money for last week." Michael ground his teeth back and forth. "I'm expecting Oscar to be six feet tall when I see him next if he's growing as much as she's saying he is."

Norman barked a laugh but quickly turned serious. "Shit, mate, I'm sorry."

"Does she think I'm a bloody imbecile?" He raked a hand through his hair.

"Did you give her the money?"

Michael cringed. "I did."

Norman gave him a flat look. "Then what did you expect, mate? You keep giving her the money she asks for."

"How could I not?" Michael balled his hands into fists. "She threatens to take Oscar away for good if I don't." He turned cold at the threat he'd heard too often.

"C'mon, man." Norman slapped Michael's shoulder. "You gotta stop being such a walkover. I get it's scary hearing those threats, but she hasn't got a leg to stand on. *You're* following the court order, and *she* isn't. Chat to your lawyer tomorrow. You'll thank me for it."

Michael ran a hand through his hair again and puffed out a sigh. "Yeah, I will. Thanks, mate. Anyway, the limo's coming back to pick everyone up at ten-thirty. I'll walk home. The fresh air will do me good."

Norman nodded and walked off to find Joanna.

Michael left. When he stepped outside, the fresh air was immediate relief from the stifling hall. He yanked off his tie, shoved it in his trouser pocket and unbuttoned the first two buttons of his shirt. He raked his hand through his hair once more, loosening the hold of the gel and slowly made his way home.

He followed the footpath for the first couple of kilometres then took a set of stairs onto the sand, which he followed back home. When he reached his house, before going up to his bedroom, he stopped outside the sliding doors leading into the house when he saw Claire come out of Mum's room. She rustled around in the cupboard then went back to Mum's bedroom. He slid the doors open and stepped inside, closing them after him.

His phone vibrated in his pocket, and he removed it. Crap, another message from Addison.

I need another $100, Michael. Oscar's clothes are expensive.

Cursing under his breath, Michael clenched his teeth and breathed through his nose as he typed a response.

You're not getting another cent from me.

Who the hell did she think she was? Her reply came through seconds later.

Fine. I'll contact my lawyer tomorrow. Don't expect to see Oscar these holidays.

He gripped his phone tightly, his other hand balling into a fist. From Mum's bedroom, he heard Mum and Claire talking. He couldn't hear much of what they said, but clear as day, he heard Mum say, "You're divorced, aren't you?"

He scoffed and stuffed his phone back into his trouser pocket. Bloody typical. Bet Claire was like Addison.

The room closed in on him, making his head pound. It began to swim before his eyes, and something snapped inside him. When Claire left Mum's room and started washing some dishes, he was pretty sure he wasn't even himself. It was as though someone else was controlling him.

***

"I didn't peg you as the sort to wash dishes. Good to see you've got your priorities right," Michael sneered.

Startled by the voice, Claire shrieked and spun around, dropping the wet plate she was holding. It landed on the floor and smashed into large pieces. Heart racing, her hands trembled, and it took all her willpower not to give in to the attack she expected to follow.

God, I can't even break a plate without reminders of that bastard.

Ignoring the broken crockery, she looked up to find Michael standing in front of the French doors. He was home earlier than expected. The room, apart from the light in the kitchen, was in darkness. She could only make out his wide silhouette.

When his words sunk in, anger bubbled through her veins, dousing the panic like water to a fire. "Excuse me?"

"You heard me." His words came out in a growl.

Claire pulled her shoulders back and held her head high. If Ryan had taught her anything, it was that she *wasn't* a doormat. She could and would stand up for herself. "What do you mean by my 'sort'?"

He moved forward and stepped into the light. His mussed-up hair looked as if he'd run his hand through it too many times. His tie was gone, and the top two buttons of his shirt were undone, displaying a smattering of fine, dark hair. If he hadn't just insulted her, she'd be tempted to run her fingers through it.

This is so not the time.

Claire swallowed and allowed her gaze to drift up to Michael's frowning face. Dark bags cast shadows under his eyes. Her anger ebbed away enough to let sympathy begin to form. He had a story, one he probably had to deal with tonight. She didn't condone his behaviour or implications, but if she could figure him out, she'd be able to excuse them.

A bitter smile graced his lips. "I assumed you'd leave these to Von."

"Not that it's any of your business, *Mr Karalis*," she used his surname to poke him, knowing no one liked such an informal address, "but this has nothing to do with priorities. I'm helping out a woman who took it upon herself to get me settled and make me feel welcome. I can't say as much for you."

He gave a careless shrug. "It's not my job. She's the housekeeper. It's expected of her."

Claire stumbled back. "She's been with you for years, doing your dirty work, and you repay her by saying that?"

She could handle insults thrown at her, but she wouldn't tolerate him insulting Von, who thought so highly of him. *I'm yet to see why.* Von would be devastated if she ever learnt what he'd said. His misogynistic opinions were *not* on.

Claire levelled her gaze to meet his. If the storm brewing in his hazel depths was anything to go by, she'd hit a raw nerve. His nostrils flared, and he took a step forward.

If Ryan had done this, she would've taken a step back. She'd be a blubbering puddle on the floor. With Michael though, she didn't once lose her composure. She held her head high and even took another step forward, maintaining his gaze. Her instincts said he was angry, but not violent.

His next words hit her like daggers. "All bloody women are the same."

Claire's tongue lashed back, "And you're like every other man I know."

What happened to not judging?

Michael scoffed. "Yeah, I bet you know a few. Is this your first divorce? Or your fifth? I overheard you talking to my mother." She jerked back, unable to respond before he steamrolled ahead. "I bet you're like every other woman. You marry some poor, unsuspecting bastard until you break them and leave them licking their wounds."

His words stung, and her cheeks flushed. He'd taken one step too far. "You know *nothing* about me, Mr Karalis. *This* is my first divorce and my last. I don't intend to get involved with any other man, especially if they're anything like you."

Michael folded his arms. "Anything like me? What are you implying, Ms Stone?"

Oh, so he's playing the formality game too, is he?

She smiled bitterly. "I'm implying that men like yourself have no respect for women. You think you can control us and mould us however you want. Well, I have news for you. You don't, and you never will."

She stared at him for a long moment. Then, ignoring the broken plate and dirty dishes, she stormed past him to go to her room. Claire didn't even reach the door before he grabbed her wrist and spun her around. He wasn't rough, but it was unexpected, and the suddenness of it sent a jolt of panic to her heart.

Everything happened so fast. She was facing Michael, but the image of Ryan's face grinning demonically was all she could see. Cold, steel-grey eyes stared back at her. It was so real, as if he was in the room with her. Her chest heaved, her breathing coming out in rapid breaths. She was paralysed, trapped with Ryan once more.

She gasped for air, somehow managing to writhe free from Michael's grasp. She squeezed her eyes shut in a desperate attempt to come back from the darkness.

He's not Ryan. He's not Ryan. He's not Ryan.

She repeated it like a mantra until the image disappeared. When it did, she opened her eyes again and found herself staring into Michael's concerned hazel ones. An expression she couldn't grasp crossed his features, followed by realisation, then guilt.

Oh no. No, no, no. He can't have figured it out. Why the hell am I so transparent?

Michael's eyebrows drew together. "Who's Ryan?"

Claire's eyes widened in horror. Had she said that out loud? *Cover blown.* Rather than responding, she ran outside, up the stairs and into her room.

She threw herself on to the bed and curled up into foetal position, rocking back and forth. What was going on? It was as if the last eighteen months of recovery and therapy had never happened. She had made the wrong choice accepting this position.

Chapter 5

The angry cloud hovering over Michael's head lifted, his anger disappearing in a puff of smoke. He collapsed on to the sofa and held his aching head in his hands. *Could I have been a bigger bastard? I sounded like the misogynist women accuse me of being.*

That wasn't the real him. Yet wasn't that the problem? The only people who knew the real him were his parents, Von, Norman, and Joanna. His distrusting nature meant no one else got a glimpse of his true self. He was so focused on protecting his heart, he'd come across like a bastard instead.

While there was no excusing his terrible behaviour, if the evening hadn't been so disastrous, he probably would've caught himself in time, and none of this would've happened.

Bloody Addison.

Norman was right. Michael had to ring his lawyer first thing. His ex-wife brought nothing but trouble.

To hell with her.

He released a weary sigh then slapped his hands to his knees and stood. He cleaned up the dishes and broken plate then dragged his feet upstairs. When he entered the second floor, he stopped outside the spare room. Claire's room. The door was closed, and he stared at it for a long moment, guilt eating away at him.

He owed her a massive apology, and an explanation, but he couldn't do either. Not tonight. The explanation would be hard because it'd mean exposing his vulnerabilities and delving into his past. Was he ready to do that with a stranger?

No.

He went to his room and closed the door after him. He'd have to settle for an apology for now. And to do something about his attitude if he ever wanted Claire to forgive him and view him as a half-decent man.

Removing his suit, he hung it up, then threw his shirt and boxers in the washing basket and went into his ensuite for a long, hot bath. Once immersed in the steaming water, he rested his pounding head back on the tiles. He needed the headache gone if he was going to deal with his lawyer tomorrow.

The image of Claire's fearful eyes came to life in his mind. He'd had no intention of hurting her. All he'd wanted to do was apologise and didn't get a chance to speak the words before she'd run away.

That was when it slotted into place. Her extreme reaction to his touch, followed by the name 'Ryan'. The fear. Her skittish behaviour. The signs were all there.

She's been a victim of physical abuse.

Was it by this Ryan person? Was that why she was divorced? He'd arrogantly assumed she was like Addison—only interested in her interests, no one else's—but he'd been wrong. *So* wrong.

Of course, this did nothing to appease his guilt.

Groaning, he ran his wet hands down his face. *Why do I care anyway?*

They'd barely spoken, let alone civilly, so his care factor should be zero. Yet for some reason, he was drawn to Claire Stone. A beautiful, broken stranger.

Still unable to answer the question, he pushed it away. Closing his eyes, he emptied his mind altogether. For a few blissful moments, it was him alone in a hot bath with the faint sounds of waves coming in through the bathroom window.

***

"Despite what you think, you're not going backwards. If anything, you're making progress."

Claire sniffled and wiped the tears away from her cheeks with her spare hand. The only person she could speak to after the disaster downstairs was her therapist, Laura. Despite the two-and-a-half-hour time difference between them, and the fact Claire had woken her up, Laura was still happy to talk.

"How can you be sure?" Her bottom lip quivered. She hadn't been able to stop crying. "I completely freaked out when he touched me. I saw Ryan's face, Laura. It scared the crap out of me. This can't keep happening. I have a job to do, and I can't let my past affect it."

Claire stretched her legs out in front of her. She sat on the balcony, a cool, salty breeze kissing her skin, creating a smattering of goosebumps in its wake.

"It won't." Laura's tone was soft, soothing. "Today was a day of new things, so it's no surprise it's been so stressful for you. And from what you've told me, it seems like Michael might've had a bad evening himself. You said you saw a picture of a little boy, possibly a son. Who knows what he's battling? You both need a bit of time to get comfortable around each other."

I hope you're right.

Claire stared out over the ocean. With no moon, it was dark, and all she could see was a buoy flashing on and off on the horizon. She took a deep breath, held it for a few seconds then released it.

"Are you okay now?" Laura asked.

Claire thought about this for a long moment. *Was* she okay? That was the million-dollar question. When she couldn't come up with a proper answer, she simply said, "I will be."

"Yes, you will, don't expect too much of yourself at once. This is a massive adjustment for you. Give it time. The sea is very therapeutic. If you have a spare moment, try sitting on the shore for a few minutes."

Claire smiled. "Oh, I intend to. It helps having a balcony overlooking the sea too. If I can't get onto the sand, this is the next best thing."

"Stop it. You're making me jealous."

Claire chuckled. "I should let you get back to sleep. I'm so sorry for bothering you. I'll pay you for—"

"Don't you dare. I'm not only your therapist, Claire. I'm also your friend, and as a friend, I'm here for you all hours."

A warm glow formed in Claire's chest and spread throughout her body. Even though she knew Laura had become a friend, hearing it out loud solidified it in her mind.

"Thanks, Laura." Her voice broke, and fresh tears pooled in her eyes. "Damn it, I'm so emotional."

"It's perfectly natural. We'll chat soon, okay?"

They hung up, but Claire stayed out on the balcony for a while longer. It was getting late, but she was no longer tired. Weary from the day of travelling and the emotional rollercoaster ride, if she tried to sleep, she'd only stare at the ceiling. Time to think things over. Perhaps it would do some good to get her thoughts in order.

If her argument with Michael proved anything, it was that they had one thing in common. They were both broken. It didn't take a genius to figure out he'd been burned by a woman, turning him bitter. While she didn't know the details, it shed enough light on the situation to extinguish her anger.

They were both in the wrong, and they'd both said nasty things. She only hoped one day, when the time was right, they could start again.

Why did she care? Was it because they both had demons? In hindsight, a miracle had occurred that day. Despite the events, Claire was drawn to him. She wanted to learn more about him. Help him. This was a huge step for her.

What if he needed help from someone who understood heartbreak? They could overcome their bitterness toward the opposite sex together. Help each other heal.

Her cheeks flushed, and she stood quickly, the chair scraping along the cement floor. Her mind was heading in a dangerous direction, and it had to stop. Now. *I'm way too emotional to make rational decisions.*

A glance at her watch told her it was nearly time to check on Daphne, so she made her way downstairs. Before going inside, she took Laura's advice. Removing her shoes, she held them and wandered toward the water's edge. The sand massaged her feet, the cool breeze rustling her hair and caressing her skin.

When she was a few metres away from the water, Claire dropped her shoes then sat on the sand and lay back. With no moon and little light pollution to dull the brightness, the bright smattering of stars across the sky twinkled brilliantly. She'd never stargazed before. Something was calming about it. All that vastness made her troubles seem so minute in comparison. For a brief moment, her problems disappeared.

Laura was right. It *was* therapeutic.

When it came time to go inside, she got to her feet and brushed herself off. She suddenly felt light, like the weight of the world had lifted from her shoulders. How long it would last, Claire didn't know, but she embraced it all the same.

When she reached the front door, she dropped her shoes next to the mat, then brushed the sand from her feet and wandered inside. With everything in darkness, she fumbled her way to the kitchen and felt along the wall for the light switch. She flicked it on, shielding her eyes from the brightness. The broken plate was gone, the dirty dishes washed up.

Michael must've done it.

She cringed at the memory of their less-than-pleasant encounter. She needed to apologise but she'd let the dust settle first.

Wandering to Daphne's room, she snuck in. Once she was happy her patient was comfortable and sleeping peacefully, Claire backed out again. She decided to try for some sleep, knowing she needed a few uninterrupted hours to function the next day. Switching off the kitchen light, she closed the main doors and snuggled down on the sofa. Claire couldn't bring herself to go back upstairs in case she saw Michael again. For the time being, she'd be civil but keep her distance.

She pulled the blanket splayed over the back of the sofa around her. Resting her head on a cushion, she closed her eyes.

The lightness she'd experienced while on the beach had gone and now an overwhelming emptiness smothered her. Here she was, an abuse victim, with no home, no friends, no life. She had a fresh start, something she'd once been excited about, but now she was terrified. She had complete control of her life now, but what if she wasn't cut out for this? What if she was fooling herself into thinking this was her big break when she was setting herself up for failure?

She'd never know until she tried, but hell, it was hard, and the fear of failure hung over her like a thunder cloud. Turning over, she hid her face and let a few hot tears drip onto the cushion, lulling her into a deep sleep.

Chapter 6

Michael lay on his bed, hands behind his head, staring up at the ceiling. Sleep was a long way off. His headache had cleared, but now all he could think about was Addison. Anxiety knotted in his stomach at the thought of speaking to the lawyer in the morning.

The fear of losing Oscar ran deep, and Addison had the ammunition to make it possible. She knew he couldn't fight for full custody yet and she'd do anything to beat him to it. Could he act now? No, his circumstances weren't right, but he couldn't keep giving in to her.

When he wasn't thinking about Addison, he was thinking about Claire. The argument ran around in his mind, and he berated himself for his disgusting behaviour.

Damn, why won't my brain switch off?

After half an hour, he was still wide awake, staring into the darkness. He sighed and got up to go downstairs.

Perhaps a nip of brandy will do the trick.

When he got to the French doors, he spotted Claire's shoes by the mat. Peering through the door, he saw her lying on the sofa. He hesitated before going in.

Is she afraid of me?

His stomach lurched. Michael didn't like who he'd become, but how could he change? His mother and Von always told him to let go of the past, of what Addison did, and move on. The problem was not knowing how. She'd destroyed every inch of him.

Michael quietly pulled the door open and stepped inside. When Claire didn't stir, he pulled it closed again. Noticing the blanket had fallen off, he placed it back over her again, making sure her shoulders were covered. It was an instinctive reaction, one he couldn't quite understand. He stared down at her for a long moment, admiring her. Her dark blonde hair splayed across the pillows. Her pale face was content and peaceful.

There was something different about this woman. What was it?

She wasn't Addison, that much was obvious. Her looks alone proved that. Addison was high maintenance. She dressed to impress in expensive designer outfits and always wanted the best of everything.

Claire had come to Busselton in jeans and a t-shirt, with nothing more than a handbag and a suitcase. Yet he sensed she had a story, one he wanted to know. This was a surprise, because he hadn't wanted to get to know another woman for years.

No, there was something more. Maybe in time, he'd figure it out.

Staring too long, he shook his head and tore his eyes away. Silently making his way over to the cupboards, he reached in for a glass. In the process, his hand knocked another, and it came crashing to the floor.

A shriek filled Michael's ears. He spun around to find Claire sitting bolt upright, the blanket tight around her shoulders. He'd never seen anyone so terrified in his life, even the countless times he had to save someone from a fire. Those people trusted him. They knew he was there to save them.

Oh, if only this were as simple. And, hell, a raging inferno *was* simple compared to the life he'd created for himself. He'd let himself turn into a bitter, untrusting bastard who Claire now saw as the enemy. This was another reminder that something had to change.

He swallowed hard and instinctively advanced, wanting to help Claire in any way possible. When she scuttled back into the corner of the sofa, Michael stopped and held up his hands. "I'm sorry. I didn't mean to scare you."

Her eyes were wide, her breathing rapid. Seeing her in such a state caused a sharp pain to spear his chest. If he'd been more agreeable to her from the moment she arrived, taking the time to talk to her and get to know her, even five minutes, he might be able to offer comfort now.

Michael wasn't entirely sure why, but he took another step forward. Doing so only resulted in Claire jumping from the sofa, the blanket falling to the floor.

"Please don't come any closer." Claire's voice trembled. She took a couple of steps back toward the door.

He planted his feet on the floor so he wouldn't move again. "I want to help."

She took another step back. "*You* want to help *me*? The last I heard I was like every other woman. I marry men until I break them."

Michael hung his head in shame. He *had* said that, hadn't he?

The last thing he heard was the sound of the door sliding shut. With a sigh, he turned back to the broken glass and proceeded to clean it up. It was a night for breakages.

He glanced over his shoulder, unable to stop the gnawing worry. The knowledge that someone hurt such a beautiful and fragile woman sent him into a blind rage. *I hope the bastard is in jail for life.*

Since he was the wrong person to approach her, should he consider telling Von or his mother? Or maybe it was better to leave it alone? What if she accused him of interfering?

Placing the broken glass in the bin, he forwent the brandy and went to sit by Mum's side. He'd often do this on nights he couldn't sleep. He didn't want to waste any precious moments with her.

The reminder of her impending death sent a cold chill through him. No one prepared him for this. He ignorantly assumed both of his parents would be always there. The prospect of death had never crossed his mind. How was he supposed to deal with it?

Opening the door, he entered and sat on the chair next to the bed. Taking her hand, Michael stared at his mother's peaceful form, wishing things were different. He loved Mum more than anything, and seeing her deteriorate day by day was heartbreaking. The only way he coped was because of her positivity and contagious smiles.

He sat there for a long while, paying no attention to the time. When she began to stir, he sat up straighter and waited for her to come to. Her eyes fluttered open and landed on him.

"What time is it?"

Michael looked at his watch. "After two-thirty."

She frowned. "You shouldn't be up this late. You've got work tomorrow."

"It's Saturday tomorrow, Mum." He smiled sadly. The concept of time came and went with her. Sometimes she'd be fine, other times she didn't know what time or day it was.

"Oh well, okay then. Make sure you get some sleep soon though, don't tire yourself out on my account."

She shuffled to get comfortable, and Michael asked, "Do you need anything? I can get the nurse for you."

He wasn't sure why he referred to her as 'the nurse'. It seemed he and Claire were both more comfortable with formalities than accepting they had names.

As if reading his mind, Mum chided, "She has a name, Michael. And no I'm fine, she needs a good night's rest." She looked at him for a long moment then said, "I know you're difficult to get on with sometimes. I hope you haven't made her feel unwelcome."

His spine stiffened, and he sat back. "Mum."

She only blinked at him. "You know it's true." She squeezed his hand. "I understand why, but she doesn't. Don't go scaring her off, I like her."

Michael relaxed. "You barely know her."

"Mother's intuition. Trust me, I know a good egg when I see one, and she's someone special. Maybe you should get to know her too." In a softer voice, she added, "She's not another Addison."

He gritted his teeth at those words and stared at the door, not seeing it. It always came down to Addison. He needed her gone from his life, but while she had custody of their son, it wouldn't happen. Somehow, he needed to find a way to stop her controlling ways and man up to her.

"She hasn't told me much, but she's had a rough life."

Michael's brow furrowed. *Addison?*

Mum laughed softly. "Claire, I mean. Addison wouldn't know what 'rough' meant if it bit her in the behind."

Michael snorted. "That's the understatement of the century." He almost told her his suspicions about Claire but held his tongue, still not comfortable doing so. Perhaps another time.

"The poor girl doesn't even have any family." She sighed sadly.

He conjured up an image of Claire all alone and frightened. It made his heart ache. *Why the hell do I care so much?*

The question taunted him again, but he couldn't answer it. He let go of Mum's hand and leaned in to kiss her cheek. "You need to sleep." He stood. "I'll see you in the morning."

He left the room and had that long-awaited brandy.

Chapter 7

Claire slept, but it was restless. Her dreams were filled with Ryan, and she woke up in a panic around five-thirty in the morning. There was no way she'd go back to sleep, so she kicked back the covers and stared up at the ceiling. Even though the balcony doors were closed, she could still hear the faint sound of waves lapping at the shore.

After a few moments, she got up and made her way to the bathroom, her feet dragging along the carpet. Her head was stuffy as if someone had filled it with cotton wool. A hot shower should liven her up.

Turning the taps, she adjusted the water to the correct temperature and began to undress. Dreams about Ryan had stopped a few months ago, and she was sure the one from last night was a result of Michael breaking the glass.

When it'd happened, she'd been in such a deep sleep, the sound had crashed through her subconscious like a wrecking ball to a building. In the aftermath, she hadn't missed how genuinely sorry he'd appeared, but her logical thoughts were blurred, her reaction instinctive. She'd had no control over her tongue and regretted her words.

With a sigh, she stepped into the shower. The hot needles massaged her skin and head. She closed her eyes and relished in the pleasure for a few moments. She'd go about doing her job and would apologise to him when the time was right.

Turning off the taps, she stepped out and wrapped a towel around herself. The shower had rejuvenated her, and she felt clean and refreshed. If she did get tired, she'd be able to nap when Daphne did.

Entering her room, the towel still wrapped around her, her eyes landed on the clock on the bedside cupboard. Quarter to six. It was nearly time to check on Daphne.

While she dried herself, she heard the screen door leading to the first-floor slam closed, but there were no footsteps in the hallway. Michael must be heading downstairs. She finished getting ready in record time, and after tying her hair up in a ponytail, left the room and descended the stairs. It was still dark out, and the cool breeze scattered goosebumps across her arms.

Light from inside shone through the French doors, illuminating the stairs. Peering in, she spotted Michael sitting at the table with a coffee. She wasn't ready for a confrontation, but she couldn't avoid the man forever. Taking a deep breath, she slid the doors open and walked in. He looked up when she entered. Dark bags had settled beneath his eyes, indicating his sleep was also limited.

Today he looked…normal. His ebony hair was slightly dishevelled from his morning wash, but it suited him better than the messy-after-work look or the formal-gelled-back look. He also wore track pants and a snug t-shirt, which outlined his broad and defined chest. Yes, he was a handsome man, and her heart did a little flutter in agreement.

Damaged or not, she appreciated eye candy like any other woman. Her problem was trusting men.

Seeing him on a new day, and in a new light, he didn't appear aggressive at all. If anything, he looked sad. A wedge of guilt lodged itself in her gut, unmoving. She'd wrongly judged him, exactly what she *didn't* want to do.

The tension between them was thick, but she managed a brief good-morning smile as she closed the door behind her. She strode past him to Daphne's room but then stopped, feeling the urge to say something about the situation. Show him she wasn't completely cold or heartless.

Stumbling to a stop, she turned to him and surprised herself by saying, "I'm so sorry about your mother, Mr Karalis. I understand how difficult this is, and I promise to keep her as happy and comfortable as I can."

Michael's lips twitched at her formal address, and she bit her lip. Saying it in anger was one thing. Saying it in polite conversation was weird. Yet she still couldn't bring herself to use his name.

"Thank you, Ms Stone. And thank you for coming all this way to look after Mum."

She winced at his formal address, her spine stiffening. *Touché, Michael Karalis, touché.* A wicked grin graced his lips at her reaction, and his eyes shone a vibrant hazel.

He's poking fun at me.

The axis shifted between them. A bubble of laughter rose in her throat, threatening to send her into hysterical giggles. Her lips morphed into a slow smile. Their gazes met. Huge butterfly wings sprang to life in her stomach, filling her with a warmth she hadn't experienced in years.

She released a shaky breath and tore her eyes away, seeking refuge in Daphne's room. Claire leaned against the closed door for a moment, breathing heavily, her heart performing drum beats. Once composed, she checked on Daphne who was still asleep. There was little Claire could do if she didn't want to wake her patient too early. After adjusting the covers, she left the room.

When she exited and heard Von's cheerful, "Good morning, Michael," from the kitchen, she breathed a little easier.

Impeccable timing.

Claire entered the kitchen and smiled at the older woman. "Morning, Von."

Von's face lit up, and she bustled over to Claire, embracing her in a warm hug. "Good morning, Claire. Did you sleep well?"

In her periphery, Michael shifted uncomfortably in his seat. "Fine, thanks," Claire replied.

Michael stared at her with a look she couldn't decipher. He turned away when he caught her looking and stood. "I'm going for a run."

Before anyone could respond, he left. Von looked at Claire quizzically. "Have you spoken to him this morning? He seems very off."

"No." Claire didn't want to lie, but Von didn't need to be involved in what was going on.

While Von started breakfast, Claire got to work organising the medication she hadn't got around to doing the night before. They chatted while they worked, Claire liking her more and more. Von was bubbly and easy-going but firm when need be. A couple of times, she mentioned Michael's son, Oscar, but never went into detail. The only thing she let slip was Oscar's visit soon.

How would Michael act around his son? Claire couldn't picture him being good with kids. He seemed so stuffy and—

Stop it.

She bit the inside of her cheek and shook her head, scolding herself for judging him yet again. If the previous evening had proven anything, it was that making judgements about someone she barely knew was a bad idea. Somehow, she needed to find the confidence to clear the air and take the time to get to know him. Until that time, she had to exercise patience and stop thinking of him badly.

When Claire finished sorting the medication, she went in to check on Daphne again, finding her sitting up in bed with a book. She appeared perky and upbeat. A smile lit up her face when she saw Claire approaching.

"Good morning," Daphne greeted. "How was your first night?"

"Oh, it was fine." It was her motto to never go into any of her woes with her patients. They had their own worries and didn't need to know hers.

Daphne raised a knowing eyebrow. Rather than persisting, she said, "You know, my son was in here last night."

Claire froze. What did he let slip? Not wanting to push, she simply said, "I hope he didn't wake you. You need as much sleep as you can get."

"Oh, it was nothing like that. He often comes in and sits by my bed when he can't sleep. I tend to wake up during the night anyway, so when I did, he was there. Had no idea how long he was there though. Bless him. I know he can be difficult, and while he didn't say anything, I got the impression you two didn't have a smooth start."

"Is that so?" Claire feigned surprise. "We're not best mates, but we've been civil."

I'm going to be struck down for lying.

Daphne gave her a look that told her she knew better. "My dear Claire, I may not know you well, but I can tell when something's not right. Now I know my son, and I know he can be a pain in the rear end, so if he's done something to upset or offend you I'd like to know so I can give him a good kicking."

Claire sat on the chair next to the bed. She didn't want to confess everything because he had his reasons, but maybe Daphne could shed some light on the situation. "Perhaps we didn't have the best start, but it was nothing major. He seems quite bitter to the opposite sex, but I've learnt he has his reasons."

Daphne scowled and muttered something under her breath. In a louder voice, she said, "Yes, he has his reasons, but he should know how to treat someone with respect. He's a good man deep down, but he has a few problems he's struggling to part with."

"Well, at least we have *that* in common." Claire meant to say it to herself, but Daphne appeared to have excellent hearing.

She glanced at Claire with a curious expression. "What was that?"

"Oh, nothing."

Claire went to stand, but Daphne reached out to stop her. "Claire, I know you don't know me well, but if you ever need to talk, I'm a good listener."

"Thank you." Claire forced a smile. "But right now, you're my focus. Any problems I have aren't a priority."

She gently removed Daphne's hand from her arm and stood. Sensing Daphne wanted to say something else, Claire busied herself with menial chores. After a few moments of silence, Daphne sighed and said nothing.

Claire checked Daphne's blood pressure, jotted down the results on the clipboard and then checked her temperature. The whole time, Daphne's questioning gaze followed her movements.

When Claire began packing up, Daphne asked, "Claire, please answer me honestly. Did you sleep well last night?"

Claire's brow creased in confusion. Why was Daphne making such a big deal about it?

"You have bags under your eyes, dear." Daphne's tone oozed concern.

Claire looked away to hide them, but it was useless. In the end, she settled with a half-truth. "I guess it's the stress of the last few weeks. It was hard work trying to sell the house and contents in such a short time."

"You sold everything to come here?"

Claire nodded and turned to the dresser. Selling everything was a no brainer, but it wasn't easy. After all, it *was* her childhood home. The happy memories that were once there had been tainted by Ryan.

At least now she'd permanently cut ties to anything connected to him.

Once this job ended, she'd planned to use the proceeds from the sale to settle in Western Australia. Where, she hadn't yet decided, but at least she had the freedom to go wherever she pleased.

Placing the clipboard down, she turned back to find Daphne frowning.

"You do realise this isn't long term, don't you?" Daphne asked.

Claire chuckled. "Of course I do, but it was time for me to move on so I decided I might as well embrace the challenge. When I'm done with this job, I'll find another. Who knows, maybe the local hospital will need nurses."

Daphne's face flooded with relief. "The wife of one of Michael's friends is a nurse. They often visit so maybe you'll get a chance to ask her about the job market."

"Maybe I will." She cleaned her hands with antibacterial gel. "Now, more importantly, how are *you* feeling today?"

"I'm wonderful." Claire raised an eyebrow, and Daphne laughed. "Okay, perhaps wonderful is overdoing it, but I do feel quite good today. If you don't mind, I'd like to eat breakfast at the table."

"Of course, if you're sure you're up to it. How about we get you showered and ready?"

Claire expected the process to take a while, but with Daphne in better spirits, she was able to do a lot for herself. Claire was only there for support if needed. She loved days like these because it brought so much life back into the patient.

Forty-five minutes later, Claire had a firm hold on Daphne's arm as she assisted her out of the room and into the kitchen. Michael had returned from his run and sat at the table reading the newspaper while Von cooked at the stove. The smell of bacon made her stomach rumble.

"Good morning, lovey," Von gushed when Daphne came into view. "You look as beautiful as ever today."

Daphne chuckled as Claire helped her into the seat. "And you're a charmer as always, Von. What do you think of our Claire?"

Our Claire?

Sensing Michael's questioning gaze, Claire avoided eye contact with him. She hadn't been there for a day, and already Daphne treated her like one of the family. It was nice, something she pined for with the loss of her parents. Wanting to enjoy it, she kept her gaze averted, not wishing to see how Michael felt about the comment.

"Oh, she's a good egg." Von winked at Claire. "A blessing in disguise. She even washed your dinner dishes last night. It was a grand surprise to come in and see the sink clear."

Claire's face heated up. Remembering she didn't get to finish them, she said, "Oh, it wasn't only me, Mr Karalis helped too."

The room fell silent. Claire looked at everyone in confusion, unable to avoid Michael this time. Although he *did* have an odd, almost approving look in his eyes. Von and Daphne looked shocked. She wasn't sure if it was because she addressed him as 'Mr Karalis' or whether he rarely washed dishes.

"Well, thank you both." Von smiled at them then brought a plate of bacon and a bowl of scrambled eggs over. "Now eat up before it gets cold."

Claire ate in silence while the other three conversed. Daphne didn't struggle with feeding herself this time, and it brought a smile to Claire's face.

Watching how comfortable Michael was around everyone, her opinion changed once again. He wasn't all bad, was he? He was a diamond in the rough, in need of refining. Their disastrous run-in from the day before was nothing more than getting off on the wrong foot.

When breakfast was over, Claire grabbed Daphne's morning medication and handed it to her. Daphne playfully rolled her eyes but took them all at once with a mouthful of water.

"Now open wide," Claire instructed.

"See what I have to go through?" Daphne joked but did as she was told so Claire could make sure the pills were gone.

When Claire heard Michael's genuine laughter for the first time, her heart gave an unexpected flutter. It was a low, sexy laugh that caressed her like a gentle breeze. She looked at him. His face was bright, his eyes lit up, displaying flecks of gold around the irises. He seemed a completely different person this morning.

She turned back to Daphne and nodded, satisfied. "Good. Now, what would you like to do today?"

Daphne's gaze drifted to the French doors. "Would you mind taking me outside for a bit?" She looked back at Claire with hopeful eyes. "I don't get to go out often."

"Of course I don't mind. I'll make sure I bring some extra warm clothes as the wind is quite chilly. We better not stay out too long, though."

Daphne nodded and patted her hand. "You're a real gem, Claire."

She smiled in response. "I'll grab your things. Will you be okay out here for a few minutes?"

"Yes, dear. I think I can sit up straight in the chair for a few moments." Daphne winked, and Claire laughed. She liked how easily they could banter with each other.

Sensing someone staring at her from behind, she turned and saw Michael with a small smile on his face. When he noticed her looking, rather than turning away, his smile widened and he gave her a single nod as if to say thank you. She returned the sentiment then went to Daphne's room to grab what she needed for the beach.

Chapter 8

Michael disappeared into his room after breakfast and rang his lawyer, Lance. He answered on the second ring.

"Mick, what can I do for you?"

"Sorry to bother you on the weekend, mate, but I have a slight problem." Michael went out onto the balcony and stood in front of the railing. He spotted Claire setting up a chair and an umbrella. He smiled, raking his gaze over her slim, feminine form. It was still early, a little after eight, and the sun wasn't very high in the sky, but she was taking every precaution to protect her beautiful skin.

Hell, where did that come from?

"You're never a bother, mate." Lance's voice interrupted his reverie. "What's Addison up to this time?"

In recent weeks, Michael had been on the phone to Lance more and more as Addison made his life more difficult.

"Last night she rang needing another hundred bucks for Oscar. He needed more clothes apparently."

Lance swore loudly. "You didn't give it to her, did you? I've got kids too, Mick, and yes they grow, and yes they ruin their shoes and clothes, but I never need to buy as much as Addison supposedly does. She's diddling you, you know that, don't you?"

Michael winced and turned his back to the ocean. "I know, but she threatened to take Oscar away. I couldn't take that risk. That's not all though. She texted me again later in the evening requesting *more* money, stating the clothes she wanted were more expensive."

"Holy shit, Mick, unless you're a millionaire, no kid should need two hundred bucks for clothes they're going to grow out of in a few months. Please, please don't tell me you gave in again."

Michael couldn't help but laugh at his lawyer's exasperated tone. "Not this time but she's onto her lawyer this morning. She's trying to take him away completely, Lance." His throat closed up, and tears stung his eyes. "I can't lose him. She's trying to throw around words like abuse and neglect. I'm terrified, mate."

He shivered, remembering Addison's cold words when she first called him the night before: *"I'll tell them you abuse him. I'll have full custody in no time."*

He'd tried to argue there was no evidence, but he knew as well as she did that when it came to children, the courts could and would make decisions without evidence if required.

"Now you wait right there, Mick." Lance's tone hardened. "You and I both know they're words and not fact. She can try, and she probably will, but it won't stick, I can guarantee it. We can get character reference from friends, family, and colleagues if we need them. Besides, her lawyer is a level-headed woman. While some lawyers will fight without evidence, she won't, and you know that."

Michael turned back and looked out onto the sand once more. Mum sat on the chair under the umbrella, Claire on the sand next to her, reading her a book. His heart twinged at the image, warmth spreading through him.

"What should I do?" Michael turned and headed back into his room.

"Leave it to me. I'll get onto Addison's lawyer, and we'll have a chat. Enjoy your weekend and don't let it worry you. It may take a few days, but I'll get back to you soon with an update."

They hung up, and Michael released a long, slow breath. His shoulders dropped, some of the tension vanishing from his body. He made his way downstairs and onto the beach, having a sudden desire to be near Mum and Claire.

When he drew closer, Claire's voice drifted on the soft breeze, melodious and soothing. It caressed him, waning away any remaining stresses he had. She had a beautiful reading voice. He stopped beside Mum and smiled down at her then at Claire. She put the book down and to his surprise, smiled easily at him.

"Michael." Mum beamed up at him. Even under the umbrella, she wore a large floppy hat and sunglasses. A cardigan rested on her lap, but her arms were bare.

"Do you mind if I join you?"

Even though he directed the question at Claire, Mum answered, "Of course not."

Michael didn't sit until he got the okay from Claire. Of course he didn't need her permission, but he was all too aware of her fragility. He didn't want her to feel intimidated or threatened in any way.

He stared at her for a long moment, waiting. She appeared shocked that he wanted an answer. A flash of something—was it apprehension?—flashed on her face, but she smiled her acceptance. "Don't let me stop you. I'm not here to interfere. Besides, you're the one who has to listen to my boring reading voice."

"Oh hush, you." Mum reached out and patted Claire's shoulder. "You read beautifully."

"I agree." Michael levelled his gaze to hold hers. "I heard you as I approached."

"Oh." A light pink coloured her cheeks. "Thank you." She averted her gaze and picked up the book, the pink in her cheeks deepening to a fierce red.

Michael laid back on the sand, hands behind his head and closed his eyes as Claire began reading again. With the sound of seagulls squawking overhead and waves lapping at the shore, he couldn't remember a time he'd been so relaxed. There was something about Claire Stone, something special, and he wanted to find out what it was.

The prison walls around his heart lowered enough for it to flutter to life, reminding him it was there…that one day he wanted to find love again.

***

A week passed, and Claire had settled well into the job. While she and Michael hadn't spoken much, they hadn't argued either. She supposed it was progress. There were occasional looks of curiosity, a sign that he was interested in her, and surprisingly, she wasn't scared. It made her heart race every time and only made her curiosity grow. It never went beyond glances, and it never would until they cleared the air once and for all. Neither of them had apologised yet, the timing never right.

It was a warm day, so while she had a couple of hours free, Claire decided to go for a swim, something she hadn't done since she was seventeen.

Up in her room, she dug around in the dresser for the bathing suit she'd bought before she left Adelaide. It was the only item Claire had purchased when she found out she'd be by the sea.

It'd been so long since she'd even dipped a toe in the ocean, she could barely contain her excitement. Once clad in her bathing suit, she turned to the mirror to pull her hair back. She began plaiting it when her eyes landed on the angry red scar above her left breast. Claire dropped her arms to her side, hair coming loose and falling in tendrils around her shoulders. Strands covered the scar, and with a trembling hand, she pushed it back over her shoulder.

Inching closer to the mirror, she inspected it closely. Cold fingers came up to touch it, and her breath caught. The memory was clear as day—the pain of the blade slicing through her like butter, a pain she'd never experienced before. It was Ryan's final attempt to end her life, but thanks to his bad aim, he'd missed her heart by a sliver.

Shivering, she dropped her hand and started plaiting her hair once more. Usually, she'd wear tops to cover it, not wanting to answer questions, but today she wouldn't. Firstly, with Michael off visiting a mate, Von busy with chores, and Daphne sleeping, there was no one around to ask. Secondly, she refused to hide behind her fears anymore. If someone *did* ask, she'd find a way to answer.

The scars were a part of her now, and it was time to embrace them. Her self-image had been in tatters for so long, she'd look for any excuse to bring herself down, but it had to stop. If she ever wanted to be the girl she was before Ryan, Claire had to accept herself for who she was, scars and all.

A week has changed a lot in my outlook.

She smiled and finished the plait, twisting a hair tie around the end. The freedom she'd experienced when she left Adelaide heightened. There was no fear, no panic attacks, no nightmares. She was...*normal*.

Slipping on a dress over her swimmers and thongs on her feet, Claire picked up a spare towel from the bathroom and left the room. Daphne was asleep, probably for at least another forty-five minutes, so Claire set an alarm on her phone.

The warm afternoon sun in the cloudless sky beat down on her. Seagulls flew overhead, squawking as they went searching for their next meal. A warm, gentle breeze caressed her skin in a whispered kiss, making her smile in contentment.

Passing the spot where she'd set up with Daphne a week earlier, her heart skipped. It'd been a surprise when Michael appeared, and an even bigger surprise when he'd sought permission to join them. There was no way she would've stopped him. He could spend as little or as much time with his mother as he pleased, but the fact he'd asked had shifted something between them again.

His presence had been surprisingly comforting. She'd enjoyed the hour they ended up spending together with Daphne. Claire read, while Daphne and Michael listened, sometimes laughing at a scene or giving opinions on the characters' actions. It'd been a surreal yet beautiful moment. While it hadn't happened again, it was still clear in her mind, as if it'd only happened that morning.

When she left Adelaide, she'd been terrified she wouldn't adjust to being around a man again. That she'd always be afraid. Yet, in a short week, she'd lost that fear around Michael—*despite* their words on her first evening at the house.

Claire felt she was finally able to finish healing.

Stopping a few feet away from the water, she laid her towel out. Removing her dress and thongs, she placed them beside it then meandered to the water's edge. She stood on the wet sand, waiting for the waves to come to her.

Her heart leapt when the first wave approached. Excitement skirted along her skin, and she gasped in glee when the water wrapped around her ankles. Colder than expected since the weather had been quite mild. The best thing to do would be to dive straight in. So, without further hesitation, she rushed forward and dived into the aqua water.

Coming up for air, she brushed her hair away from her face and giggled in glee. She felt like a child experiencing the ocean for the first time. She'd forgotten how wonderful it was to be in such a huge expanse of water. It was like looking up at the night sky. Her problems seemed so minor compared to the expanse around her.

For the next half hour, she swam, enjoying the freedom of being herself once again. She'd lost her identity when she was with Ryan but being here, in this beautiful town of Busselton, she began to remember the things she once loved. The ocean was one of them, and she decided that no matter where she ended up, she needed to be by the water.

When the sun got a bit too warm, and she worried her sunscreen might've washed off, she swam back to shore. As she did, Michael's silhouette came out of the house towards her. Her heart raced. When had he returned?

Have I done something wrong?

It was an irrational fear, one she couldn't stop. Swallowing hard, she let the waves assist her back to the shore. He stopped by her belongings, a hand held up to his forehead to block out the sun. When her feet touched the sand, she took long strides out of the water, suddenly self-conscious.

Stopping in front of him, she avoided his gaze while she composed herself. A couple of deep breaths did the trick, then she lifted her gaze to meet his. He smiled at her, making her breath catch in her throat. The sun shone directly on him, his eyes shining vibrantly.

His smile slipped but his gaze grew intense as they took their fill of each other. Claire felt like she recognised Michael for the first time. Not as *him*, but as a man. Strong and handsome. Someone she could fall for if she allowed it.

His gaze moved from her eyes and swept over her swim-suited body, leaving fire in its wake, burning her up. And it *wasn't* from the sun's intensity either. Butterflies came to life in her belly. When his gaze made its way up again, it lingered longer than necessary on the scar.

She drew in a breath and restrained herself from covering it with her hand. Her fingers twitched in anticipation. Embracing her new self, scars and all, meant she couldn't make it known that she was still affected by them.

When his eyes met hers, an overwhelming sadness filled them. He wasn't a stupid man. No doubt he'd suspect abuse by her earlier behaviour. Perhaps now, seeing such vicious evidence, it had affected him. His mouth opened, then closed again, as if he wanted to say something, but he shook his head instead.

Unsure what to say, she blurted the first thing that came to her mind. "I'm sorry."

He blinked and furrowed his brow.

Now that she'd started, she couldn't stop. "I only went for a swim because your Mum was still sleeping when I checked on her about half an hour ago. I set the phone alarm for—"

It was still instinctive to defend herself—that much hadn't changed. Not yet, at least. It was a work in progress.

"Hey." His voice was soft as he reached out to place a soft hand on her arm. "It's okay. I wasn't checking up on you." Rather than his touch sending her into an instant panic, it did the opposite. She shivered in pleasure.

When his words sunk in, her cheeks coloured. "Oh." She dropped her gaze.

Michael removed his hand, and it fell to his side. "I wanted to let you know I've got some friends visiting. They wanted to meet you. One of them, Jo, is a nurse."

Her ears pricked up at this. *Jo? A nurse?* Her brain was still fuzzy from Michael's touch, but there was a connection somewhere that she couldn't quite figure out.

She entwined her hands, unsure of how to answer. Inviting her in to meet his friends, did that mean something? And *why* did he want her to meet them?

Stop second-guessing everything.

Biting her lip, Claire lifted her gaze once more and met his. She relaxed when she saw nothing but honesty in his eyes. She nodded. "Okay, I'd love to meet them. I should shower and change first. I'll be about ten minutes."

Michael nodded then turned and made his way back to the house. Claire released the breath she didn't realise she'd been holding and bent to pick up her things. She switched off her alarm, then dashed up to her room.

Ten minutes later, she was showered and dressed. Her wet hair hung in a fresh ponytail. Making her way downstairs, she glanced through the French doors before entering. Michael and his friends, a man and woman, sat at the table. Von continued to bustle around the kitchen. *That woman never stops.*

Sliding the door open, she walked in. Michael, who sat at the end of the table, stood and turned to her when she entered. "Norman, Jo, this is Mum's nurse, Claire Stone."

It was the first time he'd said her name, and while it wasn't to her face, the sound of it rolling off his tongue so naturally made her shiver.

For some reason, they still hadn't addressed each other informally. In fact, they now avoided using names altogether. *This is getting ridiculous.*

She shook the thoughts from her head.

The woman spun around with a gasp. When their eyes met, Claire's heart tripped. *Jo? Oh my god, it's Joanna.* Tears pooled in Claire's eyes as she took in the familiar sight of her best friend from high school. They'd even studied at university together.

"Joanna is a nurse at the local hospital," Michael continued, oblivious to the two women gawking at each other, speechless.

Joanna's light brown eyes were warm and inviting, exactly how Claire remembered them. Although today, they sparkled with tears. Her hand came up to cover her mouth, her shoulders shaking with silent sobs.

No one spoke. Claire stood frozen to the spot. Memories of the day she wrote the fateful text message ending their friendship came flooding back. Joanna was a loyal friend, and if she'd known Claire had been in trouble, she would've done anything to help her.

Ryan had demanded Claire end their friendship a week after they were married. She could still hear his cold, hate-filled tone. Her hand came up of its own accord and fingered the scar on her neck, hidden by her hair. Ryan had threatened her life that day, and it was the only reason she'd sent the message. It had been the hardest thing she'd ever done.

A tear slid down her cheek, jolting her back to reality.

Joanna jumped out of her seat. "Claire? Oh, my god."

Still unable to move, Claire almost lost her balance when Joanna's full body weight slammed into her, embracing her in a rib-breaking hug.

Joanna broke away and held Claire at arms' length. "Claire, what are you doing here? Where's Ryan? Why did you never reply? What did I do? Please, you have no idea—" Tears ran down her freckled cheeks, her eyes searching Claire's as though they held answers to her questions.

Claire's breathing turned irregular, and her hands trembled. Panic bubbled up inside, and her throat grew thick and dry. Sensing the curious gazes from Michael and Norman didn't help. She had to leave. Immediately. As she backed away, Joanna's hands fell to her sides.

"I'm sorry," Claire whispered, "I can't—" Shaking her head she turned, ran out the main door and upstairs to her room.

Chapter 9

No one spoke. Michael turned to Norman, who shrugged.

What was that all about?

Joanna stood with her shoulders slumped in defeat. Norman made the first move, approaching his wife and placing an arm across her shoulders.

"Do you know Claire?"

She sniffled and nodded, wiping her eyes with the back of her hand. "We were friends years ago." She shook her head as though ridding herself of a memory. "One day she said we couldn't be friends anymore. I never found out why." She looked across at Michael and gave an apologetic smile. "I'm sorry, Mick. You don't need to see me break down."

He smiled and waved a dismissive hand. "It's okay. I'm sorry if this is intruding, but you mentioned the name 'Ryan' before. Who is he?"

Michael was sure he knew the answer, but he needed confirmation. Perhaps he shouldn't ask, it wasn't any of his business after all, but he couldn't stop himself.

"Her husband," Joanna replied. "Well, if she's here alone, then maybe he's her ex now. I don't know. It wasn't long after they married we lost contact."

Michael drew in a sharp breath. *I knew it.*

"People often lose contact when they marry, honey." Norman ran his hands up and down her arms. "I'm sure you don't keep in contact with all of your friends."

"No, of course not, but this was different." She shook her head again. "Anyway, don't worry about me. I should talk to her." She turned to Michael. "Where's her room?"

"Upstairs, first on the right."

She nodded and walked out the door.

Norman sat back down opposite Michael. "How are you finding Claire? Do you like her?"

The look Norman gave him had Michael rolling his eyes, recalling their conversation from the night of the gala.

Unsure how to answer, he settled for a diplomatic one. "She's a great nurse, flawless in fact."

Norman raised his eyebrows. "I sense a 'but' coming."

Michael shrugged. Harsh, depreciating words formed. Words he once would have said without thinking. But, he supposed, if the last week with Claire had taught him anything, it was that because Addison was bad didn't mean all women were. He tried to stop his cruel words from forming, as they sat on the tip of his tongue, taunting him.

He took a deep breath, swallowed the words he wanted to say, and pulled his shoulders back. "She's okay, I guess. The jury's still out."

Norman eyed him curiously and placed his hands on the table. "Just okay?" He grinned and pushed himself to a standing position, his chair scraping along the floor. "Coming from you, though, that's bloody high praise. She really must be something. I'm impressed." He stepped aside and pushed in his chair. "Right, I need to pick Juanita up from my parents' place." He laid a hand on Michael's shoulder. "Look, mate, I know what Addison did to you, and I know she hurt you badly, but you can't keep dissing other women because of it."

Michael held his arms out, meeting Norman's stern gaze. "Why the lecture? I didn't say anything."

"You didn't have to. I know you were thinking it. Don't even think it, okay?"

Michael looked into Norman's stern eyes and sighed. Of course, Norman was right. He'd always been a good mate, and never held back in giving Michael a good kick up the arse when he deserved it. And at that moment, he well and truly deserved it.

I'm definitely a work in progress.

Norman advanced to the door, ready to walk back toward town. He turned to Michael. "Tell Jo where I've gone, will you?"

Michael nodded but said nothing. Once his friend had left, Michael stood and paced the room. His mind went over the conversation a dozen times.

His thoughts were interrupted a few moments later when Joanna barged through the door, determination written on her face. "Do you have a rope?"

Michael frowned. "A rope?" He thought he'd heard wrong. When she nodded in response, he shook his head.

She sighed in exasperation. "How about a ladder? Something that will reach the top of the balcony?"

He ignored her question. "What exactly are you trying to do?"

"I'm trying to get into Claire's room so I can make her talk. That damn girl is still as stubborn as ever and won't talk to me. So, do you have a ladder?"

"I don't think this is a good idea. Claire obviously needs to come to terms with seeing you again."

Joanna looked at him incredulously. "*I'm* the victim here, Michael. *She* ended our friendship without any explanation. I have a right to see her."

"Jo, listen to yourself. This isn't like you. Since when were you the victim?"

She ran a hand through her short, dark brown hair and sighed. "It's…well, we were close, Mick. When she cut me off, I was devastated. Seeing her now brings everything back to the surface."

"I'm sure she had her reasons."

Nodding, she intertwined her fingers and stared out the door. "I know, and that's why I'm so desperate to talk to her."

"Maybe she needs time. It's bound to be a shock for her as much as it is for you."

Turning back to him, she offered him a small smile. "I know, you're right." She glanced at her watch. "I guess I should go. I need to pick up Juanita."

"Norman's already left, said he's doing it." He walked her to the door and slid it open.

Joanna cast a wistful look to the second storey and sighed.

An idea formed in his mind. "Tell you what, why don't you come around for dinner on Monday? It'll give you and Claire two days to come to terms with this. Maybe she'll be more willing to talk."

Jo smiled and kissed his cheek. "You're a good man, Mick. Thank you, that sounds wonderful. See you then."

With a quick wave, she turned and walked down the stairs and onto the beach. She and Norman lived a few streets closer to town, well within walking distance.

Once she was out of sight, Michael closed the door and turned back as Von reappeared from doing chores in the laundry.

"They gone already, love?" Von asked as she wiped down the table.

"Yeah. They came to see Mum, but she was sleeping."

"That's a shame. Why don't you get them around for dinner one night?"

He chuckled. "Funny you say that. I invited them over on Monday."

"Lovely, your Mum will love to see them again. I'll make sure I cook extra."

The sliding door opened, and Michael turned. Claire entered, her eyes puffy and bloodshot. His heart constricted. What'd happened between her and Joanna? Was it connected to Ryan? Having found out his connection to Claire, he'd bet his life on the fact that he was the abuser.

Claire offered a tight smile then disappeared to Mum's room with her head down. He wished he could do something to ease her pain. Help her somehow, but how? There was still a barrier between them. The only way to remove it once and for all was to clear the air and apologise. They'd pussyfooted around it long enough.

Von returned to work, and Michael sat at the table to wait for Claire. There was no time like the present. The moment she was free again, he'd pull her aside.

His phone rang, and he answered it. It was Lance telling him everything was okay—Addison's lawyer had talked Addison down, and she wasn't going to take legal proceedings. Michael thanked Lance and hung up, a smile stretching across his face. He'd dodged a bullet this time, but he'd remain on guard. Addison wasn't one to give up easily.

Still, he *would* be seeing Oscar in two weeks, and he couldn't be happier.

Did Claire like children? How would she react to having Oscar around? Was it wrong that he wanted her and Oscar to get on?

He shook the thoughts from his head and glanced at Mum's door, hoping Claire would exit so he could talk to her.

She didn't.

Tapping his fingers on the tabletop, he recalled the image of her coming out of the ocean earlier. He couldn't remember ever seeing such a stunning vision in his life. With water dripping off her, glinting in the afternoon sunlight, she looked so majestic. When she stopped in front of him and met his gaze, he'd forgotten how to breathe. Her blue-green eyes matched the colour of the ocean.

She'd always struggled to meet his gaze, fear always lingering, but it wasn't there today. He even had the chance to touch her without her flinching. This made his heart swell with pride. She was learning to trust him.

Somewhere in the last week he'd grown attracted to her. It wasn't appreciation and respect for her either. It was a full-blown romantic attraction. It came out of nowhere, but to his surprise, he welcomed it. The prison walls around his heart lowered some more. While he still didn't know Claire well, what he was confident of was that she *wasn't* Addison.

With that knowledge, more than ever, he wanted to hold Claire in his arms and feel her soft lips against his. He couldn't yet, though. He sensed she reciprocated his feelings, but he wouldn't rush it. She was fragile, and because trust had begun to grow, it didn't mean he could take advantage of it—or her. He wouldn't make a move unless he was one hundred per cent confident it was what she wanted too.

He snapped out of his thoughts when Claire exited Mum's room. *This is it. Time to apologise and prove I'm a half-decent human being.*

When Claire walked past the table, he opened his mouth to say something, but the words lodged in his throat. She stood with her back to him, shuffling through the medicine cupboard. Michael took the opportunity to piece together what he wanted to say.

She turned back again and began walking back to Mum's room. It was now or never.

He stood. "Uh…Claire?" The words flew off his tongue. He might've used her name to introduce her to Joanna and Norman before, but it was the first time he'd used it to address her. It rolled off so naturally too. Why had he struggled to say it before now?

She came to an abrupt halt and turned to him, shock marring her features. "Yes?"

"Um…I was…uh…wondering if…" He rubbed the back of his neck. He prided himself on always knowing what to say and saying it confidently. This day he prattled away like an idiot. Taking a deep breath, he blurted, "I was wondering if you were okay."

She stared at him for a long moment, her brow creased in confusion.

This is what happens when you leave it too long. She doesn't know how to react.

He was tempted to keep talking and throw in the apology, but he held off. *I want her to know I'm genuinely worried about her.*

Claire broke out into a sunny smile, washing away the shock and confusion on her face.

She's so beautiful.

"I'm fine," Claire said, "thanks for asking Mr Kar—uh, I mean, Michael."

Her soft voice speaking his name sent waves of pleasure over him. His heart skipped in a manner he hadn't experienced in years. This was a major turning point, only the simple use of each other's names had broken the invisible barrier. It shattered around their feet, exposing their vulnerabilities.

Claire's cheeks reddened, and she hid her face behind her hair. He had an insane urge to stride up to her and tilt her face so he could look into those stunning blue-green depths.

When she looked up at him again, their gazes met and held. A heartbeat passed, and Michael remembered the first time they met. He'd been attracted to her even then but hadn't realised it. Or perhaps he couldn't bring himself to admit it? He didn't know. In the past week, a lot had changed, and it was all because of her. They'd barely spoken yet her presence had eased his bitterness and made him want to be a better man.

His eyes flicked to her lips, then back up to her eyes again. Her chest heaved up and down. Did she feel it too? Oh, how he wished he could scoop her into his arms and ravish her with kisses, prove to her he wasn't like the bastard who hurt her.

The temptation was too much. Michael was the first to look away. If he didn't, he wouldn't be able to trust himself and the last thing he wanted to do was scare her off.

"I'm sorry for causing a scene." Claire's soft voice drifted across the room and caressed him like the warm ocean breeze outside. "It was very unprofessional of me. It won't happen again."

Before he could say anything, she turned and disappeared into Mum's room. He raked a hand through his hair and released a long, slow breath. If only she knew he didn't think of it as 'causing a scene'. If only she knew he cared and he was worried about her. There were *so* many things he wanted to say but couldn't. Maybe one day he'd be able to.

Chapter 10

Claire disappeared into Daphne's room, medication in hand, tumultuous emotions raging through her veins. Still disoriented from seeing Joanna followed by what'd occurred in the kitchen, she stumbled over to the chair and collapsed into it. With Daphne still asleep, she put the medication on the bedside cupboard and rested her head in her hands.

Seeing Joanna had been a shock. In hindsight, Claire wished she hadn't panicked and asked to speak to her outside instead. Controlling the sudden influx of her emotions was an area that still needed work. She only hoped Joanna would listen next time they saw each other. If there was a next time.

Claire's heart ached. How she hoped they would see each other again. It was time to apologise and tell Joanna everything. Try and go back to where they left off. She was the only true friend Claire had ever had. Sending that text message was her biggest regret. She'd do anything to take it back. Since she couldn't, she'd do anything else to make up for it.

As for Michael...

Oh, how so much had changed in such a short time. It seemed the simple use of their names allowed the chemistry to roam freely, enveloping them, drawing them closer together. She didn't miss his eyes flicking to her lips, desire and want flashing in them. Rather than sending her into a panic, she found herself *wanting* to kiss him. How could she be experiencing such emotions? Only a week ago she couldn't imagine being with another man...now this.

She sat up straight and breathed slowly and deeply, calming her racing heart. She needed to keep her mind off it for a while. Standing, she made her way to the window and opened the curtains. The ocean glimmered like thousands of diamonds in the afternoon sunlight. As she opened the window, a balmy breeze wafted into the room.

Daphne had enjoyed a good run of health for a few days after Claire's arrival. Daphne had joined them for every meal and visited the beach for an hour every day. There were even times she stayed up later than usual to watch a movie.

Unfortunately, over the last few days, Daphne's health deteriorated. The only way she was able to enjoy the sunshine and the ocean was from the confines of her bed. Claire recognised the signs—Daphne was lacking in energy and her pain was increasing. Claire had called the doctor in, who ran some tests, but it didn't take a genius to figure out the cancer had spread.

Tearing her gaze from the window, Claire turned back to the bed. Daphne began to stir, so Claire helped her into a sitting position. After Daphne had taken her medication, Claire helped her to the bathroom. On the way back, a knock sounded at the bedroom door. Once Daphne was comfortable in bed, Claire answered, surprised to see the doctor there. He wasn't due for a couple of days.

His grave face gave it away though—he wasn't there for a social visit.

"Doctor Charlton." Claire forced a smile. "We weren't expecting you."

He returned the same forced smile. "Good day, Claire." He ran a hand through his thinning, grey hair. "I thought I'd pop by with the test results."

The look in his green eyes confirmed it wasn't good news. Claire gave a single nod then stood back and let him in. She poked her head outside to search for Michael, since he liked to be in the room when Doctor Charlton visited, but he wasn't there. He must've gone out.

She closed the door and turned back as Doctor Charlton stopped at Daphne's bed, giving her a beaming smile. Claire had met him a couple of times and liked him. He was professional but also had a way about him that put everyone at ease.

"Hello there, Daphne. You're looking younger and younger every time I see you." He lowered his tall frame into the seat next to her.

Daphne's weak laugh held no humour. "If only that were true, Doctor. To what do I owe this visit? I presume you're not here to tell me my cancer is gone and I'm going to live another thirty years."

Claire walked over to the bed and stood next to it, waiting for his response.

Doctor Charlton clasped his hands together. "I'm afraid not, Daphne. Your test results show your cancer has spread much faster than I originally estimated. A few weeks ago I said you had six months left to live. After these results—" He cleared his throat.

"Say it, Doctor," Daphne said when it became clear he was struggling with his words.

Claire reached for Daphne's hand and grasped it firmly. She was terrified of the outcome despite knowing deep down what it was. Even though she'd vowed not to get emotionally involved, with Daphne, it was impossible. She was so likeable, and Claire cared for her a great deal. The reality of her death sent a dagger through her heart.

"I'm sorry, Daphne," Doctor Charlton finally said, "but your results show you have a month left at most. The cancer is aggressive and has reached your lungs. There's nothing we can do to slow it down."

Claire turned cold. Doctor Charlton ran his shaky hands down his face. A solemn silence fell over them. Claire felt Daphne squeeze her hand, but no one spoke.

Claire took a couple of deep breaths while she focused on digesting the information. She squeezed her eyes tight to stop the tears from falling.

"Oh, dear," Daphne finally said. "Oh, dear me."

Claire opened her eyes again. Daphne held her free hand to her chest and shook her head from side to side, tears dripping down her cheeks. It was bad enough knowing she had six months left to live. Now it had reduced...how could anyone cope with that?

"Daphne, I'm so sorry," Doctor Charlton said. "I wish I could've come bearing better news..." he shrugged.

When Claire glanced across at him, there were tears in his eyes. It was apparent he too was very close to Daphne. Who wouldn't be?

Claire let go of Daphne's hand and reached for a tissue on the bedside cupboard. She handed it to Daphne, who used it to wipe away her tears.

Once she'd regained control, Daphne released a bitter laugh. "This was always my fate, Doctor. The moment you told me the cancer had reached my lymph nodes, I knew there'd never be better news. It was only a matter of time until I heard the worst."

Doctor Charlton patted her hand. "It still pains me to tell you this. The next few weeks won't be easy on you. I'll increase your dosage of medication—"

Daphne held up a shaky hand. "Please, no. If it's not going to save my life, what's the point?"

Before the doctor could respond, Claire spoke, "Daphne, I explained when I first started here, you would be in excruciating pain if it wasn't for the medication. As the cancer worsens, so will the pain. This is why the dosage needs increasing."

Daphne huffed. "I don't care."

"Daphne, please think carefully about this," Claire went on. "We can't force you to do anything, but all I ask is you think of those close to you."

Turning to look at Claire, Daphne said, "My dear girl, they're all I've thought about since I was first diagnosed. I'd rather suffer for a shorter time than prolong their suffering. If I refuse the extra medication, I'll die sooner."

A lump formed in Claire's throat. No one should ever want to die. What made it worse was hearing Daphne's begging tone. Claire opened her mouth to respond but couldn't find the words. Daphne wasn't asking them to euthanise her. She was only saying she didn't want her medication increased. It was the doctor's job to recommend it, but he couldn't enforce it.

Claire looked across at Doctor Charlton, who shrugged.

"Okay then." Doctor Charlton stood. "If this is what you wish, I respect that. But be warned, your pain will worsen."

Daphne smiled sadly and nodded. "I'm very aware of that, Doctor."

"If you change your mind, tell Claire and she'll get in touch with me. Now, I must be going. Continue with your usual medication, and I'll call back Wednesday."

"Thank you," Daphne said with a small smile.

When the doctor walked past the bed, he gestured for Claire to follow him. They walked out, and he shut the door behind them. The first thing Claire noticed was Von scrubbing the table more than required and Michael pacing back and forth. He was dressed in jogging gear, explaining his earlier whereabouts.

"Daphne's pain is going to get much worse." Doctor Charlton kept his voice low. "Keep a strict eye on her. If it becomes unbearable, contact me. I'm sure we can talk some sense into her once the news has sunk in. I don't like not increasing her dosage."

Claire nodded. "I'll try and talk her around."

"I'll tell them on the way out." He inclined his head to Von and Michael.

"Thanks, Doctor."

They said their goodbyes and Claire went back to Daphne who sat motionless in bed, staring wistfully out the window. Claire sat in the chair and folded her hands in her lap. What could she say to make this better? Nothing, that's what. Here was a dying woman, and no one could do a damn thing about it.

"How are you?" Claire asked softly.

Daphne blinked but never removed her gaze from the view outside. Her hands were entwined and her she had a crestfallen look on her face. Her shoulders shook, and tears dripped down her cheeks in large drops. Her head fell forward, and the sounds of sobbing filled the room.

Claire moved from the chair to the bed and placed an arm across Daphne's shoulders. For a few moments, she sat there rubbing Daphne's arm while she cried. There were no suitable words. Nothing could fix the physical and emotional pain Daphne was experiencing.

At one point Von came in with a cup of tea for Claire and Daphne, her cheeks streaked with tears. She left quickly.

The tea sat untouched.

Claire fell apart inside, but somehow, she had no idea how, she kept a composed exterior. This was so difficult. In all her years as a nurse, she'd learnt to switch off emotion. It was the only way she could cope. Be professional, don't get attached. That was the mindset she had when she started this job, but Daphne had blindsided her. She was so damn likeable it was impossible to fight the attachment. If Claire had known this would happen, she probably wouldn't have taken it. Then again, she couldn't imagine Daphne not being in her life. Or Von for that matter.

Or Michael.

She shivered. Well, that was unexpected.

Daphne's soft, lifeless voice cut through her thoughts. "Oh, Claire, what am I to do?"

Claire's heart shattered into a million pieces.

It's times like this I hate being a nurse.

Taking a deep breath, she said, "Live every day to the fullest. Spend time with those close to you. Make new memories."

Daphne stared at her with dark, lifeless eyes. A chill ran down Claire's spine. What if Daphne gave up? There'd be no chance of her surviving the month. She may not even get to see her grandson again.

"How am I supposed to do that?" Daphne's tone was cold and hard. "Look at me." She gestured to herself then ripped off her bandana to display a head of short, patchy, grey hair. "How am I supposed to enjoy my days when I look like this? What's the point in making new memories when I'm not going to remember them? And why would anyone want to remember me looking like this?"

The emotional change in Daphne shouldn't have been a surprise, but it was. She'd always been so composed, so calm. Seeing this side of her was unexpected.

Claire reached for Daphne's hand, but she ripped it away. "They love you, Daphne." Claire placed her hands in her lap instead. "They don't care about any of that. All they want is to spend every moment with you."

"Then why aren't they in here? If they care so much, they'd be in here now wouldn't they?"

"It's only because I'm in here. They'll come in as soon as I'm done."

"Well, leave then." Daphne threw a glare in Claire's direction. "I'd rather spend what's left of my time on this earth with family, not some senseless nurse."

Claire's chest tightened, and tears stung her eyes. The words hit her like daggers. She shouldn't have been offended. Daphne was upset, but it stung like hell. *This is why getting close to patients is a bad idea.*

Forcing a smile, Claire nodded and stood. *I must be professional. This should never have got so personal in the first place.*

"I'll send Michael in," Claire said while fluffing up Daphne's covers and pillows. "Do you need anything?"

When she looked up, there was a flash of guilt in Daphne's eyes, but it didn't last long before being replaced with anger. She shook her head and looked away.

Claire nodded and stood back. Spotting the cups of tea on the cupboard, she asked, "How about a sip of tea?"

"No." Daphne jutted her chin out.

Claire picked up one of the cups. "It'll help you feel better."

"I said no."

Taking a step forward, Claire moved the cup closer to Daphne. "One sip, please. You need to—"

Daphne's arm came flying up and knocked the cup out of Claire's hands. Claire jumped back with a gasp, the lukewarm tea splattering across her shirt and Daphne's bedcovers. The cup shattered on the far wall, the sound sending her heart racing.

The door burst open, and Michael rushed into the room. "What's going on?" He looked from Claire to his mother.

Claire clasped her trembling hands together, taking deep, shallow breaths. It was no easy feat to remain calm. Daphne looked away and didn't respond. Claire avoided the question by crouching to clean up.

She sensed Michael moving around her, probably to his mother's side.

Picking up the pieces of china, her hands shook so badly they kept falling back to the floor. Tears blurred her vision, and when she went to pick up a shard again, she sliced the skin on her palm. Blinking away the tears, she breathed in through her teeth, dropping the pieces she was holding.

Cursing under her breath, she went to try again when drops of crimson appeared on the white carpet. She froze. *Oh god, not the carpet.* Icy fear clawed through her veins. How would Michael react? Or Von?

She bit her lip and swallowed back a sob. With nothing to wrap around her hand, she had no choice but to leave the china unattended. Standing, she held her good hand under the injured one to stop the blood from dripping any further. It was difficult because her hands wouldn't stop trembling.

Michael appeared by her side. "Mum's calmer now. I'm afraid she went into shock after the news. I'm sorry—" he looked down at her hand and gasped. "You're hurt. Are you okay?"

"I...I'm sorry." She looked down at the carpet, the splotches of crimson blurring through her unshed tears. "The china slipped. I didn't mean to get any on the carpet. I...I didn't mean for it to happen. I'll clean it up, I promise. It was an accident."

His intense gaze met hers, full of worry and sadness. "It's okay." He offered a consoling smile. "There's no harm done. Let me have a look at your hand."

He gently took it to inspect the cut. The moment his fingers touched her skin, chemistry bolted through her body. It was too much to handle in such a vulnerable state. She stepped back, holding her hand away from him. "Please don't touch me."

His eyes widened, but he nodded. "I'm sorry."

"Where's Von?"

Hurt flashed across his features, but he inclined his head toward the door. "In the kitchen."

Claire nodded and offered a smile of thanks. When she walked out, she chided herself for losing control. Daphne's reaction was purely due to shock.

Chapter 11

Michael raked a hand through his hair then let his arm fall to his side. His heart pounded at what felt like a million miles per hour.

Mum has so little time left. What am I going to do?

Even before now, he hadn't been able to come to terms with her diagnosis. Now, it kicked him in the gut so hard he couldn't breathe, could barely think. Mum's sobs echoed through the room, jerking him into action. He ignored the china and blood-stained carpet and joined her, sitting on the edge of the bed.

"Oh Michael." Mum's quaking voice broke his heart even more. "I'm not ready to die."

He had no words, no way to make this better. He placed an arm around her shoulder, and they cried together. Michael hadn't once cried since finding out Mum was terminal. He'd tried to be strong, but he couldn't anymore. Not after that devastating news.

What could he say? 'Oh, it's okay, it's one of those things. You'll get used to it.' Hell no. If he could go back in time and stop her getting sick, he'd do it in a heartbeat. But there was damn well nothing he could do, and he'd never felt so wretched in his life.

He moved back and wiped his eyes. Removing a tissue from the box by the bed, he handed it to Mum, who wiped away her tears. She stared at him with regret-filled eyes.

"Michael, I'm sorry I haven't been a very good mother." Her voice shook.

He jerked back and stared at her in disbelief. "What do you mean? You've been a great mother."

She shook her head, fresh tears trickling down her cheeks. "I should've worked harder at your father's and my marriage. Raising you without him wasn't fair on you."

Where is this coming from? He shook his head and reached for her hand. "Don't talk like that. I don't feel like I've missed out. Do you know how many kids I went to school with whose divorced parents bickered all the time over who'd have who and when? You and Dad never did that. I saw him every weekend without fail. You fairly divided the holidays so you'd both get the opportunity to spend time with me. You never questioned what he did or where he took me, and he didn't either. Honestly, it could've been much worse."

Mum's bottom lip trembled. "But didn't you wish we were together?"

A small smile tugged at his lips. "Of course I did, but you and Dad made sure I understood what was going on and I understood it wasn't possible."

She sighed deeply and shook her head. "There are so many things I wish I'd done differently. I should never have left your father. He did nothing wrong."

Michael squeezed her hand. "Mum, don't do this to yourself. What's done is done, you can't change that. It's time to let it go and enjoy what's left of your life."

She managed a small smile and patted his hand. "You're a good man, Michael. I couldn't wish for a better son." Her smile slipped, and her gazed drifted to the closed door. "I wish I could see your father one last time. I don't want to die without telling him how much he means to me."

A shudder ran through Michael's body, bringing hot tears to his eyes. It was so morbid. So real. How was he supposed to deal with this? When his bottom lip trembled, he pursed his lips together firmly. *Hold it together.*

He might not be able to stop Mum from dying, but he could make her wish come true. He leaned in and kissed her cheek. "I'll make it happen, Mum."

She didn't answer straight away, and when he turned to her, she had a relieved smile on her face. "Thank you, Michael." She took a deep breath and glanced at the door with a frown. "I'm sorry about earlier. Poor Claire." She shook her head. "I was so nasty to her."

Michael didn't know what'd happened. He'd come in after hearing the smash. What he did know was that whatever Mum had said or done wouldn't have held any meaning.

"You were in shock." He got to his feet. "She'll understand."

Mum shook her head vehemently. She said nothing but he knew she'd apologise before the day was out. He went over to the broken teacup and began cleaning it up. When he spotted the drops of blood on the carpet, his thoughts drifted to Claire. The terror on her face broke his heart. He wished he could hold her and tell her everything would be okay.

Shaking his head, he stood and made his way back out to the kitchen.

***

Claire drew in a sharp intake of breath when Von dabbed at the cut on her hand, the antiseptic seeping into the gash.

"I think this is going to need stitches," Von mused. "Maybe I should get Doctor Charlton to come back."

Claire inspected the cut, then shook her head. It stung like hell, but it wasn't that bad. "No, it'll be fine. There's no need for him to come back."

Von looked up. "Are you sure? It looks quite deep."

"I'm sure. It looks deeper than it is. The bleeding has already slowed down, so if you use a few strips of surgical tape, it'll do the same thing."

Von dug around in the first-aid kit sitting on the table next to her and pulled out what she needed. "Well if you're sure. You're the nurse, after all."

They shared a smile, and Von cut off a piece of tape.

"How are you, Von?" Claire asked while Von concentrated on the task.

Von looked up and smiled sadly. "Oh you know, broken inside but putting on a brave face to keep Daphne's spirits up."

Claire used her free hand to squeeze Von's. "There's nothing wrong with breaking down from time to time."

"I know, dear. I do but usually in private."

"You know you can always talk to me, right? I know you haven't known me long, but I'm a good listener."

Von chuckled as she wiped away some blood. "I appreciate that, love. And for the record, having only known you for a week means nothing. You're like family to me."

Claire's cheeks glowed. Before she could respond, Michael exited Daphne's room. He placed the broken pieces of china in the bin then turned back and gave her a reassuring smile. She looked away, not used to seeing this side of him. In Daphne's bedroom, he'd been so attentive…so caring. He wasn't at all like Ryan.

He stopped at the table. "Is your hand okay, Claire?"

In her periphery, she didn't miss Von's smile. Was it because of how easily Michael used her name after all this time?

Claire looked up at him and offered a shy smile. "Yes, fine, thank you. I'm sorry again for—"

He shook his head. "Please don't apologise. It's not a problem." He looked to Von and asked, "Von, do you have anything to remove blood from carpet?"

Claire sucked in a breath. She hadn't mentioned the carpet yet. Von didn't seem the type to overreact, but it was instinct to fear the worst.

"Yes, I do." Von placed the items she was holding on the table and stood. "I must get to it immediately though. It can be difficult to remove if left unattended. Can you take over what I'm doing here, Michael?"

Claire's stomach lurched. "I'm sure I can do the rest."

Von gave her a curious look. "Don't be silly. He's not going to bite." She chuckled then moved away from the table and briefly explained to Michael what she'd been doing.

I don't think I'm ready for this sort of closeness.

When Michael took Von's seat a few seconds later, his knee brushed Claire's, and her heart raced. She took slow, deep breaths to ease the anxiety. Moving her hand away, she held it close to her chest.

When Michael had himself sorted, he looked across at her and smiled. "I can't do this if you keep your hand to yourself."

She tried to smile in response, but it felt more like a grimace. This was her chance to escape. He didn't have to finish the job. She kept a first aid kit in her room for emergencies, which had everything she needed. It would be awkward, but she'd manage.

She bit her lip. She'd come this far in not being afraid around Michael. Why go backwards now? Slowly she moved her hand back to the table and spread it out. To anyone else, it would be a small accomplishment, but to her, it was huge.

Michael peered at her hand. "That looks nasty." He looked back up at her with a frown. "Are you sure these strips will be enough to hold it together?"

Claire's shoulders slackened, and her breathing began to regulate. "Yes, they'll be fine. It looks worse than it is."

His frown deepened. "You're sure?"

She nodded.

He took a deep breath. "Okay, then."

He picked up a piece of tape Von had previously cut and stuck it in place. Claire jumped. Every time he touched her, he left her skin scorching. His touch was gentle, his skin soft. Considering his career, Claire thought it would be calloused.

He looked at her with worry-filled eyes. "Are you okay?" He grabbed another piece of tape. "I didn't mean to hurt you."

He said the words with such sincerity. "No, it's okay." She relaxed some more. "I'm afraid I don't handle pain well." This was a lie, but she didn't know how else to explain away her behaviour.

He raised a questionable eyebrow. "How do you manage to be a nurse then?"

"I'm not the one experiencing the pain."

As soon as the words came out, Claire gasped. *Talk about inappropriate.* She opened her mouth to apologise when Michael erupted into laughter. She'd never heard him laugh so heartily before. It was a soothing and comforting sound. The mood had grown cold since Doctor Charlton's visit, but Michael's laughter brought some life and happiness back into the room.

"I'm sorry," Claire said. "I probably shouldn't have said that."

Michael shook his head and stuck another piece of tape down. "No need to be sorry. I'd never thought of it in that way."

With the last piece of tape in place, Michael dabbed at the cut to remove any excess blood. The tension left Claire's body, and she breathed easier.

Sticking the last bit of tape in place, Michael sat back in his chair. "Now what?"

Pointing, she said, "Place that pad there on top of the cut then bandage it."

He nodded and proceeded to do so.

When the bandage was clipped in place, Claire spoke. "Thank you, I appreciate your help."

Michael smiled. "You're welcome." His eyes gained an intent look when he added, "Claire, I owe you an apology."

Her breath caught. Their gazes met, and she saw nothing but sincerity in his. On the first day she met him, there was a coldness in his eyes, but it'd disappeared.

"Me too." She didn't break the gaze. "I suppose we started off on the wrong foot."

He looked away and winced. "Yes, I suppose we did. But the way I spoke to you was out of line." He looked back at her again, his brow knitted in concern. "I hope you won't hold it against me. I formed the wrong opinion of you, and I'm sorry."

She shrugged. "I'm afraid I did the same thing, and I'm sorry too. Perhaps we can start over?"

"I'd like that." He grinned then held out his hand. "Michael Karalis, local mechanic, divorcé and somewhat a bitter man."

Claire arched an eyebrow and accepted his hand using her good one. "Nothing like being honest."

He smirked and gave her hand a firm shake. "I figured it might help you understand why I'm sometimes a little hard to get on with."

Their gazes met again. Time stood still. Michael didn't let go of her hand. At that moment in time, they were the only two people in the world.

"Well if we're doing that," Claire said with a tremble, "I suppose I should be equally as honest. Claire Stone, live-in nurse, also a divorcée, and an extremely bitter and untrusting woman."

We have more in common than I realised.

Michael's gaze softened and connected with hers. "Thank you, Claire."

He still didn't let go of her hand. Instead, his thumb made small circles along the skin, sending her pulse skyrocketing. The pounding of her heart echoed in her ears. Chemistry buzzed around them, caressing, hinting, encouraging. She half expected a pang of fear to bubble forth, but it didn't.

Despite her best efforts, her fear still had a stranglehold on her when she left Adelaide, but after a week in Busselton, it'd disappeared for good. Now she'd come to know a man who wasn't Ryan. A man she was interested in romantically. Someone special.

Was he her new future? It was too soon to answer, but what she did know was that she wanted to find out.

Michael shuffled to the edge of his seat, his knee brushing hers again. Her breathing hitched, and her body trembled. Rather than warning bells going off, waves of pleasure washed over her. Without realising it, she found herself shuffling forward too.

Michael let go of her hand, but he leaned closer and cupped her cheek. Her eyes fluttered closed, and she leaned into his touch. How could this be happening? The trembling in her body increased, but it wasn't from fear. Neither of them spoke, but chemistry crackled around them.

"Claire?"

Her eyes open and clashed with Michael's vibrant ones, staring at her so intently she felt like the most important woman on the earth.

"Yes?" Her voice was a whisper.

His thumb ran over her cheek, his eyes questioning. "Why are you trembling?"

She blinked. How could she answer that? "I don't know." Perhaps it was simply because this was foreign territory.

Michael's brow creased. "You're not afraid of me, are you?"

To her surprise, she didn't even have to think about it. "No."

The worry lines on his face cleared and he broke out into a brilliant smile. "You have no idea how much that means to me."

He moved his hand to the back of her neck, caressing it. He leaned in so close now, and his warm breath fanned her face. Was he going to kiss her? Did she want him to?

Yes.

Pulse racing, her lips parted in anticipation, her breathing irregular. Michael leaned in further and placed a kiss on her cheek. Then the other. Her head spun, a soft whimper escaping from the back of her throat.

Michael pulled back, his eyes capturing hers in silent question. Could he kiss her? She gave a single nod in response, surprised at how much she wanted this. He leaned in again, and this time his soft lips pressed against hers. It was a whisper of a kiss. Tentative. Questioning. Safe. But it was enough to send her heart racing so fast, she feared it'd jump out of her chest.

When Michael pulled away, his eyes capturing hers once more, she craved more of his lips. Wanted to experience them fully in a heart-stopping, nothing-held-back kiss. But deep down she knew she wasn't ready and she appreciated that he didn't push her. His silent question was proof of that. It was better this way.

Michael opened his mouth to speak, but the moment shattered when Von came out of Daphne's bedroom. Michael sent her an apologetic smile and sat back. Disappointment threatened to wash over her but didn't get a chance to. The memory alone of his lips on hers was enough to push it away.

Von stopped at the table, oblivious to what'd transpired. "Claire, Daphne wishes to see you."

Recalling their last encounter, Claire's heightened state dimmed. A flutter of apprehension came to life in her chest. Pushing her worries aside, she smiled in thanks then stood and walked away. Daphne was a suffering, sick woman, and Claire couldn't blame her for her actions.

When she entered the room, Daphne was sitting up in bed with a book. Compared to an hour earlier, she'd perked up a lot.

The bedcovers were replaced, and the mess cleared up. Von had done a remarkable job removing the blood. There was no reminder of what'd occurred. *Well, apart from my clothes.* She looked down at her blue shirt and cringed at the brown stain, not having had time to change.

Claire cleared her throat to announce her presence, and Daphne's head snapped up. The guilt in her eyes told Claire she felt bad for her earlier outburst.

"How are you feeling?" Claire stopped at the foot of the bed and shuffled from foot to foot. There were no tasks for her to undertake unless Daphne had a request.

Daphne shrugged and placed her book on the bed. "Better, I suppose, considering the circumstances."

"I'm very sorry for your news, Daphne."

"No." Daphne shook her head vigorously. "I don't want to hear 'sorry' anymore. This has been my fate for a long time."

"Perhaps, but it's still news you don't want to hear."

A silence fell upon them. For the first time since starting the job, Claire didn't know what to say or do. When her nurse duties finished, she'd often sit with Daphne and talk. Today she was hesitant about doing so. She picked up the clipboard and scanned over it. Of course, nothing had changed, but it made her feel like she was doing something useful.

There was only one question she needed to ask. Now that Daphne had come to terms with the news, the words needed saying.

"Are you still firm in your resolve not to have your medication increased?"

Multiple emotions flittered across Daphne's face—anger, frustration, uncertainty—but in the end, defeat settled in place. "I don't want those close to me to suffer," she said, sounding dejected, "but I don't want to be in chronic pain either." She gave a sad smile. "I've never had a high tolerance for pain. Is that very selfish of me?"

"Of course not. No one would think it selfish. No one wants to see you suffer."

"I suppose I have to stop being stubborn then, right?" Daphne winked, and the awkwardness in the room eased.

"Yes, I'm afraid you do," Claire said with a laugh. "I can't force you to take the higher dosage, but I recommend it, and so does Doctor Charlton."

Daphne turned her gaze to the window and in a defeated tone, said, "Then do it."

Claire breathed a sigh of relief. "This is for no one's benefit but your own, Daphne. You have to be as comfortable as possible."

Daphne nodded but said nothing.

"I'll ring Doctor Charlton now," Claire said after a moment's silence.

She turned and walked away. When she reached the door, Daphne called her name. She turned back to her. "Yes?"

"I'm very sorry for my outburst earlier. There was no excuse for it."

"You were in shock. You had every excuse."

Daphne shook her head. "No, I disagree. It was out of character for me, and I feel terrible. I hope I haven't offended you."

"Of course not." Claire meant it. It was a shock at the time, but she understood.

Relief crossed Daphne's face. "Thank you, Claire. Now when you've called the good doctor, would you mind too much taking me to the beach? I feel I'm capable of spending a few hours outside today. It'll do me good."

Claire nodded her acceptance. "I'm more than happy to. I'll be back soon."

Chapter 12

Michael pushed himself out from under the car he'd been working on and stood, stretching his back. It'd been a dull morning at the garage, as only a handful of jobs were booked in. Between him and Norman, they were up to date.

"I'm heading off for lunch," Norman said, entering the garage. "You want to join me?"

"Sure, I'll wash my hands."

As he scrubbed at his blackened hands with abrasive soap, Michael's thoughts drifted to Claire. Since their brief kiss two days earlier, he'd struggled to think of anything else. Even Mum's impending death didn't suffocate him like it once did. It was like Claire took the pain away.

He wanted nothing more than to kiss her again, properly this time. The fact she'd let him kiss her at all was a huge feat and he'd purposely held back from trying again. He couldn't wait much longer, though. Those soft, pink lips were on his mind all day every day.

While their talk had mended the rift between them, she'd now become painfully shy around him. Every time he spoke to her and held eye contact for the briefest second, her cheeks would turn a violent red, and she'd look away. He found it adorable but wished he could help her not be so awkward.

He wanted to encourage her to open up to him, to trust that he wouldn't hurt her, but he didn't want to push either. Knowing she wasn't ready to talk to him, he'd finally confided in Mum the day before, telling her of his suspicions. She promised she'd get Claire to talk.

Turning the taps off, Michael smiled to himself. Mum could draw blood from a stone. She'd get Claire to talk, no doubt about it.

He wiped his hands on the hand towel then he and Norman left the garage and took a right at the footpath. Riley's Burger Place was *the* takeaway hotspot in Busselton, not only because it had a perfect location in the main street, but it also had a one-hundred-year reputation of 'the best, mouth-watering burgers in the country', as was splashed across the sign hanging on the veranda.

It'd gone midday when Michael and Norman stepped inside, so the mad rush hadn't begun. They placed their orders then stood out of the way for other customers who'd started to arrive. While Norman took a call from Joanna, Michael checked his emails. When Addison's name popped up, his stomach dropped. She was the last person he wanted to deal with right now.

He tapped on the email, and his heart became a lead weight in his chest when he read her one sentence.

You can't have Oscar these school holidays.

Michael slapped his hand against his thigh and stormed out of the shop to call her. "What do you mean I can't have Oscar?" he demanded the moment Addison answered.

"I thought it was quite clear."

"There has to be a reason."

"You know I don't want him flying alone yet, Michael. He's only five."

He groaned. They'd gone over this so many times and had agreed for Addison's eighteen-year-old niece, Kristen, to fly with him.

"What happened to Kristen?"

Michael would normally fly to New Zealand to see Oscar, but after learning Mum had little time left, he had to make the heart-wrenching decision not to travel this time. When he spoke to Addison about it, the rare occasion she was reasonable, they both agreed for Kristen to fly with him since they both trusted her.

"She's going to England for six weeks," Addison said nonchalantly.

"England? She knew she'd have to accompany Oscar, didn't she?"

Addison hesitated. "No. I hadn't told her yet. She's recently graduated from high school, Michael. It's a graduation gift from Mikayla and me. She flies out tomorrow."

Michael's grip on the phone tightened. *Graduation gift*? His chest heaved up and down. It was no easy task keeping his cool.

"A *graduation* gift? You demand money from me, even though I pay maintenance and yet you can afford to pay for a trip overseas? This isn't on, Addison."

He'd had enough of Addison's controlling. It'd taken him too long to get to this point, and he wasn't giving up without a fight. Oscar was his son, and he *would* see him, one way or another.

"Don't play that card," Addison argued. "You got me pregnant, and it's your duty to pay for anything else our son needs."

Michael laughed bitterly. "We've been through this a dozen times, Addison. You know exactly what our court agreement states. It's high time you stopped ignoring it."

The court agreement between Michael and Addison was nothing out of the ordinary. It stated Michael was required to pay child support, which he did, but they each had to cover their expenses when Oscar was in either of their care. A clause Addison ignored at leisure, which was why she came to him for more.

Addison scoffed. "He's your son. If you *honestly* cared, you'd be willing to pay extra."

Michael ran a hand through his hair. Norman appeared holding two Styrofoam containers. He inclined his head toward the garage and started walking. Michael followed.

"Don't do this to me." It took all of Michael's willpower to keep his voice calm. "I don't appreciate you blackmailing me. I love my son, and I'm happy to provide for him, but it's only fair we both pay our individual expenses."

Addison's sigh was audible. "This is a pointless argument, Michael. Unless you can make arrangements to see Oscar, you can't have him these holidays. End of story."

"Fine, I will." Michael ended the call and shoved the phone in his jeans pocket.

When they reached the garage, he stopped and ran his hands down his face. Slumping against the wall, he closed his eyes and took a couple of deep breaths. Speaking to Addison sapped every last ounce of energy. He hated that she always managed to have the upper hand.

"You okay, man?"

Michael's eyes snapped open at Norman's voice. He thought he'd gone inside already.

"Fine," Michael snapped, standing up straight. "Let's have lunch."

He strode inside and made his way to the kitchen in a small room at the back of the garage. He lowered himself into the chair, then rested his elbows on the table and placed his head in his hands. *Is it too much to ask for a quiet and happy life?*

The smell of food made his stomach rumble. He lifted his head and looked into the concerned eyes of his friend.

"You can't let a Riley's burger go to waste," Norman said with a smile.

Michael returned a weak smile and opened the container. He could never resist a burger even when boiling over with anger. For a few moments they ate in silence, Michael mulling over the conversation with Addison.

Norman's voice interrupted his thoughts. "I can only presume it was Addison on the phone."

Michael took another bite of his burger and nodded. Once he'd swallowed, he said, "Oscar's due to arrive on Saturday. I couldn't go to NZ this time, so we'd planned for Kristen to fly out with him. She's holidaying there at the moment and was supposed to leave the same day as Oscar. Now Addison's saying Kristen can't do it as she's going overseas."

Norman scoffed. "Sounds bloody convenient if you ask me."

Michael looked up in surprise. "What makes you say that?"

"Come on, mate, you had this all planned. Is it possible Addison did this on purpose so she could try and stop you from seeing Oscar?"

He'd been so overcome with anger, it hadn't crossed his mind. "She did say she and Mikayla organised it as a school graduation gift. Kristen leaves tomorrow apparently, probably flying out from Auckland to save backtracking to Australia." He shrugged.

Norman's face turned dark, and he shook his head in disgust. "See what I mean? Bloody convenient. Kristen graduated last year, nearly a year ago now, I remember you telling me."

How had Michael forgotten that? Losing his appetite, he placed his half-eaten burger down and pushed the container away. "I hadn't thought of that." He sighed and slumped down in his chair. "What should I do, Norm? I can't not see my son, but I can't go over there either. I can't leave Mum for two weeks. She's only got a month left to live." He shook his head vehemently. "No, I can't do it, and I know how much she wants to see Oscar again."

Norman, who was midway through taking a bite of his burger, stopped and put it down. His face paled. It was only then Michael realised he hadn't told him of the latest diagnosis.

"Shit, I'm sorry mate," Michael said. "I forgot to tell you. We only found out after you and Jo left on Saturday. As I'm sure you can imagine, it's been a bit of a shock."

"Crikey, mate, I'm sorry."

"So am I. The doc says the cancer has reached her lungs."

"How's she coping?"

Michael reached for a napkin and started shredding it. "Surprisingly well considering. You know what she's like. She had a meltdown when she found out, but it's to be expected."

Norman shook his head, and he too pushed his food away. "Bloody hell, I don't know what to say."

"There's nothing to say. We have to face the inevitable truth."

They both stared at their hands, the remainder of the food sitting untouched. A lump formed in Michael's throat. Since finding out, Mum had kept on a happier face than normal. Michael wanted to scream and throw things, but it wouldn't solve anything.

Why is life so damn unfair?

His thoughts were interrupted by the bell at the front counter. Norman got to his feet and went out to greet the customer. After binning the lunch rubbish, Michael joined him, thankful for the diversion from his thoughts.

***

"Are you and Jo still on for dinner?" Michael asked as they packed up for the day.

"Wouldn't miss it, mate." Norman closed and locked up the small office. "You don't mind if we bring Juanita too, do you? We couldn't get hold of our babysitter."

"It's not a problem, you know we don't mind."

Michael exited into the late afternoon spring air. It'd been a warm day, a reminder that summer was only two weeks away. He turned and took in the surrounds. Located on the corner of the main street, and with petrol bowsers out the front, they were in an ideal location. The afternoon picked up from the morning, with a steady flow of customers.

Glancing at his watch, Michael tutted and turned back to the garage, poking his head inside. When he couldn't spot Norman, he called out, "Norm? You coming?"

Norman appeared from the back, wiping his hands on a rag. "I'm coming, I'm coming. Why the rush?"

Michael didn't answer, but the truth was, he was eager to see Claire.

His heart fluttered, and he released a shuddering breath. How was it possible he'd become so smitten so quickly? After the number Addison did on him, he'd been so against women for so long. Then Claire came along, trustworthy, honest and oh so likeable, and the bitterness ebbed away.

When Norman exited the garage, Michael pulled down the roller door and locked it. Together they turned and commenced their walk home. Michael lived within walking distance of the garage, so he rarely took his car to work unless the weather was bad. He'd stop at Norman's place, and the two of them walked to and from work together.

"How's Claire doing?" Norman asked as though reading Michael's thoughts. "Are you on speaking terms with her now?"

Since he didn't know exactly what was happening between him and Claire, he decided not to tell Norman what'd transpired yet.

"I suppose she's not so bad," he quipped with a smirk.

He could feel Norman's eyes boring holes into him. "You're serious?"

Michael chuckled and shrugged. "We talked the other day and cleared the air. I guess I can safely say I like her."

"Get outta here." Norman punched Michael's arm good-naturedly.

Michael threw his mate a wry grin.

"Wait a minute." Norman came to a stop and grabbed Michael's arm to stop him also. "This isn't a passing comment, Micky. This is *huge*."

Michael lowered his gaze and rubbed the back of his neck. The fact his best mate acted so surprised was proof of how much of a bastard Michael had been in the past. It was a hard pill to swallow, but he vowed to do better from now on. In such a short time, Claire had already changed him. Helped him see that because Addison broke him didn't mean every other woman would.

A heavy silence hung between them, but Michael didn't know what else to say. In the end, Norman huffed and asked, "Do you mean 'like' as in she's a nice woman and perhaps a good friend? Or 'like' as in something more?"

Michael wished he hadn't asked that. He wanted to tell him all about their sweet, albeit brief, kiss, but he couldn't. Not yet.

Deciding to be semi-honest, he looked up at his mate and shrugged. "There's a bit of something more there."

God, he felt like an awkward schoolboy all over again. All this talk of 'something more' rather than coming right out and saying, 'I fancy her'. Admitting it out loud was harder than it should be.

Norman's eyes widened, a slow smile spreading across his face. "That's great, Micky." When Michael winced, Norman narrowed his eyes. "It is great, isn't it? Or do you think she doesn't feel the same way?"

He was making this so hard. How much could he say?

Michael looked up at the clear sky and breathed out slowly. There was nothing wrong with confessing his feelings, was there? He didn't have to go into detail about the kiss.

Looking back at Norman, he said, "I'm sure she does, but it's complicated." Deciding it won't hurt to at least share his suspicions he added, "I've noticed some things, Norm. Her reaction to certain things, broken glass, being near men, clamming up about her private life."

"Well, the latter sounds a lot like you." Norman smiled then shrugged. "As for the rest, what are you thinking? Some people are nervous."

"Perhaps, but I think there's more to it."

Norman's smile slipped. "You're not thinking—" He looked around then lowered his voice. "You're not thinking abuse, are you?"

Michael kicked at a stone. "I'm certain. All the signs are there."

"I dunno, mate, this is a big assumption to make." Norman ran a hand over his head. "Has she hinted at anything?"

"Not as such, but like I said, it's obvious. Besides, I saw a scar the other day. It looked suspiciously like a stab wound." Saying the words out loud caused bile to rise in his throat. How had she survived that?

Norman's face paled. "Shit."

"I told Mum something was bothering Claire," Michael continued, "but I didn't go into detail. Maybe she'll figure it out."

Norman nodded but his brow knitted together in concern. "And you're afraid of scaring her off?"

Petrified is more like it. Michael nodded in response and cast his gaze down the street. Other shops were closing for the day, and the main street grew quieter by the second.

"Well, I think you need to spend some time with her. If what you say is true, you need to let her get to know you and vice versa. Prove to her you're not like that."

I would if she wasn't so shy around me now. He bit back a smile and started walking again, Norman following.

For a few moments, they walked in silence. When they turned onto Norman's street, Michael asked, "Did Jo mention anything about how she knew Claire?"

"Not a lot. Only that they used to be close friends and Claire ended their friendship."

"Why would anyone do that?" Michael mused.

"Who knows? These things happen, I suppose."

Michael hummed in response, certain that he actually knew the answer. He only hoped one day Claire learnt to trust him enough to confide in him. If she could do that, then he *could* prove he wouldn't hurt her. Hell, of course he wasn't a perfect husband in his first marriage, but he'd never once laid a finger on Addison. The idea of hurting anyone, especially a woman, made him sick to the stomach.

Norman came to a stop, breaking Michael out of his thoughts. Michael blinked a couple of times, realising they were in front of Norman's house.

"Okay, so we'll see you later?" Michael asked. "Six o'clock okay with you?"

Before Norman could answer, the front door swung open and five-year-old Juanita ran out. "Daddy. Daddy."

Norman turned around as Juanita ran into his legs and wrapped her arms around them, giggling excitedly. He picked her up and kissed her cheek. "Hello, princess. Have you had a good day?"

Her light brown pigtails bounced when she nodded. "I went to kindy, and I baked cookies."

"All by yourself?"

She frowned and shook her head. "No, the nice lady helped." She turned to look at Michael, giving him a beaming smile. "Hello, Uncle Michael."

"Hello, Juanita. Will I see you tonight?"

Juanita looked at Norman quizzically who whispered in her ear, then she nodded. "Dinner with Dappy."

When she was learning how to talk, she couldn't say Daphne so said Dappy instead. Even though she could say it now, the nickname stuck.

"Can we make it a quarter past six?" Norman asked.

Michael nodded. "See you then." He waved at Juanita. "See you, sweetie."

She waved her chubby hand erratically as he walked away. On the way home, Michael's thoughts drifted to Addison's call, and his shoulders slumped. There was no way he could visit New Zealand, but how else could he get Oscar out?

Perhaps I'm going to have to forgo seeing him for one set of holidays. It was the last thing he wanted to do, but what other option did he have?

Chapter 13

Claire paced back and forth in front of the house, running an agitated hand through her hair. The day was sunny and perfect, with barely a breeze. Even the ocean was quiet. This, mixed with the rough sand on her feet, would usually be enough to calm her.

Not today.

With Joanna coming for dinner tonight, she wasn't holding up well. Claire had wished for a second chance to see her again, and now that she had the opportunity, she was suffocating in guilt. How would Joanna react when Claire told her the truth? Would she be willing to be friends again after everything?

She stopped pacing and ran her hands down her face.

Turning, she stared out at the ocean. The water shone brilliantly in the afternoon sun, waves lapping at the shore in a gentle and relaxing motion. Placing her hands on her hips, she closed her eyes and let the warm, salty breeze caress her and whip through her hair. With the soft sounds of the lapping water and the occasional squawk of a seagull, her anxiety began to ease.

How had she lived so long not being near the ocean? She couldn't imagine ever leaving.

"Claire?"

Claire's eyes snapped open, and she spun around. Daphne stood at the top of the stairs, leaning on the wooden rail. Fearing the worst, Claire bolted into action and ran to her aid, grasping her arm securely.

"Daphne." Claire took a deep breath to calm her pounding heart. "What're you doing out here? I thought you were sleeping. Am I late?" She checked her watch and frowned. It had only been an hour since she left her patient to rest. "I don't think my watch has stopped."

Daphne chuckled and patted Claire's hand. "Don't fret, dear. Today's a good day, that's all. I feel like I can take on the world, so

I want to take advantage of it. For once I didn't want to sleep. I've spent an hour staring at the ceiling. My feet have been itching to get up and about. I didn't want to bother you when you were on your break, so I decided to give it a go. This is as far as I got."

Claire smiled. "You scared me. I'm not used to seeing you walking about on your own. How wonderful."

"Help me sit down. I want to talk to you."

Looking around, Claire saw nothing to sit on but the step. "I'll go in and get your wheelchair. I don't want—"

"I don't need my wheelchair," Daphne said. "The step is fine."

Shrugging, Claire helped her down then sat next to her. For a few moments, they sat in silence, staring out over the ocean.

"I had the most interesting conversation with my son yesterday," Daphne said after a few moments.

"Oh?" Claire continued to stare out over the ocean. A dog ran into her line of vision, barking joyfully and splashing in the shallow water.

"Yes. It seems he's worried about you."

Sitting up in surprise, she turned to Daphne. "It's not about my job, is it?"

Daphne chuckled and shifted to face Claire. "No dear, nothing like that. We're both delighted with you. Like me, he's observant, Claire. I've noticed something's been bothering you for some time, and it seems he has too." She shook her head and smiled. "I never thought I'd ever see my son show any concern for a woman who wasn't Von, Joanna or myself."

Claire looked down at her hands. "Oh, well…" Her heart swelled with pride at the realisation that Michael cared enough about her to speak to Daphne. The feeling didn't last though, when it occurred to her Daphne was asking her to tell her about her past.

Am I ready to do this?

Unable to answer, she forced a smile. "I appreciate your concern, but everything's fine. It's taking me a while to settle, that's all."

That's a pathetic lie, Claire.

She grimaced when Daphne said, "You expect me to believe that?"

Seriously, why do I bother? Daphne's the most switched-on woman I know. Of course she's going to see right through me.

Claire's shoulders slumped forward, and she hung her head and sighed. Was she ready to open up to someone else? Move forward in life? It was what she'd dreamt of for so long, but that would lead the way to tell the truth to Michael, then Von. Joanna was already a given. Claire would be opening her heart and exposing her vulnerabilities. Could she do it?

Her thoughts drifted back to her brief kiss with Michael. She'd wanted nothing more than to kiss him again, explore what could become of them, but she didn't think she could face him. Not out of fear, more out of embarrassment. She didn't know what to do, how to act. She hadn't been in this situation for so long.

I have so much baggage. Do I want him to deal with that? Claire's niggling little common-sense inner voice prompted her.

Isn't that for him *to decide?*

When a hand covered her own, Claire looked up into Daphne's kind eyes. They were sparkling and full of life. The knot of dread in the pit of her stomach told her the sparkle wouldn't last long.

"I'm sorry if this is difficult for you," Daphne said softly. "But after all you've given up to look after me, putting up with my outbursts and listening, I want to repay you. It's time *you* had someone to talk to." She hesitated. "I know you don't have anyone else."

All of a sudden, Claire's mind filled with unwanted memories. Identifying her parents' bodies after the car accident. Ryan promising to look after her forever. The first time he hit her on their wedding night. Losing her friends one by one as Ryan's abuse worsened. The final night when he'd nearly killed her.

Tears seeped from the corners of her eyes and rolled down her cheeks. Yes, she was ready to open up. But was Daphne the right person?

An arm slid across her shoulders. Through tear-filled eyes, she met Daphne's determined gaze.

"You can talk to me," Daphne said softly. "I don't mind."

Claire sniffled and removed a tissue from her jeans pocket to wipe her tears away. "I don't think I can," she whispered.

"Why not?"

She thought about what to say. "Because what I have to tell you isn't very nice. You have your own worries, and I fear what you hear may..." She mulled over her next words. "I've dealt with cancer patients before, Daphne. For many of them, their condition has worsened after terrible news. Some of them even give up on life because they can't handle what they've heard. I can't do that to you. Your family needs you."

A silence fell upon them. Claire wiped away her tears and turned her gaze back to the ocean.

"I want to know," Daphne finally said. "You made me realise something the other day, Claire. You told me to enjoy every day while I can and make new memories. One thing I want to do in my last days is to be here for you. I want to know I can die peacefully knowing I've made you realise some people do care about you."

Claire's bottom lip trembled, fresh tears pooling in her eyes. "Why me? What's so special about me?"

Daphne squeezed Claire's shoulder. "You've brought a lot of happiness into this house without even realising it. Michael was always such a bitter man, but now it seems he's found a way to care for another woman. So much so, he spoke to me voicing his concerns. I don't know what you did, but *you've* changed him."

Claire shrugged awkwardly then stood and stretched her legs. She went down on to the sand. How could she respond to that? Had she changed him that much? If anything, she thought they saw each other for who they were. Equals.

"Then there's Von," Daphne continued from behind her. "She has her sparkle back. For a long while, she struggled with my cancer. She stuck by me, but I could tell it was wearing her down, especially after the death of her husband. Helping her, talking to her and being *you* has made a huge difference."

A blush formed at the base of Claire's neck and slowly crept up until her cheeks burned. She'd never accepted compliments well.

"Then, there's me." Daphne's voice broke, and Claire turned around. Daphne's eyes filled with tears, but she had a smile on her face. "You've spent countless hours looking after me, talking to me and helping me see I can still enjoy the time I have left and not be afraid of dying."

When she struggled to her feet, Claire ran to her aid and helped her up. Once standing, they went onto the deck near the door, and Daphne took Claire's hands. "My dear, you're a blessing in disguise to this family, and you don't even realise it. I want to repay you for all you've done. I want you to feel you can talk to me about anything. Whatever you have to say, it won't kill me."

Turning back, Claire and Daphne shared a smile. She took a deep breath and released it slowly. It was time to stop keeping her past hidden and let people into her life again. She'd been alone for too long.

Claire nodded then inclined her head toward the door. "Shall we go inside, then? I think I need a strong coffee before I open my heart."

Chapter 14

Sitting at the kitchen table, Claire wrapped her hands around the coffee mug, drawing comfort from its warmth. Von was taking a well-deserved break, giving Claire and Daphne time to talk. Staring into the brown liquid, Claire sighed and willed the muddled words in her mind to come together. Where did she start?

"How did you meet your ex?" Daphne asked, guiding the conversation.

One simple question and the words morphed into memories. "In high school." Claire smiled and sipped her coffee. "I was no one special." Claire stared at the wall, letting the past take her away. "Just your average teenager who had a crush on the 'hot jock.' I was gawky, pimply and hormonal, but he saw through that." She blinked and turned her gaze to Daphne. "He was so kind back then, made me feel beautiful, said all the right things that a teenage girl wanted to hear."

"You were together a long time then?"

Nodding, Claire took another sip. "We were high school sweethearts. I was convinced we were meant to be. When Mum and Dad died, he even moved in with me. Life was great, *he* was great." She sighed into her coffee, unable to figure out what went wrong.

"What changed?" Daphne asked softly.

Tears pooled in Claire's eyes, blurring her vision. "To this day I still don't know." She blinked, the tears slipping down her cheeks. "The day we graduated Uni he proposed. A week later we had a registry-office wedding." She shrugged, wiping the tears away on the back of her hand. "That night, everything changed."

"He hit you?" Daphne's hand came out to squeeze hers.

A shudder ran along the length of Claire's spine. "Yes. It was as though having that piece of paper gave him a skewed sense of power." She laughed bitterly. "He apologised, of course. Always said and did the right things to make me believe he was sorry, made me believe he'd change." She shook her head and sighed.

"But he never did," Daphne finished.

Claire looked up and smiled sadly. "No. I mean there were good days. Days when we'd go back to how we were before we got married." She stared at the knots in the table, running her finger over one of them. "They were the days I was so hopeful he was finally changing. Sometimes we'd go a week or more when he wouldn't hit me, and we'd be happy. I could pretend like we were a normal happy couple."

Gulping down her coffee, Claire placed the mug on the table and slumped back in her chair.

"Did you ever try to escape?" Daphne asked.

Sitting up straighter, Claire nodded. "So many times, I lost count. I never succeeded though because he had this uncanny way of always knowing where I was. I learnt very quickly there was no point in trying to escape because each time he caught me, things got so much worse." She hunched her shoulders.

"But you did escape eventually, right?"

Claire didn't answer at once, she merely stared out the front door where the afternoon sun shimmered on the ocean. "I'll never forget the day. Ryan was insanely jealous, and his anger was getting worse and worse. But we had been having a good day, probably the first one in months." Her tears had dried but the ache in her heart pounded as memories flooded her mind. "Ryan and I went out for a picnic. The day was much like today, sunny and perfect."

The next words lodged in her throat. Gloomy silence fell over them as Claire lived the nightmare once more.

"What happened?" Daphne asked softly.

It took a long moment for Claire to build up the courage to say this. "While we were out, I ran into an old Uni friend. He was there with his wife and newborn baby. We chatted briefly as friends do, hugged to say goodbye and that was that. But Ryan being Ryan, he read too much into it. Even though he saw the guy was married and had a baby, he decided I'd cheated on him. No amount of denying it would change his mind, he was too far gone in his own twisted world. He'd threatened my life many times before, but later that day, once we went back home, was the first time he followed through."

She pulled her shirt down enough to show the angry scar. Her tear-filled eyes rose to meet Daphne's horrified gaze.

"He barely missed my heart." Her lip trembled as she let her shirt go. "I vaguely remember the door being knocked down and Ryan being dragged away by the police, but everything else is a blur."

"Oh my dear girl." Daphne reached for Claire's hand and squeezed it for dear life. Tears coated her cheeks. "I can't even begin to imagine what sort of pain you must be going through. I'm truly sorry."

Claire managed a weak smile and rested her other hand on top of Daphne's. "Thank you. Some days I feel like I'm doing better, like I can take on the world. Other days, like today, it's all too much and I feel like I'm going around in circles, not making any progress."

She moved her hands away and ran them down her face, frustrated that all she seemed to do was take one step forward and ten steps back.

"Claire, don't be so hard on yourself. Recovery takes a long time and it takes a lot of patience. Moving here, being in the same house as a man again, it's a big adjustment, and you've done wonderfully."

Claire laughed and hiccupped at the same time. Sniffling, she removed a tissue from her pocket and wiped her nose. "Wonderfully? I beg to differ. I'm afraid there have been times my emotions have got the better of me when I should've been professional."

"Pfft." Daphne waved a dismissive hand. "You can't control how you're going to feel each day. It hasn't impacted your work, you've taken good care of me and that's all that matters." Daphne gave Claire's hand a squeeze again. "The past is the past, Claire. It defines you as a person, but you get to choose what sort of person that is. You're frightened and broken for valid reasons, but is that who you want to be for the rest of your life?"

Claire looked up with a furrowed brow. No one, not even Laura had ever put it so simply before. It was the million-dollar question, wasn't it? The answer should be simple, but Claire couldn't find it. Not right now.

"My father abused me as a child."

"What?" Claire's head snapped up, eyes widening.

A sad smile tugged at Daphne's lips. "It took me years to recover. He instilled such a sense of fear in me. When I met Michael's father, I almost lost him because I was too scared to let him into my life."

Claire opened her mouth to ask how she recovered and where Michael's father was now, but the sliding doors opened. Michael walked in, once again covered in dirt and oil from a day at work. Claire was beginning to like this look.

He smiled broadly at them then came over and kissed Daphne on the cheek. He turned his attention to Claire, smile softening, his gaze drifting to her lips. Cheeks flashing hot, Claire smiled shyly and looked away.

"I'm not interrupting anything, am I?" Michael asked.

"No, not at all. We were gossiping, weren't we?" Claire turned to Daphne who smiled.

"Exactly right, women's stuff, you wouldn't want to know."

Michael wrinkled his nose. "No, you're probably right. Well, I should duck upstairs and shower."

"I wouldn't mind a lie down myself," Daphne announced, sounding tired.

Claire stood. "Of course, let me help get you settled."

***

Claire lay on her bed, staring up at the ceiling. A sense of calm had descended upon her after her talk with Daphne. It was no surprise she was so approachable and consoling. Daphne cared enough to cry over her, something Claire never expected to experience again after losing her parents.

While a weight was lifted, she knew this was no miraculous recovery. Events or memories would still be triggers, but talking about it meant over time, they'd lessen.

Rolling to her side, Claire stared out the open doors. The sun dipped lower in the sky. It was edging on to dinnertime. A smile tugged at her lips when she recalled Daphne's words of wisdom. Claire couldn't answer them earlier, too wrought with emotion to think clearly. Now she asked herself the question again: did she want to be defined by her past by living in fear forever?

Absolutely not.

Daphne's confession had helped. Even though she hadn't gone into detail, the knowledge was enough, and the mutual confessions had drawn the two women even closer.

The one lingering worry Claire had was seeing Joanna. *What will we say to each other?*

Pushing the thought aside, she sat up and checked the time—six-fifteen. She gasped and scrambled off the bed. Removing her usual jeans and blouse, she dashed to her wardrobe to find a more suitable outfit for dinner. Flicking straight to the dresses, she went through each one with care, wanting to look extra lovely for Michael.

Butterflies came to life in her stomach, and a smile broke out on her face. She'd never expected to be in this situation so soon, but she was ready to embrace it. Michael was genuine. He'd witnessed her at her most vulnerable, and rather than scaring him off, he'd treated her with kindness. That itself proved he was nothing like Ryan. She was willing to take the risk.

Will he do the same with me?

Even though she knew little about his past, she hoped he'd learnt to trust her enough to confide in her. For their relationship to go anywhere, they needed to be open with each other.

Donning a pretty pale-yellow sundress with small white flowers, she went searching for some shoes. She dragged out a pair of white sandals as a knock sounded at her door. Opening it, she stumbled slightly seeing Michael standing there.

"Hi." Warmth rose to her cheeks, and she ran her hands along the skirt of her dress.

He greeted her with a heart-stopping smile. Her heart skipped, then raced. "Hi, thought I'd let you know Norman and Joanna are here."

She swallowed hard and nodded. "Thanks for letting me know. I'll be down in a few minutes. I need to finish getting ready."

"It's okay, Von won't be dishing up until six-thirty so you have time." He stared deeply into her eyes as though searching her soul. After a long pause, he asked, "Will you be okay? I know this must be difficult for you."

His concern touched her. She shrugged one shoulder. "To be honest, I don't know. I suppose I won't know until I see her."

Michael appeared thoughtful for a moment. A smile played at his lips when he asked, "How about a code word then?"

"A what?"

"A code word. You know, if you decide you need to get away, you say the word, and we can go for a walk."

She laughed lightly. "That could get awkward. If there's a lull in the conversation and I suddenly say, I don't know, 'spaghetti' for example, can you imagine the looks I'd get?"

Michael threw back his head and burst into laughter, his Adam's apple bobbing up and down his throat. A lock of jet-black hair fell across his forehead. Hypnotised by him, Claire swallowed hard and rested a hand against the doorframe to steady herself, not trusting her trembling knees to hold her up. The tips of her fingers tingled, wanting nothing more than to run along the length of his smooth, tanned throat.

He stopped laughing, and their gazes clashed. A soft smile stayed on his lips as he took a step closer. His hand reached out and cupped her cheek, his thumb running along her skin. Her breathing hitched as he lowered his head, his lips now only inches away. He paused, his warm, minty breath caressing her cheeks. Eyes searching hers, he asked, "May I kiss you, Claire?"

Her breath caught. An inkling of fear grabbed her deep inside and rose, swiftly upward, panic threatening to surface. Where was this coming from? She wanted this, god alone knew that, yet something stopped her. She blinked rapidly and shook her head, confused as to why she was so scared all of a sudden. She opened and closed her mouth, praying for sensible words to come forth but instead she was left speechless.

Michael's hopeful gaze held hers, but the hope began to fade. He moved back, disappointment flashing across his features so quickly she questioned whether it was all in her head. Of course, it wasn't. He *was* disappointed and let's face it, so was she. She'd wanted to kiss him since their last one.

"Michael, I'm…" She shook her head. What could she say?

He smiled, and even though it didn't reach his eyes, she silently thanked his efforts to be understanding.

"It's okay, Claire. I understand." He stepped back, and she immediately missed his closeness.

Her brow furrowed and she shook her head again, trying to make sense of her jumbled thoughts. "I appreciate it. I don't know what came over me. I'm sorry."

His smile brightened, more naturally this time. He levelled his gaze with hers and sincerely said, "Honestly, it's fine. I know you're dealing with stuff, and I respect that. If you ever want to talk…" He shrugged and buried his hands in his pockets.

She'd wanted to tell him everything earlier, but now she wasn't so sure. Why the sudden step back?

She forced a smile and blinked back threatening tears. "Thank you," was all she could say. She cleared her throat and clasped her hands behind her back. "I need to finish getting ready. I'll be down shortly."

Michael took another step back. "Of course. I'll meet you downstairs." With a nod, he turned and walked away, the screen door closing after him seconds later.

With a sigh, she closed her bedroom door and leaned against it for a few moments. Closing her eyes, she focused on breathing to ease the panic. Maybe after she'd chatted to Joanna, she'd be able to make sense of things.

Shaking her head, she opened her eyes and pushed away from the door. Time was ticking, and she didn't want to be late for dinner. She disappeared into the bathroom and turned on the taps. Her gaze landed on the hand she'd injured a few days ago, the bandage now gone. It wasn't a deep cut, and it'd begun healing already, only a red line with a scab forming.

After splashing her face with cold water and running a brush through her loose hair, she slipped her sandals on. Before leaving her room, she looked in the full-length mirror. The dress hugged her feminine curves and settled above her knees. The angry, red chest scar was visible, but for once, she didn't mind that it was there. At least in *that* area, she'd improved.

Smiling at her reflection, feeling happier for the first time within herself, she turned and left the bedroom. Overall, life was looking up. She was still finding her feet with Michael, but deep down, confidence began to grow…confidence that this would work out.

Exiting the second level, she stopped at the top of the stairs. Holding onto the rail, she closed her eyes and breathed slowly. *It's going to be okay. I'm going to see Joanna again. I've wanted this for a long time.*

Remembering the countless times Claire had thought about her friend, and even tried to text her, she knew she had to embrace this moment. It was time to make up for lost time.

When she reached the bottom of the stairs, she took a deep breath, then stepped forward and opened the door. The moment she did so, a little girl ran up to her and skidded to a stop. She looked up at Claire curiously, large brown eyes squinting.

"You're Claire, aren't you?" she asked matter-of-factly.

Claire smiled down at the girl. She was the spitting image of Joanna. She glanced up briefly, her gaze catching Joanna's. They shared a smile, and she breathed a little easier. *Well, this is a better start than last week.*

"Yes I am," Claire answered, looking back down at the girl. "What's your name?"

"Juanita."

"That's a pretty name."

Juanita giggled then grabbed Claire's hand. "Mummy told me all about you, and she said I'm allowed to like you. You're sitting next to me."

Juanita had a firm grasp on her hand, and Claire had no choice but to follow. When they reached the table, Juanita excitedly pulled out an end chair and tugged on Claire's arm in an attempt to get her to sit.

"Be patient, my love," Joanna said with a laugh, coming up and taking Juanita's hand. "Claire may not want to sit down yet."

Juanita pouted and looked up at Claire with hopeful eyes. "I'm sitting right here." She patted the chair next to the end one. "You *must* sit next to me."

"I need to see Daphne first." When Juanita's pout turned into a frown, Claire quickly added, "But if you don't mind saving this seat for me, I'd love to sit here when I get back."

Juanita's frown deepened as she contemplated this then she grinned and nodded. "Okay." Then she ran off to Norman on the other side of the room.

"Claire." Joanna stood next to her. "How are you?"

Turning, Claire found herself staring at her long-time friend, heart pounding against her ribcage. Here she was. Her best friend. The one she'd lost so many years ago.

Tears stung her eyes. "Jo," her voice broke, "I can't believe it's you."

They flung themselves at each other in a warm embrace. Tears flowed as they were once again reunited. Oh, how she'd longed for this moment. When they pulled apart, they laughed happily and embraced again.

"It's so good to see you," Joanna said into Claire's hair. "I'm sorry about the other day."

They pulled away, and Claire wiped away her tears, shaking her head. "No, *I'm* sorry. It was unexpected, and I freaked. I didn't mean to give you the cold shoulder."

"It's fine. Oh, look at you." Joanna looked at Claire up and down. "You look amazing. Beautiful as ever."

Claire's face heated up. "Don't be silly." She took in Joanna's petite form and shook her head good-naturedly. "You were always the better-looking one and you still are."

Joanna threw back her head and laughed. "You haven't changed a bit, Claire. My god, I can't believe you're here." Her face turned serious as she added, "I would love to catch up properly. We have so much to talk about."

"Maybe after dinner? Daphne won't be up late so I'll have some time free."

"I'd love that." Joanna's gaze turned to Juanita, who was sliding open the door. Joanna gave Claire an apologetic smile then ran up to her daughter. "Sweetie, you can't go out there alone."

While Von got the plates out for dinner, Claire took the opportunity to check on Daphne. She wasn't sure if she'd be joining them since her good days often meant her nights weren't as good.

Once in the room, she found Daphne wandering around aimlessly.

"Are you okay?" Claire asked.

"Oh, my dear." Daphne spun around, a hand over her heart. "You scared me." She looked around and added, "I seem to have lost my other shoe."

Claire went to help her, enjoying seeing her in such good spirits. *If only it were permanent.*

"Here it is," Claire said a few moments later, standing up from looking under the bed.

Daphne chuckled and lowered herself into a chair. "Thank you. I have no idea how it got under there."

"They tend to have a mind of their own." She knelt and placed it on Daphne's shoeless foot. "I'm presuming you're okay to join us for dinner?"

"Yes, dear, I wouldn't miss it. I haven't seen Jo and Norm for so long."

"I'm glad." Claire stood. "Now if you're ready, let's head out." She offered her arm to Daphne, who took it and stood. Before they left, Daphne patted Claire's arm and asked, "How are you?"

Claire thought about this then turned to Daphne with a smile. "You know something? I'm feeling pretty good."

Daphne nodded and smiled back. "I'm so happy to hear that. Talking often does wonders."

"You're right. I want to thank you again for being a listening ear today. It was so good to get it off my chest."

"Of course it was. You can't keep these things to yourself. I did once upon a time, and it didn't do me any favours."

They turned and left the room. The moment they entered the kitchen, Juanita shrieked in delight and ran up to them.

"Dappy," Juanita squealed. "Dappy's here."

"Juanita, be careful," Joanna warned as her daughter tore toward them.

Claire stepped forward, ready to stop Juanita if she needed to but it wasn't necessary. Juanita stopped in front of Daphne and wrapped her arms gently around her legs.

Daphne chuckled and stroked Juanita's hair. "Hello, Juanita, how are you?"

"You're sitting next to me too," Juanita exclaimed, ignoring Daphne's question. "Claire is sitting next to me, and so are you."

As they made their way to the table, Daphne chuckled and said, "Seems you're an instant favourite, Claire."

"I have no idea why," she muttered mainly to herself.

Daphne raised an eyebrow. "Oh, I think I know. Remember what I told you today. More people care for you than you realise. I bet Joanna's told her daughter a lot of good things about you."

Claire shrugged but said nothing else. When they reached the table, Juanita fussed about, making sure everyone sat where she wanted them. By the time everyone was in their assigned places,

Juanita was on Claire's left with Michael on her right. When he took her hand under the table, she breathed in sharply. Her heart fluttered madly in her chest, butterflies doing loop the loops in her belly.

She turned to him and their gazes locked. The same bubble of panic from earlier tried to rise, but she pushed it away. She *wanted* something to happen between them. She wouldn't let fear win. In his eyes, she could see he was trying to tell her something. Searching his face, she could tell by the open and honest expression that he was telling her he'd never hurt her.

She believed him, and the panic disappeared. She squeezed his hand to convey this silent message. His face lit up with a smile, and he squeezed back.

Chapter 15

Michael sat back in his chair and watched on with interest at the scene playing out before him. Joanna's cheeks were a bright red as Claire laughed with her.

"Joey?" Norman asked from beside him. "Your nickname was Joey in high school? As in baby kangaroo?"

Claire nodded and laughed even harder while Joanna shrugged and looked away.

Joanna faked a pout. "I hated that nickname." Looking across at Claire, she added, "No fair, that was our secret, Claire."

"We never spit and shook on it, so it's no secret."

Joanna gasped in horror.

Michael raised an eyebrow. "Spit and shake? I hope it's not what I think it is."

"It probably is." Claire grinned. "If you promise to keep a secret, you both spit in the palm of your hand then shake so the saliva mixes together. It's a pact."

"Not one of my proudest moments," Joanna muttered. "I think I have more of Claire's cooties than Norm's."

"Oh, thanks," Norman said, folding his muscled arms across his chest. "I'm not sure how to feel now."

Von, who'd been deep in conversation with Daphne, stood and began clearing the table. Claire shook her head and said, "Don't worry, Norman, all the secrets Jo and I have won't affect your marriage."

He scratched his head in confusion. "Thanks, I think."

Claire stood. "Von, let me help you clean up."

"And me." Juanita exclaimed, jumping out of her chair.

Michael witnessed the raised eyebrows Joanna and Norman exchanged.

"This never happens at home," Joanna said. "We should come here more often."

Norman laughed. "It's Claire's influence, I think."

Michael stood and sat in Juanita's seat next to Mum. It was good to see her back to her old self. It was a moment he'd cherish because he knew it wouldn't last.

"It's nice to see you and Claire getting on," Mum said in a low voice.

Michael looked across at Claire. She, Von and Juanita had a production line happening. Von washed, Juanita rinsed with the aid of Von and Claire dried.

He turned back to her. "I think I like her, Mum." The moment it registered what he'd said, he cursed under his breath.

Mum's eyes shone when she smiled. "How wonderful. See? Not all women are bad. I always told you."

Trust her to get the wrong meaning of 'like'.

"No, I mean…" *Should I tell her?* Apart from Norman, no one else knew. Deciding it wouldn't do any harm, he awkwardly added, "I mean *like* her as in…you know, more than friends."

He wiped his hands along his jean-clad legs. Putting his feelings into words was still impossible. How the hell would he ever tell Claire without screwing it up?

Mum's face turned to surprise. "Oh, I see."

Running a hand through his hair, he shrugged and looked at Claire again. She was chatting and laughing with Von and Juanita at the sink.

He wasn't ready to dive headfirst into a relationship, but he was willing to get to know another woman. The more he thought about it, the more he wanted that woman to be Claire. The only thing stopping him from pushing was her vulnerability. He'd seen the terror in her eyes earlier, when he asked if he could kiss her. He couldn't deny the rejection stung, but how could he hold it against her?

Deep in thought, he jumped when Mum spoke.

She reached for his hand and squeezed. "Michael, I'm so proud, but be careful, I beg you. You asked me to speak to Claire, and I did."

He held his breath. "And?"

"And I think talking helped her a lot. The poor girl has no one else."

"What did she say?"

"It's not for me to say, Michael. If and when she's ready, she'll tell you. In the meantime, be careful. She's fragile for a reason."

He huffed out an annoyed sigh and folded his arms.

Mum's eyes narrowed at his childish behaviour. "Is that necessary, Michael? It's not up to me to share her story."

He winced, and his annoyance faded, guilt taking its place in a heartbeat. He shook his head. *What the hell was I expecting? Of course, it's Claire's story to tell.* He offered a weak, apologetic smile. "Sorry, Mum." He ran a jerky hand through his hair. "I guess…" He shrugged, dropping his hands into his lap.

Mum looked at him, deep into his soul, and nodded knowingly. "You do care for her, don't you?"

He flicked his gaze up to her and nodded. "Yeah, I think I do, Mum."

"Then be patient. Let her tell you in her own time." She smiled and stared at him for a moment before adding, "I'm proud of you, Michael. You've come a long way since Addison, and even if you don't realise it yet, I know Claire's helped a lot. If Claire feels the same way, I'd be thrilled if you two made this work."

Michael's heart swelled with love, not for Mum, but for Claire too. It came out of nowhere, and like a bolt of lightning, he realised he was in deeper than he realised. Rather than terrifying him, it only encouraged him to continue proving himself to Claire, and eventually, hopefully, they could both trust each other. Maybe it was time he confessed about his past too?

"Thanks, Mum."

She smiled at him then leaned back in her chair with a sigh, suddenly appearing exhausted. It was only eight, but it'd been a big day for her.

"I think it's time I went to bed." She glanced back. "Claire, would you mind helping me?"

Claire immediately stopped what she was doing. "Of course." Her gaze met Michael's briefly, and she gave him the sweetest smile. His heart beat a little faster, and his stomach fluttered. Yep, he was definitely in deep.

When Claire disappeared into the bedroom, he turned away and caught Norman looking at him with a smirk, nodding knowingly. Michael flushed and looked away.

A few moments later, Claire returned and went to help with the remaining dishes. She was shooed off by Von, and Juanita copied her. Michael laughed.

Joanna shook her head and chuckled. "She's a real little miss. She's started mimicking everything we do."

"It's the age," Michael said. "Oscar's doing the same thing."

"When do we get to see him again?" Joanna asked.

He sighed, remembering Addison's earlier call. It'd been nice not thinking about it for a while, but now he had to. "He was supposed to arrive on Saturday, but it seems there's a problem."

By the time Claire joined their little group, they'd migrated to stand in front of the open French doors. A gentle, salty breeze ruffled his hair as he relayed the story. When no one could offer a solution, Michael was left feeling deflated. He'd resigned himself to not seeing Oscar these holidays when Claire spoke up.

"I might be able to help."

Michael blinked in surprise. "How?"

"Well, you said you don't want your mother or Oscar missing out on seeing each other, and rightly so. It seems the only option is to go over there and bring him back with you."

Michael shook his head sadly. "I'm afraid it's very costly, and I don't have the funds to pay for three return trips." He shrugged one shoulder.

"Well, this is where I can help." Claire bit her bottom lip and entwined her fingers. "Can I lend you the money? It's not fair your son should miss out on seeing his grandmother, especially in her state, and I know you don't want to be away from her for so long either."

Michael stared at her in shock. The selfless act melted his heart. Yet despite how tempting it was, how could he accept? It felt wrong, as if he was taking advantage of her. And that was why he found himself saying, "Claire, thank you, but I couldn't accept. It's a lot of money, and I wouldn't be able to pay you back for some time."

Claire shook her head. "I don't care. You've done me a huge favour letting me stay here, and I wouldn't expect repayment. However, I have a feeling you're the sort of person who would insist on it anyway."

Michael shrugged and smiled. "You're right there."

"Well if so, take your time. I'm in no rush to have it back."

He couldn't tear his eyes away from her. Her offer was a generous one, and he caved in. It was the only way Oscar would get to see his grandmother one last time.

Claire laughed. "I can tell you're relenting. Say the word, and we'll make a plan for me to transfer the funds to you."

Michael shook his head, then reached out and took her hands. They felt so warm in his, making them tremble. Not even Addison had affected him this way. "Claire, this means the world to me." He rubbed his thumbs over the tops of her hands. "Thank you."

She smiled in response, and he dropped her hands.

Juanita ran up at that moment, interrupting further conversation, taking away Claire and Joanna's attention.

Michael ran a hand through his hair and released a shaky breath.

"She's a keeper," a voice said in his ear.

He snapped his head around to find Norman standing next to him, a knowing smile on his face. Not knowing how to respond, Michael offered a small smile. He was rapidly learning she indeed was.

In a louder voice, Norman turned to Juanita and said, "Right, it's way past your bedtime, missy. Let's go home."

"Do we have to, Daddy?" She stuck out her bottom lip. "I want to stay with Claire."

"It's nearly Claire's bedtime too," he countered. "You'll get to see her again soon."

Juanita's pout stuck out further, but it was smothered by a large yawn as she reluctantly agreed.

Norman turned back to Michael. "Let's catch up while Oscar's here. Juanita's excited to see him again."

Michael's smile stretched across his face. He was still unable to believe had a solution now, all thanks to Claire. "Sounds good, mate."

"All right," Norman said, clapping his hands, "say your goodbyes, Juanita."

Juanita ran around like a whirlwind, waving vigorously, saying goodbye to everyone as she left with Norman.

Michael waved goodbye, and once they were out the door, his brow furrowed when he noticed Joanna was still there. "I assume there's a reason you're still here?"

Joanna looped her arm through Claire's. "I told Norm I'd be home later. Claire and I have some catching up to do. We didn't want to say anything in front of Juanita otherwise it would've been impossible getting her home. She won't notice I'm missing until she's back at the house."

"How's that even possible?" Michael shook his head. "Oscar notices I'm missing within seconds."

Joanna tapped her nose. "It's called being sneaky. If we can get her preoccupied with something, like saying goodbye for example, it gets her excited enough to get out the door. Norman will keep her talking all the way home so she won't even notice."

Michael laughed. "That's conniving, but I'll have to try it."

"Trust me, it works. Now if you'll excuse us, Claire and I are going for a wander on the beach."

When they left, Claire walked close enough so he could reach out and brush his fingers along hers. She glanced back as she passed, and their gazes connected. They smiled at each other then she disappeared out the door.

That gentle touch alone was enough to make his knees buckle. He shook his head. *I've got it bad.* He stepped out the door and onto the landing, watching the two women disappear down the beach. Claire's laughter caught on the breeze. It was a musical laugh, one he could listen to every day.

He continued to stare after them wistfully. Claire's dress caught on the breeze and blew up. She used her hands to hold it down, and she and Joanna burst into laughter. They broke into a run along the beach. Their laughter could still be heard even though they were a fair distance away by this point.

They settled down on the sand, barely visible now, and Michael took this as his cue to turn away. He went back inside, a smile fixed on his face and closed the door after him. He loved seeing Claire so happy. Would she ever be like that around him?

Chapter 16

Claire glanced out over the ocean and sighed in contentment. The quarter moon shed a small amount of light on the rippling water. Her hair caught in the gentle, balmy breeze and flew across her face. For a blissful second, she was happy and free. She lifted her face to the sky and glanced up at the blanket of stars. It was a wondrous night, and being with her best friend once again made everything perfect.

When she and Joanna left the house, they'd spent the first half-hour talking generalities, enjoying the easy banter they could once again share. Now, silence had fallen upon them, and Claire knew the big question wasn't far off.

Joanna broke the silence between them. "So you sold the house and all your possessions to move here?"

Shuffling on the spot, Claire nodded but didn't respond straight away. It was difficult to know where to start. Talking to Daphne had been easy because she was an outsider with no personal attachment to Ryan. Joanna, on the other hand, knew Ryan well. It was even safe to say they were friends in high school.

"It was time to move on," Claire finally said. "I know this isn't a permanent job, but I figured I'd find somewhere in WA to settle after it ends. There'll be hospitals with positions vacant, I'm sure."

"No doubt about it. If you decided to settle here, the Busselton hospital alone always has vacancies. They're so understaffed. If you went there now asking for a job, they'd snatch you up. I'm only part time because of Juanita."

"Is that why Michael couldn't find a live-in nurse locally?"

Joanna nodded. "All the female nurses had jobs already. You know what, he mentioned he'd found someone from Adelaide, and I didn't even think it'd be you."

"I had no idea you were here."

Another silence fell upon them, but it was only for a moment or two. Finally, Joanna asked, her voice strained, "What happened, Claire? Why'd you cut me off?"

There it was. Claire stared out over the ocean, picking up fistfuls of sand and letting it filter through her fingers. A flutter of apprehension appeared in her gut. They'd had so much fun laughing and talking, what if her confession broke them apart again?

Don't hold off any longer, Claire. Joanna of all people deserves to know.

After taking a deep breath, Claire said, "Ryan told me I couldn't be friends with you."

Joanna sucked in a breath. Tension radiated off her. After a few agonising seconds, she spoke. "Why?"

Claire closed her eyes to hide the tears pooling behind them. In a trembling voice, she said, "He abused me, Jo. He threatened to kill me if I didn't cut you off. He knew if you found out, you'd try and help me."

There, it's out.

A longer silence followed, but Claire didn't say anything. She sat motionlessly and waited, giving Joanna time to process.

Opening her eyes, she stared up at the blanket of stars once more. One shot across the sky, and rather than making a wish, she made a resolve. From now on, she wouldn't let the past dictate her. She'd let Michael in and stop the fear from taking over. And finally, she'd embrace her second chance at life and make the most of it.

Contentment washed over her, and deep down, she knew things would be okay.

Sensing movement next to her, she turned to see Joanna's shoulders shaking. Seconds later a strangled sob escaped and her friend broke down.

"Oh, Claire, I had no idea," Joanna cried between sobs. "I resented you and I hated you...oh, god, I can't believe it. I should've known there was something wrong, but I was too hurt even to think straight. I'm sorry, Claire. I'm so sorry. I should've known, I should—"

Claire placed an arm across her friend's shoulder and held her close. "You weren't supposed to know," Claire said softly, a tear sliding down her cheek. "Why do you think I wrote the message? I was trying to hide what was happening. I missed you terribly, Jo, but I didn't want you involved. I didn't want you getting hurt."

"I would've done anything for you, Claire."

"I know, but I'm glad you never knew. If you found out, something terrible would've happened to you, I know it. Then you would've never met Norman, and you wouldn't have Juanita."

Joanna hung her head. "I know, but…I still wish I'd known. I wish things were different. I wish you'd never met Ryan."

Claire laughed bitterly. "You and I both, Jo. You and I both."

They were silent for a while longer as Joanna pulled herself together. When her tears had dried up, she looked to Claire and asked, "Where's Ryan now?"

"In jail."

"Oh, god. On what charges?"

"Attempted murder."

Joanna gasped but said nothing. Now was the time to confess the whole horrifying truth. Again. Telling Daphne was easier because she was an outsider. Joanna would feel the pain more deeply. But there was no point in hiding it any longer. It wasn't doing anyone any favours, especially herself.

While she mulled over how to tell Joanna the sordid details, memories of her last day with Ryan came back with force. The day she nearly died. Safe now next to Joanna, her body shook uncontrollably, images of Ryan's hate-filled eyes prominent in her mind. She began crying, her gut-wrenching sobs cutting through the night, drowning out the ocean.

Claire covered the scar above her breast with her right hand then wrapped her left arm around her waist, rocking back and forth. *What has he done to me? The bastard has turned me into a freak.*

Joanna's voice cut through the fog. "Claire? Claire? Are you okay?"

When a hand touched Claire's arm, she recoiled. Drawing her legs up to her chest, she wrapped her arms around them and buried her tear-stained face.

"Hey, it's okay." Joanna's hushed tones washed over her. "It's me, it's Jo."

When Claire felt a tentative hand on her arm again, her breathing hitched. She lifted her head, her gaze connecting with the concerned one of Joanna's. Dropping her guard altogether, she threw herself into Joanna's arms, sobbing into her shoulder.

"The memories won't go away," Claire cried.

When Joanna's arms wrapped around her, she relaxed fully. Neither of them spoke while Claire cried. Joanna rubbed small, soothing circles on her back, speaking in soft, consoling tones. After a few moments, Claire regained control. The sound of waves lapping at the shore was prominent again, acting like a natural healing balm.

Claire pulled away and pushed strands of soggy hair away from her face. She smiled weakly at Joanna. "I'm sorry." She crossed her legs and rested her hands behind her.

"You don't have to be sorry for anything." Joanna moved to the side a little so she could stretch her legs out. "I'm here for you, Claire."

Claire nodded slowly and glanced out over the ocean again. It'd come in cloudy all of a sudden and the light of the moon disappeared. There were no other lights nearby, creating an eerie atmosphere.

"Do you want to talk about it?" Joanna asked. "You can talk to me, Claire. I promise I'm not going anywhere."

Taking a deep breath, her emotions now calmer, she said, "It started on our wedding night. I stood up for myself the first few times, threatened to leave him, but he played on my emotions. Told me he'd kill himself if I left. He'd apologise every time too, but then he'd say it was my fault because I was a bad wife." She shuddered and wrapped her arms around herself to ward off the sudden chill. "He was so convincing. I believed him."

Joanna placed a hand on Claire's arm. "Oh, Claire."

She swiped away at a tear and shook her head. "When I finally escaped, people asked why I didn't leave him sooner. Why I believed him. And the truth is, it's not that easy. I wanted to believe there was good in him. I'd seen it before, so had you." She cast a look at Joanna, who nodded. "It's why we got married. I wanted to believe the 'good Ryan' would come back, and with the number of times he apologised, and so convincingly too, I was so sure this was it. Ryan was back. But he never was. I lost him when we said 'I do'."

After taking a deep, shuddering breath, she continued, "Then after a while, I was too scared to leave and instead I became obsessed with proving I could be a good wife. I suppose it was a way to prove to myself that going through hell was worth it. But no matter how hard I tried, it was never enough, and by the time I realised that, the damage was done."

"Do you know what happened? Why he changed?" Joanna asked.

Claire shook her head. "I honestly have no idea. It felt like it was a control thing, like having that piece of paper that legally bound me to him gave him some kind of weird, twisted power trip. I don't know."

"Did you ever try to leave?"

Claire stared off into the distance, remembering the countless times she'd tried and failed. "Yes, but he always caught me. I wasn't smart enough for him. He had tabs on me all the time. I'd meticulously plan it, but he'd still find out." She laughed bitterly and thumped the sand with her balled-up fist.

Joanna placed a hand on her fist and asked, "How'd you escape then?"

Blinking a couple of times, Claire turned to her friend and gave a sad smile. "To this day, I'm convinced I had some kind of being, or"—she shrugged—"I don't know, *something*, looking out for me. In all the years we were together, our neighbours never reported anything amiss. But this one day, he stabbed me." She ran her finger subconsciously over the scar. "Almost killed me, but they heard my scream and called triple zero."

Joanna's eyes flicked from Claire's face to the scar. "Holy shit, Claire." When their eyes met, they broke down and cried, collapsing into each other's arms once more.

"Oh, Claire," Joanna sniffled and pulled away. "I feel so terrible for you. How on earth did you cope all this time?"

Claire ran her finger through the sand. "When I was with Ryan, I was so desperate to prove I was worth something and that was enough to give me a will to live. After I woke up in the hospital though, I didn't want to live anymore. The damage he'd done to me was so immense, I didn't think I'd ever be able to cope. Ryan destroyed me, physically, emotionally, and mentally. I can't deny I contemplated suicide. It was fortunate I was in the hospital and under strict watch."

Joanna shook her head and looked at Claire admiringly. "But look at you now. You're beautiful and full of life."

Claire threw Joanna a fleeting smile. "What I look like doesn't reflect the internal battles I'm constantly struggling with, Jo. I've come a long way in the last eighteen months but it's still no easy feat. Facing men hasn't always been easy."

Joanna's eyes widened. "How did you do with Michael? You two seem to be getting on fairly well."

"It wasn't easy at first, but we found our feet in the end. It took some time and soon enough we both realised we had histories."

"I confess I'm surprised," Joanna said with a light laugh. "Michael hasn't got a great opinion of women. He's warmed to *you* quite well."

Claire shrugged. "I suppose we have more in common than people realise. We're two broken individuals who understand the pain suffering brings."

"Has he told you about his past?"

"No. I only know snippets, but it's not my place to ask."

"I think he'll tell you one day."

Claire looked at her friend curiously. "Why do you say that?"

Joanna smiled and waved a dismissive hand. "I have a feeling. Anyway, if it doesn't bother you too much, I want to know everything."

"Are you sure? I'm happy to talk about it, but I don't want to upset you."

"You won't, Claire."

Looking at her watch, Claire said, "I have to check on Daphne first. Why don't we chat in the living area? Then I can keep an eye on her too. She's due her four-hour medication soon."

Joanna nodded then stood. Claire followed, but before they walked away, they both looked up at the night sky as another shooting star flashed across it.

"Make a wish," Joanna whispered.

This time Claire did. She wished that she'd never lose contact with Joanna again.

****

***

"Oh my god, I can't believe it's three in the morning." Joanna yawned and stretched her arms above her head.

Claire tiredly looked across at the clock. "Time has flown. I think I'll be napping when Daphne does today."

Joanna dropped her head to the back of the sofa and sighed. "I should go home. Juanita will freak if she wakes up and I'm not there."

Remembering one thing they hadn't discussed, Claire asked, "How'd you meet Norman?"

Joanna's smile lit up her face as she sat up. "After you and I lost contact, I moved to WA and was offered a job at the local hospital. I'd see Norm around town, and even though we never spoke, there was something about him I was attracted to. Then one day we had a bomb scare—this was before he left the department. Norm was one of the firefighters on the scene along with Michael. When they'd finished their job, I asked him for his number."

Claire burst out laughing. That was the Joanna she knew. Never shy around men and able to get any phone number she wanted.

"You hit it off, obviously."

A blush coloured Joanna's cheeks. "We did. So well, in fact, we were married within six months. I suppose me falling pregnant was all the encouragement we needed."

"You had a shotgun wedding?" Claire smirked.

Joanna's face reddened, and she shrugged. "I suppose you can call it that. We knew it was right though and didn't regret it. We clicked, you know?"

Claire nodded in understanding.

"I think I should go," Joanna said.

"I'll walk you back if you like?"

"No, it's okay." Joanna stood. "I'm only five minutes away."

Claire walked her to the door. They embraced once more and grinned as they pulled apart.

"It's so good to see you again, Claire, and I'm so sorry for all the times I thought badly of you. I'm especially sorry for what happened with Ryan."

"Please don't be sorry, Jo. As Daphne said, the past is the past. If I want it to define me positively, I can't let it control me anymore."

"Next thing you know you'll be married with a dozen kids."

Claire laughed nervously and folded her arms. "I don't think I'm ready for that sort of commitment yet."

Joanna's eyes sparkled knowingly. "Perhaps not right now, but I have a feeling a certain someone might be attracted to you."

Claire's heart skipped. Was it that obvious? *Of course it is, silly.* Yet despite this knowledge, she still found herself saying, "I don't think so."

The disbelief on Joanna's face made it clear she didn't believe her. "Don't give me that. I saw the way you two acted around each other earlier." Joanna turned serious. "I know you both have things to work through, but don't ignore the obvious, okay? When the time is right, if anything happens, let it happen naturally. I've known Michael for as long as I've known Norman, Claire. He's a good man."

Even though Claire had come to the same conclusion, there was still an element of relief hearing it from someone else.

With their conversation at an end, they waved goodbye. When Joanna was out of sight, Claire went back into the living area. She wanted to get some sleep but Daphne's next four hours were up soon, so there was no point.

Sitting on the sofa, she smiled to herself and reflected on the evening. She was genuinely, one hundred per cent happy. It was a nice change. *If I can be this positive all the time, I might actually be able to move on from this.*

Chapter 17

Claire's feet sunk in the soft sand as she paced back and forth, waiting for Michael to return from work. It was late Friday afternoon, and she desperately needed to speak to him. He'd been extra busy and she'd barely seen him. They chatted daily, but romantically he'd backed away after she rejected his kiss a few nights ago.

While she appreciated he didn't push it, it was time he knew she was ready. That she wanted to explore what they could have as a couple. She'd tried a few times before now but always chickened out at the last second. Today she wouldn't. With Oscar due to arrive tomorrow, this was her last opportunity to speak to him without distractions.

Holding a hand against her stomach where butterflies swooped in large circles, she drew in a deep breath, held it for a moment and then released it slowly. *I can do this.* Sitting on the sand, legs stretched out in front of her, she stared out over the ocean.

It'd been a long time since she'd told any man how she felt about them and she was out of practice. With Ryan, they'd clicked when they met in high school. With Michael, they had a rocky beginning, and they both had dark pasts. A small part of her feared rejection. Yes, it was clear he felt the same way she did, but what if she was being presumptuous?

There's only one way to find out.

She drew in another breath and held once more, closing her eyes and enjoying the salty breeze kissing her skin.

"Mind if I join you?"

Her eyes snapped open and her breath came out in a whoosh. She looked up to see Michael standing beside her, the sun behind him making him appear like a silhouette.

Where'd he come from?

She managed a small smile. "Sure."

He sat close enough so his arm brushed against hers, sending sparks of pleasure right to her toes. Once upon a time she would've shied away from his touch, but not this time. She looked up at the clear, blue sky as though willing it to give her the confidence she needed to speak to him. After taking a large gulp of air, she turned to him.

"Did you have a good day*?" I might as well ease into it and start off with the basics.*

Michael pulled his knees up and rested his arms over them. "Busy." He threw a small grin her way. "It's been a hectic week."

Raking a hand through his hair, he puffed out a breath then shuffled closer and rested his arm over her shoulders. Claire's heart rate spiked but she didn't move, wanting to prove she wasn't afraid. He was rigid at first, but after a few seconds, he relaxed and gently tugged her closer.

Adrenalin rushed through her veins but no fear. She sighed then blurted, "I'm sorry."

He looked down at her, eyebrows drawn together. "What for?"

She pulled her knees up this time and wrapped her arms around them. She stared out over the ocean, sparkling in the late afternoon sun. "Monday night…before dinner."

"Monday…" He trailed off as though casting his mind back, then snapped his head around to her, eyes wide, "Oh." He removed his arm but shuffled around so he faced her, taking her hand. "Claire—" His gaze met hers, understanding shining in his hazel depths. "You have no reason to be sorry."

She shrugged and lowered her gaze. "My emotions were all over the place. Seeing Jo again, it brought back—" She cut off and shook her head.

How could she tell him? She needed to, *wanted* to, but words failed her.

Michael squeezed her hand and she looked back up at him. "Claire, I'd love it if you could open up to me, but if you can't yet, I—"

She shook her head. She wasn't about to let fear win *again*. He deserved to know, and she needed to if this was going anywhere.

"No." She removed her hand from his and stood, brushing sand off the back of her jeans. "I want to. It's…" She stared out over the ocean once more, sifting through the array of words buzzing through her mind. So many to choose from. In the end, she wrapped her arms around herself and simply said, "It's not easy."

Michael got to his feet and stood next to her, his arm finding its place around her shoulders again. *I can get used to this.*

"How about I ask you a question then?" he asked. "You don't have to answer if you don't want to, but maybe it'll make it easier for you to talk."

She looked up at him and nodded. "Go ahead."

He looked away, his face expressionless. After a couple of moments, he looked down at her again and asked, "Ryan, he's your husband, right?"

"*Was.*" She gritted her teeth but managed to look up at him with a smile. "I'm divorced, remember?"

He grimaced, his cheeks colouring. "Of course. Sorry, wrong choice of words." He rubbed her left shoulder with his hand.

Taking a few slow breaths, she shook her head. "It's okay. I don't mean to be so brusque about it."

"It's okay." He took a deep breath then asked, "He abused you…didn't he?"

In with the kicker.

Surprisingly, she wasn't afraid to answer. "Yes." The words came out as a whisper but the wind caught them. She knew he'd heard them when his arm tightened around her shoulders.

"Claire, I'm so sorry." He released her but turned to face her, emotion dancing in his eyes. He reached for her hand, running his thumb along the top. "You know I'd never hurt you, don't you?"

That was an easy question to answer. It might not have been a couple of weeks ago, but a lot had changed since she started her job. Michael was untrusting, occasionally angry and bitter, but he wasn't violent. So when she answered, she didn't have a single doubt in her mind. "I know." She reached up with her free hand and caressed his cheek. "I trust you, Michael."

He leaned into her touch, his eyes never leaving hers, shining with appreciation. "Thank you. Will you tell me more?" He smiled awkwardly. "I mean, if you want to."

Her heart skipped. "You want to know?"

He nodded. "Why wouldn't I?"

Biting her bottom lip, she dropped her arm and averted her gaze to the ocean. A flock of seagulls flew overhead. Why was she surprised? Of course he'd want to know. The same way she wanted to know about his past…if he was willing to share. *I hope he does.*

She shrugged and looked back at him. "It's not very pleasant. It might—"

"Don't say it might scare me off." He reached out and tucked her hair behind her ear. "I like you a lot, Claire. It means a lot to me that you're willing to talk at all. It won't scare me off, I promise."

She smiled up at him and nodded. "Well, okay then."

Where do I start?

For a few moments, they stood in silence while Claire mulled over what to say. There was so much. Her mind filled with thousands of words, all of them crowding for space.

She looked up at Michael while he stared out over the ocean. His brow was creased, his mouth tugged downwards in a frown. What was he thinking? Shaking her head, she turned away and closed her eyes, breathing in the salty sea breeze.

One thing became clear. One thing she needed to do before she told Michael everything. Was she brave enough?

Yes.

Butterflies that'd settled down came back to life with a vengeance as she looked back up at him, two words on the tip of her tongue. Dare she?

Yes. Do it.

"Kiss me?" The words came out before she could stop them. Her cheeks flamed and she averted her gaze. *I can't believe I asked him that.*

She started counting the grains of sand but failed. Anything to—

"Claire."

A finger lifted her chin and she found herself staring into his beautiful eyes, so full of real, genuine emotion.

"I'd love more than anything to kiss you." His eyes searched her face. "Are you sure?"

She stared deep into his eyes, hoping he could see she wasn't hiding anything. She wasn't afraid. All she wanted was him. Truly. Completely. Honestly.

"Yes, I'm sure."

What would it be like to be kissed with passion instead of anger? If the smile spreading across his face was anything to go by, she'd find out very soon.

Her breath caught in her throat when he leaned in, his nose brushing hers, warm breath fanning her face. Before their lips touched, his hands cupped her cheeks and he whispered, "You're so amazing, Claire."

Pulling her flush against him, Michael held her securely in his arms. He closed the gap, his soft lips caressing hers in the most beautiful, thoughtful and careful way. Her body exploded with desire. Bolts of electricity started in her lips and zigzagged to every nerve ending. She melted into him, her arms wrapping around him, her fingers scorched from the feel of his tight muscles through his shirt. *Well, now, this I can get used to.*

Winding her arms up and around his neck, she held him close, their warm breath mixing with the salty spring breeze. She held on so tightly, almost afraid of letting go. This kiss was so different to their first one—rather than being tentative, it was lively. Passionate. It spoke of promises, of a future with no fear, no pain, no suffering.

She sighed into the kiss and Michael tightened his hold. His soft lips caressed and massaged hers in such a sensual way, sending her heart beating rapidly against her ribcage. He held her so close she could feel his heartbeat against her own. Two abandoned hearts beating together...*healing* together.

The kiss slowed and Michael pulled away, resting his forehead against hers. The waves crashed gently on the shore and seagulls squawked overhead. She breathed slowly and deeply, her heart swelling with...*something* for this man. Was it love? No, it couldn't be. Not so soon.

Why not? It's not impossible.

She shivered and Michael pulled away, staring down at her with a furrowed brow. "Are you cold?"

Shaking her head, she smiled up at him. "No." There was no way she could tell him her private thoughts, not yet, so instead, she said, "I'm happy."

"Honestly?" He stepped back but held onto her hands.

She nodded, surprised she meant it even if it wasn't what she was thinking. "Yes."

Her mind cleared and suddenly talking to him was the easiest thing to do. Stepping back, she took his hand and inclined her head toward the house. "I need to check on your Mum, but once I'm done, I'd love to sit down with you and talk. If you still want to hear."

"Of course I want to." His eyes met hers, and he lifted her hand to his mouth, his lips brushing her knuckles. "I'll meet you in there? I might take the opportunity to freshen up while you're with Mum."

Claire nodded, a silly grin spreading across her face. Turning, she made her way inside, a skip in her step. Who knew she'd ever be so happy again? Not her, that's for sure, but she wasn't complaining. If this was what her future entailed, she could get used to it.

Chapter 18

When Claire was out of sight, Michael turned back to the water, a large grin spreading across his face. He closed his eyes, remembering every single detail of their kiss. It was pure perfection. The feel of her soft body against his, her lips working in sync with his, the way she gave back so openly, without an inch of hesitation or fear.

He'd never experienced anything so thrilling. His pounding heart was only beginning to slow to a normal rate.

What a welcome home.

His grin widened, and he opened his eyes again, staring out over the water. He hadn't given her rejection on Monday night a second thought, not wanting or expecting an apology. If it'd bothered her, he was glad she'd been confident enough to confide in him.

His smile slipped as her confession about her abuse rang in his ears. While he wanted to hear her story, he needed a long, hot shower first. A slow anger began to boil deep down…anger towards Ryan. He didn't want to show any signs of that towards Claire.

Running a hand through his hair, he turned to make his way to the stairs. He stopped and stared at the house in front of him—his home. A wistful sigh escaped his lips and sadness overwhelmed him. It wouldn't be the same once Mum was gone.

A lump lodged itself in his throat. He turned back to the water again, blinking back tears. Bloody hell, his emotions were all over the place. One second he bathed in the euphoria that Claire had finally lowered her guard, the next he mourned Mum's impending death. Not to mention other emotions—excitement at seeing Oscar, agitation at Addison's control and what trick she might pull next, stress from being overworked.

It was never-ending. The hardest of them all was Mum's impending death. He couldn't lose her, but he had no bloody choice. How the hell was he supposed to live without her?

Hanging his head, a couple of tears escaped, dripping down his cheeks and onto the sand. Deep, raw emotion bubbled up inside, tightening his chest, gripping onto his heart for dear life, threatening to break it in two. His hands curled into fists, untrimmed nails digging into his palms. Why was life never fair? Why did all the good people die? Why couldn't Ryan be struck down with terminal cancer? *He* deserved it. Not Mum.

Lifting his head, through blurry, tear-filled eyes, he caught the sun kissing the horizon, turning the clouds a vibrant gold.

When did it get so late?

Shaking his head, the beginnings of the stunning sunset calmed him, almost as though it were telling him everything would be okay. A small smile graced his lips, and he breathed in a deep lungful of salty sea air. When he was confident he'd had control of himself once more, he turned and took a step toward the house.

Maybe talking to Claire was exactly what he needed. Perhaps he'd finally find the courage to tell her everything about *his* past too. Could this be their new beginning?

He'd barely taken another step when the front door slid open and a small, dark-haired figure emerged, scanning the area. Michael's heart leapt, and he stood stock-still, losing all ability to move.

"Daddy."

Oscar.

Michael's chest rose and fell rapidly as he watched the figure run toward him, sand kicking up behind him. It *had* to be an apparition.

"Daddy." The childlike voice carried on the breeze, music to his ears. The voice he didn't hear as often as he wanted.

Oscar grew closer, and Michael realised it wasn't an apparition at all. Oscar *was* only a few feet away, hazel eyes lit up in excitement, a wide, toothy grin spread across his face. Falling to his knees, Michael held his arms out wide. Within seconds, Oscar flung himself at him and Michael wrapped his arms around him in a tight embrace, shedding silent tears. God, how he'd missed him.

Quickly wiping his tears away, he stood and spun around. Oscar giggled gleefully, his arms wrapped securely around Michael's neck.

When the emotion died down, and Oscar had released his grip, the reality of the situation hit home. Oscar was *here*? Michael's flights were already booked to leave in the morning.

"What a surprise," Michael said with a laugh, placing Oscar back on the ground and ruffling his thick, dark brown hair. "I was going to pick you up tomorrow."

Oscar grinned and shook his head vigorously. "Mummy said we *had* to come today."

"Why today?"

Oscar's attention was already elsewhere. "Can we build a sandcastle? Please, Daddy. I want to build a sandcastle."

Of course Oscar won't be able to answer that, but what the hell is going on?

"Maybe later, but we have to go inside now. It's almost dinner time."

"But I want to build a sandcastle *now*." Oscar stamped his foot on the sand and stuck out his bottom lip.

Michael pursed his lips and drew in a calming breath. His son certainly had Addison's temper. He crouched in front of Oscar. "We can't now, buddy. It's getting late, and dinner will be ready soon. Besides, don't you want to see Nanny?"

Oscar's eyes widened, and he nodded.

"Well let's go inside then." Michael stood and held out his hand. "We can build a sandcastle tomorrow."

When Oscar had hold of his hand, Michael walked towards the house. The closer he got, the more agitated he became. He was ecstatic to see his son again but how had he got here? Where was Addison?

His agitation soon turned to anger. After all he'd been through to get Oscar out, it'd be typical of Addison to go behind his back and do this.

What about the bloody plane tickets? I bet it didn't even cross her mind.

"Daddy?" Oscar's voice interrupted his thoughts.

"Yeah?" Michael glanced down at him.

"I miss living with you."

Michael's heart tugged. "I miss it too, buddy."

"Can I live here forever?"

If only. "As much as I'd love that, Osc, you can't right now."

"But I'm always with Mummy. I don't like being with her."

Cold fear clutched at his heart. Why would Oscar say something like that? "Why don't you like living with her?"

Oscar didn't respond immediately. Michael stopped in front of the stairs and turned his head to him only to see him frozen in place. Oscar took a step back and hid behind Michael's legs, gripping onto his trousers tightly.

"Hello, Michael," a sickly sweet voice greeted.

Michael whipped his head around and stared into cold, dark green eyes. "Addison," he greeted curtly. She stood at the top of the stairs. "What are you doing here? I was flying across tomorrow to pick Oscar up."

Addison paused for a nanosecond, uncertainty crossing her features. It passed quickly and she waved a dismissive hand, her bangles jangling. "That's neither here nor there. We're here now."

"I've paid for the flights, Addison." His anger rose by the second, and it was hard work keeping his voice even. "Are you going to pay me back?"

"I don't think we should have this conversation in front of Oscar." Addison looked back at the house, a frown masking her petite face. "So, is she dead yet?"

It was no wonder she'd given up nursing. Her bedside manner was appalling.

Body shaking with rage, Michael balled his hands into fists. If it weren't for Oscar being so close, he would've exploded. "You don't have to be so disrespectful." He glared at her then added, "And no, she's not."

Addison shrugged and inspected her manicured fingernails.

"Daddy?"

Michael turned to find Oscar cowering behind him, a wet patch at the front of his trousers. *Since when did Oscar wet himself?*

"Hey, what's wrong buddy?" Michael crouched in front of him.

Tears filled his large, hazel eyes and he looked down at the wet patch. "I'm sorry, Daddy. Don't be angry," he whispered.

Michael's heart broke, and he mustered up a consoling smile. "I'm not angry, Osc, accidents happen. You should've told me you had to go."

Oscar shook his head. "I didn't need to."

"Oh, Oscar, you disgusting child," Addison's angry voice sounded from behind them. "I don't even have a change of clothes on me."

Michael stood and turned his cold gaze to Addison. "Don't talk to Oscar like that."

Addison's eyes darkened as she hardened her gaze on Michael. "He's *my* son and I'll talk to him how I please."

"He's my son too, and he doesn't deserve to be spoken to like that."

"This has always been your problem, Michael. You're too soft on him. You don't discipline him when it's necessary."

"I discipline him as I deem fit to do so. I will *not* discipline him for something he has no control over."

Michael didn't realise his voice had risen until he heard Oscar begging him not to yell. He snapped his mouth shut, eyes widening. Hell, that wasn't intentional, but Addison had that effect on him.

A thought occurred to him, sending a wave of nausea over him. Is that what upset Oscar? Raised voices? Arguments? Anger? *What's going on at home?*

Before he could contemplate it further, Michael forced a smile and faced Oscar. "I'm sorry, buddy. I didn't mean to get angry. How about we go inside then get you showered and changed?"

Wanting to stick to his end of the bargain and support Oscar when he visited, Michael always made sure he had a couple of sets of clothes available.

"That won't be necessary," Addison said. "He's coming with me. I have his clothes at the motel. Come on, Oscar, let's go."

"No," Oscar cried, "I want to stay here."

"He's in *my* care now," Michael said at the same time, turning to Addison. "You go, Oscar stays."

Addison released a frustrated sigh and rubbed her temples. "Don't do this to me, Michael. He's not in your care until tomorrow in case you've forgotten."

"But you arrived with him today and you're at my house so obviously you had full intention on dropping him off."

Addison's icy glare sent a chill down Michael's spine. "*I* was doing the right thing by letting him see you. He wouldn't let up asking to see you, so I relented."

"Well, thank you very much," he said sarcastically, "but he wants to stay, so he's staying. I've got enough clothes to get him by until you drop off his items."

Addison looked at her watch then reluctantly said, "All right, fine, I'll come back tomorrow with them." Addison looked across at Oscar and held out her arms. "Come now, Oscar, give Mummy a hug."

Oscar's grip tightened on Michael's trousers, but he didn't move. After an impatient sigh, Addison turned and walked around the side of the house.

When she was out of sight, Michael released a held breath and shook his shoulders to release the tension. *What the hell's going on? Why's Oscar so scared?*

He turned to ask him but found he wasn't there. His heart tripped and an involuntarily chill ran down his spine. "Oscar?" His voice was laced with panic. "Oscar, where are you?"

He scanned the area, and when his gaze passed the glass doors, he spotted a head of dark hair. Walking up the steps, he found Claire assisting Mum to the table, Oscar following along, talking excitedly. Relief flooded his veins, and a small smile tugged at his lips at how full of life Mum appeared. Over the last couple of weeks, she'd been going downhill more and more. Having Oscar nearby added some life into her, but it wouldn't last.

His relief was short-lived, replaced with sadness and worry. Sadness about his mother's deteriorating health, and a new worry about Oscar.

Shaking his head, Michael stepped through the door and pushed his concerns aside for the time being. He'd talk to Oscar later. For now, he had to get both of them showered and into fresh clothes.

Chapter 19

Claire assisted Daphne to her seat at the table, ready for dinner. The happiness that'd completely overwhelmed her earlier had dimmed, but she wasn't sure why. Maybe because she'd had time to think, and thinking was bad. Every time she did, thoughts of Ryan reappeared, which brought fear along with them.

A very tiny part of her was put out she didn't get to talk to Michael before dinner, but she quickly squashed the thought. Oscar's sudden appearance had shocked everyone, and now that he was here, he was priority number one.

Why the sudden appearance?

Once Daphne was seated, Claire sat next to her. She fixed her eyes on the French doors, waiting for Michael and Oscar to reappear. She twisted her hands in her lap, her heart pounding against her rib cage and her stomach flip-flopping every couple of seconds. Everything was so different now. Their kiss had altered everything. Not that she regretted it, because she didn't, but it was newfound territory.

A cold, frail hand rested on hers, stopping them from moving. Claire looked up into Daphne's curious eyes. The sparkle of life that used to be there was gone. Her days were numbered. Yet despite this, she was still the most positive person Claire knew.

"Are you okay?" Daphne asked.

She bit her lip and lowered her gaze. What could she say? How much detail did she give? What did one kiss—oh, okay, two— mean? How would people react? How would *Daphne* react?

Stop overthinking and answer the question.

Her gaze flicked across to the cooking area where Von busily mixed something in a saucepan. Watching her work helped Claire relax. She took a deep breath and sat up straighter, throwing a smile Daphne's way. "I'm fine."

And she was. She needed time to come to terms with this new phase of her life, that was all. Lots of women dated other men after a divorce. She was no different.

"You must be excited to see Oscar," Claire added.

"Of course I am, but I'm worried. It's not like Addison to turn up out of the blue like this." Daphne's lips pursed into a thin line. "She's clearly decided to take matters into her own hands. I can only imagine what she wants in return. Spiteful girl."

Claire's eyes widened. It wasn't like Daphne to speak so bitterly about someone. Then again, she'd heard a few colourful stories about Addison. Claire's gaze turned back to the door when it slid open, and Michael entered with Oscar. He caught her gaze and gave her a weary smile. Was something wrong with Oscar?

"Nanny!" Oscar dashed over to the table and skidded to a stop beside Daphne, looking up at her with a large smile.

"Oscar." Daphne smiled warmly at him, placing a gentle hand on his shoulder. "Have you met my friend Claire?"

Oscar's smile slipped as he looked up at Claire with wide, uncertain eyes.

"Hello, Oscar." Claire gave a little wave. "I've been looking forward to meeting you."

He eyed her curiously then grabbed Daphne's arm and whipped his head away, burying it in Daphne's lap.

Daphne laughed and ruffled his thick hair. "This isn't the Oscar I know. Why are you so shy all of a sudden?"

Oscar gestured for Daphne to come closer. She lowered her head then he whispered something in her ear. For a brief second Daphne's brow creased in worry but it quickly disappeared when Oscar pulled away. Daphne whispered something back, which caused Oscar to look up at Claire with a large smile.

"You're Juanita's friend too?" he asked in a disbelieving tone.

Claire looked across at Daphne who smiled. When she began to stand, Claire jumped up to assist her, but Daphne held her hand up. "I'm fine, Claire, I need to speak to my son. You keep Oscar company for a bit."

Reluctantly, Claire sat again and kept a watchful eye on Daphne as she approached Michael, who was now sitting on a sofa by the door. He wore an anxious expression. Her worry for him grew.

Sensing a presence next to her, she looked back and saw Oscar standing next to her with an expectant look on his face. Remembering she hadn't answered his question, she nodded. "Yes, I am."

Oscar's eyes lit up as he sat on Daphne's seat. "She's my best friend. She's the same age as me."

"You're both five then?"

"Yes. I'm going to marry her."

Claire raised an eyebrow. "Are you? You're a bit young for that, aren't you?"

"No." He shook his head vehemently. "We're going to go to school together and build sandcastles and play games and—"

As Oscar rattled off a list of things he and Juanita would do when they were 'married', Claire's mind drifted. She loved the innocence of their minds. Problems were so easily fixed in their world. If adults stopped and thought as logically as children, there wouldn't be so many issues.

"—and we're going to live under the sea." Oscar's voice cut through her thoughts.

Claire smiled and shook her head. *If only marriage was that simple. Oh, to be a child again.* "It sounds wonderful, Oscar. I'm sure you and Juanita will be happy together."

He giggled and kicked his legs back and forth. He suddenly stopped and looked at her. "You're pretty."

Claire's cheeks warmed. "Thank you, Oscar."

"Daddy, don't you think Claire's pretty?"

"Yes, I do."

Claire jumped at his voice, not realising he was so close. She shifted in her seat and found him standing next to her. The worry had gone for now, and he wore a soft smile on his face. Her stomach fluttered from the compliment, her cheeks burning even hotter.

Just when she thought it couldn't get any more embarrassing, Oscar blurted, "Claire's nice to me. I wish *she* was my Mummy."

Claire's eyes widened and she whipped her head around to look at Michael. What an unusual comment for a child to say. Was Addison mean to Oscar?

She met Michael's gaze, and he smiled sadly. While he didn't say anything, deep within his gaze, she could tell he wished the same thing. She had to look away quickly so he wouldn't see the same longing in her eyes.

To her relief, the conversation ceased when Von appeared at the table with dinner. Everyone sat to eat, but Claire sensed unease. Being too busy with Daphne and Oscar, she hadn't noticed earlier.

Casting a glance around the table, Oscar seemed to be the only one who didn't have a care. He slurped away at his soup, smiling toothily at anyone who looked at him.

Something was definitely off.

Oscar's arrival was unexpected, but it shouldn't put such a damper on the night. Michael and Daphne both wore grim looks and Von looked annoyed. Casting her mind back to Oscar's comment, she couldn't help wondering what life at home was like for him.

***

When dinner was over, the unease lifted slightly and everyone chatted, but something still didn't sit right. Soon after, Michael and Oscar migrated to the sofa to watch a children's movie. Oscar had begged to watch one, claiming he never got to watch them with his mother. Claire didn't miss the look that passed between Daphne and Michael.

While Von and Daphne chatted quietly, Claire stood from the table and approached the French doors. She slid them open and stepped out on to the landing. She stood with her eyes closed while the strong, cool breeze whipped around her.

Opening her eyes again, she saw the moon hiding behind clouds, making them appear light grey. The clouds moved quickly across the sky, rolling into each other. Saltwater blew into her face as the waves crashed violently on the shore. They were in the middle of spring, but after a hot week, a forecast change was on its way.

A flash of sheet lightning lit up the night sky in the distance followed by a low rumble of thunder. Claire smiled as she rubbed at the goosebumps on her arms. She loved storms and this was the first one she'd experienced in Busselton.

For a few moments, she enjoyed the spectacular lightning display alone. Each flash drew closer and closer to the house. It wouldn't be long before it hit.

Michael joined her a little while later. He stood close enough so his arm brushed hers. A shiver ran along the length of her spine, and she leaned into him, enjoying his closeness and warmth. Michael slid his arm across her shoulders and pulled her into his side. She smiled and relaxed. This was nice.

"Where's Oscar?" Claire asked.

"Asleep on the couch," Michael responded with a laugh. "He fell asleep halfway through the movie. I'll take him upstairs shortly."

"He's a good kid."

Claire's heart constricted. She so badly wanted a family and hoped one day she could make it happen. Early on in her marriage, she fell pregnant once but miscarried. She felt like such a terrible person when she was relieved it'd happened, but how could she have brought a child into the world with Ryan as its father?

Michael sighed and she looked up at him. He stared out over the ocean, a wistful look on his face. "He is. I only wish I could see him more."

Averting her gaze, she said, "It must be difficult having him live so far away."

"He was never supposed to be," Michael muttered bitterly.

Suddenly feeling bold, she asked, "May I ask why he ended up in New Zealand?" Before now, she'd never dared to ask about his past. Now that things had shifted between them, she wanted to know more. If they were both willing to try this relationship thing again, they needed to be open with each other.

Michael didn't respond for a long while. Claire glanced up at him again. He continued to stare out over the ocean, his face masked with a mixture of fear and uncertainty. She understood those feelings all too well. Opening up to each other meant breaking down their walls once and for all, leaving them with nothing to hide behind. They'd be exposing themselves to the world—weak, vulnerable and afraid.

Can I do it? Can he do it?

Finally, Michael turned to her and took her hands. "We never got to continue our conversation before." His eyes met hers and he added, "How about you come for a walk with me in half an hour? It's time we both talked, don't you think? You can do what you need to with Mum and I'll put Oscar to bed."

Her heart leapt. This was happening. Yet despite the fear running rampant in her, she still found herself nodding. *I can do this.*

"Okay," she whispered.

He leaned in and kissed her softly before pulling back and tucking her hair behind her ear. "Okay," he repeated. It was a confirmation of sorts, that they were about to start a new journey together.

Chapter 20

Once Daphne was in bed, Claire went back to the kitchen for her next lot of medication. She found Von wiping up the last of the dishes, a worried frown etched on her face.

Taking out the medicine container, Claire placed it on the table and asked, "Von, are you okay? You don't seem yourself tonight."

Von looked up and blinked a couple of times. She smiled, but it didn't reach her eyes. "Oh yes, I'm fine lovey…" After a pause, she sighed and hung the dishtowel over the sink. "I'm worried about little Oscar."

"Oscar? Is everything okay? Is it because he arrived early?" Claire couldn't think what else would be the matter.

"Oh no, I love the little one like he's my own. You haven't met his mother yet, but she's not a very nice woman. As much as I dislike her, I can tolerate her, but today something was…off."

Claire's eyes widened in surprise. "Wait, she was *here* today?" She wasn't sure why she was so surprised. How else would Oscar have arrived so suddenly? It *did* answer a lot of her questions about why everyone was so subdued at the dinner table.

Reaching for the towel again, Von hung it on the handle attached to the stove door. "Yes." She turned back to Claire. "She visited earlier while you were in with Daphne. She didn't stay long, mind."

Claire didn't get a chance to ask further questions before a fresh breeze rushed into the kitchen, blowing the recently hung towel on to the floor. Von bent to pick it up, and Claire turned as Michael stepped through the doors, closing them after him.

He rubbed his hands together. "It's a bit chilly out. We can postpone our walk if you like?"

Once upon a time, she'd find a way to get out of talking about Ryan, but not anymore. She was eager to tell Michael the truth in the hopes they could move forward and explore their new relationship. She shook her head. "No, it's fine. I'd like to go. I need to give your mum her medication then I'll be ready." Turning back to Von, who was readying to leave for the night, Claire said, "I'll see you tomorrow, Von."

Von smiled a real smile this time and pulled Claire into a warm embrace. "Have a good night, Claire." In a lower tone, she said in Claire's ear, "Please don't tell Michael my concerns. I'll talk to him later."

They pulled away and Claire nodded. She turned back to the medication container and took what she needed.

In Daphne's room, Claire found her slumped against the bedhead, fast asleep. The events of the day had sapped the last of her energy. Claire approached the bed and gently shook Daphne's shoulder. Her eyes fluttered open.

"Sorry to wake you," Claire said. "It's time for your medication."

Nodding weakly, Daphne attempted to sit up straighter but failed. Claire didn't help immediately, knowing Daphne liked to do what she could on her own. Over the last couple of weeks, she'd been holding on to every last inch of her independence. After another couple of failed attempts, Daphne huffed out a frustrated sigh and threw Claire a resigned look.

It pained Claire to see Daphne struggle so much, but she respected her wishes. Sadly her patient was losing more and more independence as her condition worsened. Now, feeding herself was the only thing she could do, but even that was becoming a struggle.

Once Claire had helped her with her pills, done her nightly checks, and laid her down again, she said, "I'll be in again later. You get some rest."

Claire went to move away, but Daphne grabbed her hand. "Claire, I'm so proud of you."

Looking into Daphne's now dull, almost lifeless eyes, a lump formed in Claire's throat. Hot tears stung her eyes. Daphne was so close to death. It was terrifying. She was a shell—her eyes were sunken, her skin was grey, and she was only skin and bone. Every time she moved or breathed, she winced from the pain. Her breathing was turning shallow and raspy.

Based on the doctor's estimation, Daphne should still have two or three weeks left, but life expectancies could never be relied upon. It was only a matter of time.

"Why?" Claire asked.

"You're learning to trust again." Daphne gave Claire's hand a weak squeeze. "I know you still struggle but you've come so far in such a short time."

Sitting on the seat next to the bed, Claire clasped Daphne's hand in both of her own. "It's only because of you it was even possible. You encouraged me to open up about my past and made me realise I can't let it control me. So much of it still does though."

"It will for a long time, but it will get easier. I promise. Don't do what I did."

Claire's breath caught in her throat. "What did you do?"

Tears filled Daphne's eyes. "I pushed my husband away. I let what my father did to me control every last inch of me. I was so convinced my husband would do the same I didn't trust him. Eventually he left me."

"But…I thought he was dead." Claire frowned. She knew very little about Daphne's husband, only what she'd previously said, and he hadn't come up in conversation with Michael, so she'd assumed he'd died. Confused, she said, "You said you almost lost him, so I assumed everything worked out and he'd since died or something."

Daphne laughed bitterly and shook her head slowly. "I won him back once, but we didn't last long. You see, I never trusted him." She shook her head impatiently, her brow furrowing. "I should start from the beginning, I suppose."

After a moment, Daphne took a deep breath. "My mother always told me the man I married would end up being like my father. This instilled a cold fear in me from a young age. When I met Tom, I was terrified. He *was* like my father in so many ways, personality-wise at least. I was convinced he'd hurt me. I refused to tell him about my father's abuse, so he never understood why I was so closed off around him."

A tear dripped down Daphne's cheek. Claire reached across for a tissue and dabbed it away. Her heart pounded against her rib cage.

"We were together for a year but in that time, I never learnt to trust Tom. I still feared he'd hurt me despite the fact he never did. In the end, Tom had enough and he left. Said he couldn't be with someone who wouldn't be open with him. This was before we married, I might add." Daphne gave a wry smile. "He went away for a few months, and I was devastated. I loved him so much, Claire. He was a wonderful man, and I think this is what made me do something. When he returned, I told him about my father and my fear and we worked things out. He convinced me he'd never hurt me and I trusted him."

Even though Daphne hadn't finished her story, Claire already guessed how it'd end. A wave of sadness washed over her. And to think, this could've been her if she hadn't taken a leap of faith with Michael.

"We finally married, and for the first couple of years, life was wonderful." Daphne smiled wistfully. "Then when Michael was born, I had what's now known as postpartum depression. I loved Michael with all my heart, but my terror returned and I accused Tom of abusing me even though he never once did. I wasn't myself, Claire, but in my mind, everything was so real. Even though I recovered from the depression, the terror never went away. When Michael was only two, Tom finally left. Once again he said he couldn't be with someone who didn't trust him."

"Oh my god," Claire's voice came out croaky. "Daphne, I'm—"

"No." Daphne held up a hand. "Don't apologise. He was right. After he left, I knew I had the chance to pull myself together and go after him, but I didn't. He deserved a life I couldn't provide. The point is, Claire, I let my terror get to me. I let it control me, and I lost the best man I've ever known. The only contact I had with him was when we shared the care of Michael. We never properly spoke though, and I had no idea what was going on in his personal life. When I recovered, I tried to win Tom back, but it was too late. I found out he'd remarried and had a child. There was no way I could interfere. We did talk eventually, and we're on good terms now, but it's a life decision I'll always regret. I loved that man with every part of me, I still do, and I lost him because I couldn't control my emotions."

By this point, Claire had tears dripping down her cheeks. It was all too close to home. A small part of her still hadn't let go of her fear, and if she wasn't careful, it could ruin whatever she and Michael could have.

"Claire," Daphne said urgently, "I know you and Michael have feelings for each other. I know how terrifying it is to trust another man, but please, I beg you, don't make the same mistake I did. Michael is every ounce his father…a good and genuine man who would *never* lay a finger on a woman. I know he has his flaws. He's rough around the edges, but he needs some nurturing. He's wearing a broken heart because of what that heartless bitch, Addison, did to him, but I know you can help him recover."

Even though it wasn't appropriate, Claire laughed. "I never thought I'd ever hear you say 'bitch', Daphne."

Daphne chuckled lightly. "Yes, well, I could think of other colourful words to describe her but I won't. I mean it, Claire. You two could be good together. Don't let your fears stand in the way. Trust me, I know what it's like. You still hear their harsh words. The images still haunt you. But if you let them win, you'll make the same mistakes I did. You're still young, Claire. You have such a long life ahead of you, and if you try hard, your ex-husband will soon be a passing memory."

Nodding, Claire took a tissue and wiped her tears. They sat in silence while Claire let Daphne's words sink in. She *had* made a lot of progress over the last two weeks, but the fear still lay dormant. Somehow, she had to deal with her demons once and for all. Lay her fears to rest.

A knock sounded at the door, and Claire turned as it opened and Michael walked in. She hoped her eyes didn't show any evidence of her crying.

Michael looked from Claire to Daphne and smiled knowingly. "What is it with women and their incessant chatter?"

"Oh, phooey." Daphne waved a hand at him. "You know nothing. Claire and I were having a heart to heart. Now if I recall, you told me you two were going for a walk. Don't let me keep you. I must sleep anyway."

Claire leaned in and kissed Daphne's cheek.

"Don't be afraid to talk to him," Daphne whispered in her ear. "He knows all about his father and my past."

They pulled away, and Claire smiled in response. When she rose from the bed, Michael came up to kiss his mother goodnight then he and Claire walked out of the room.

When they stepped outside into the cool breeze, Michael reached for her hand and linked his fingers through hers. "Are you ready?"

Claire took a calming breath and looked across at him, nodding. "I'm ready."

Chapter 21

Walking along the beach with Claire, fingers entwined, was the most natural thing in the world. Michael listened as she told her story. She spoke fast, as if needing to get it out quickly and tucked her hair behind her ear countless times.

She finished off the story by telling him how she survived. How the blade of the knife narrowly missed her heart. His eyes flicked to the scar once more, nausea overwhelming him at the thought of what she'd been through. He stopped walking and turned Claire to him. She kept her gaze lowered. What was she thinking?

"Claire?"

She drew in a breath and looked up, her blue-green eyes shining with unshed tears. A flash of lightning lit up the night sky, making her eyes shine brilliantly.

He stared deeply into her depths when he asked, "You know I'm never going to hurt you, don't you?"

Before anything, he *needed* her to know that truth. Even in the toughest of times with Addison, he hadn't laid a finger on her. And, hell, she was a hard woman to live with. But despite the pain she'd put him through, she hadn't deserved that. No one did, man or woman.

Claire stared at him for a long moment, her eyes searching his as though peering into his soul. Finally, a small smile kicked up the corners of her lips, and she nodded.

He breathed a sigh of relief and gathered her in his arms, holding her close. He admired her strength. Yes, she still had her struggles, but the fact she was here right now, in a new job, a new life, away from Ryan, was proof of it. God alone knew he didn't have the strength she did. He'd let bitterness overwhelm him and he wasn't proud of it. He'd learnt a lot from Claire Stone, and it made him want to do better and be good enough for her. She only deserved the best.

He'd be forever grateful to whoever saved her life that fateful day. Now she was in *his* life, and he didn't want it any other way. He so badly wanted to prove that even an imperfect and flawed man like himself could treat a woman right.

A clap of thunder sounded in the distance, the storm moving away. Claire stepped back and smiled up at Michael. He reached out and stroked her cheek. He was falling in love with this woman, and as terrifying as it was, he couldn't be happier.

"Thank you for telling me all that." He moved his hand to the back of her neck and ran his fingers through her hair.

"Have I—" She paused and bit her lip. "Has it changed your opinion of me?"

She was afraid of *that*? Some men might be scared off by such a past, but not him. He shook his head, but rather than answering, he leaned in and placed a soft kiss on her lips.

He pulled back and rested his forehead on hers. "Does that answer your question?"

Her smiling eyes met his. "Maybe a little."

His eyes widened in surprise, but before he could react, she wrapped her arms around his neck and covered his lips with hers. Well, this was a new side of Claire Stone he could get used to. He secured her in his arms, wrapped tightly around her slim waist, tasting her, inhaling her delicious lemon scent, mixed with the saltiness in the air. Their hearts beat in time, two hearts healing together, growing to love another person.

He gently deepened the kiss, showing her in the most passionate way possible that he promised never to hurt her. That she was everything to him. He had images of a life together, with her and Oscar. Their own little family. Oh how he'd do anything to make it a reality. With Claire nearby, anything was possible. She made dealing with Mum's impending death bearable. Before now, he hadn't been able to cope.

The kiss slowed and they pulled away, gazes meeting again.

"Well," he said with a low chuckle, "if that didn't answer your question, nothing will."

She gave him a cheeky grin. "No, I think that's well and truly answered it."

Hell, her teasing could get her into a lot of trouble. Her smirk and the mischievous glint in her eyes that came with it only made him want to kiss her forever.

"Always happy to oblige," he said, leaning in to taste her lips again.

The rumble of thunder in the distance reminded him he still had to tell his story. Pulling away, he took a good look at Claire. So vulnerable, yet so strong. He only hoped his own story didn't send her running, but it had to be said. She'd been honest with him. Now it was time to return the favour.

"I suppose it's my turn now, right?" he quipped with a half-hearted chuckle.

Claire smiled and it was only now he noticed how much happier she appeared. No longer burdened by a secret, her eyes were full of life and sparkle.

"I'd like to know," she said, running her thumb along the top of his hand. "But only if you're ready to tell me."

He sat on the sand and patted the spot next to him, an invitation for her to join him. He pulled his knees up and rested his arms over them as she sat down. He stared up at the night sky, stars beginning to pop in and out of view as the clouds drifted away. He considered his thoughts for a long moment before he spoke.

"My wife left me because she had an affair with another woman." The words tasted bitter on his tongue. Anyone who'd suffered through the hurt of infidelity would understand his bitterness. It didn't do much for your ego when your spouse ran off with someone else.

"Oscar was only a baby when she left, still breastfeeding. He was only days old."

Claire's hand rested on his arm. "I'm so sorry."

He barely heard her, steamrolled ahead. "I found out Addison got pregnant on purpose, without me knowing she was actively trying."

He turned to Claire to gauge her reaction, knowing how ludicrous that sounded. She stared at him with wide eyes. "How's that even possible? I mean, surely you were both aware of what you were doing. You can't 'try' unless you're completely unprotected." She gasped and her hand flew to her mouth. "I didn't mean that to sound so rude."

Shuffling closer to her, he slid his arm across her shoulders. "It wasn't rude. It's a perfectly realistic question." He laughed awkwardly and rubbed the back of his neck. "Trust me, I know how ridiculous it sounds. She was on the pill, but she'd come off it without me knowing, and before I knew it, she was pregnant."

Claire shuffled on the spot, and when he glanced over, she appeared uncomfortable. She hadn't told him specifics about her personal life with Ryan, but he could only imagine he wouldn't have taken no for an answer. The familiar anger he held toward the bastard bubbled low in his belly, but he kept it buried. Now wasn't the time to bring it up. He could only vow never to do the same thing.

"What was her plan then?" Claire asked.

He raked a hand through his hair, his heart pounding against his chest as memories came flooding back. "On the way to the hospital, after her waters broke, she confessed she'd been having an affair with this woman for a year. They wanted to have a child together, so Addison used me to get it."

Claire gasped in horror.

Tears stung Michael's eyes. He stared out over the ocean, reliving the memory like a movie reel. "I was too shocked to fully understand what was going on. By the time we arrived at the hospital, everything happened so quickly I didn't have a chance to let it sink in." Michael drew in a shuddering breath. "I held Oscar when he was born." His voice broke, and he cleared his throat. "I swear it was the happiest moment of my life."

He hadn't intended to cry, but tears fell down his cheeks, his shoulders shaking. Being with Claire revealed his vulnerabilities, but for once he could confidently be himself. He wasn't ashamed or embarrassed. Claire snuggled in closer to him and rested her head on his shoulder, her arm wrapping around his back.

Once he'd pulled himself together, he continued, "For the briefest moment I forgot about everything. I was a proud father holding my son for the first time. I still remember it like it was yesterday. He was so tiny and fragile yet perfect in every way. I fell in love with him and it made me want to be the best father I possibly could. Then Addison's confession rammed home, and I was suddenly faced with the cruel reality. I was being robbed of the chance to be a father."

When Claire moved away, he turned to her. His breath caught when he saw tears on her cheeks. Tears for *him*. He shuffled around to face her, giving her a weak smile of thanks. She wiped her tears away and with a single nod encouraged him to continue.

"When Addison was discharged from the hospital a couple of days later, she left me the same day." A sharp pain shot through his heart at the memory. He'd been in a bad place when that happened. If it wasn't for Oscar, god alone only knew what he would've been capable of. "We went to court, but they viewed me as a single father who couldn't offer Oscar what he needed. They favoured Addison because a child his age needed his mother, and there was no question about it being a same-sex relationship. It didn't do me any favours. Who needs a dad, right?" he scoffed. "*She* cheated, yet she won custody of him. Then I'm left looking like the bad guy even though I did nothing wrong. Where's the bloody fairness in that?"

Claire shook her head in disgust. She reached for his hands and held on to them tightly. "Michael, I'm so, so sorry. I can't begin to imagine the pain that would've caused you." She smiled then leaned in and kissed him softly. She caressed his cheek and quietly said, "Although I don't think you were entirely robbed. You still get to see Oscar, and he clearly loves you."

Michael shrugged and glanced down the beach, over her shoulder. "I had to fight even to get that. Addison was determined to get her way, and she pretty much did. Still does. In a way, I *was* robbed because I'm not a full-time father. I only get to see him four times a year. How can I be a good father?" He shook his head and looked back to her, her face crestfallen. "It's simple. I can't be. I try, I do, but my time with him is never enough to make a difference."

"Michael, I understand where you're coming from, I do, but you don't seem to realise how much of an influence you have on him. In one night alone, I've seen how much he adores you. If you weren't a good father, he wouldn't want to visit. He wouldn't look at you with adoration in his eyes the way he does."

Michael's heart swelled with pride.

Claire continued, "You're still a part of his life, and that's a huge win. While having him closer and seeing him often is important, the fact you don't have that luxury doesn't make you a bad father. I've met enough people in my nursing career to know that having a father around twenty-four-seven doesn't always make them a good father."

Michael thought back to his father. While he saw him more often than he saw Oscar, he realised Claire was right. He shook his head and smiled at her. "I'd never thought of it like that." He squeezed her hand. "Thank you, Claire."

He let his thoughts drift for a moment, thinking about what to say next. Finally, he said, "I've wanted to fight for him for so long, to be a full-time father, but…" His shoulders dropped as the reality of his situation hit home.

"Why haven't you?" Claire asked when he'd been silent too long.

"I did when the decision was first made, but I didn't get anywhere. Then Mum got sick, and she became my priority. As much as I want Oscar here, it's not a stable life for him, and the courts would agree. So I've had to wait."

"What about now?"

Michael let go of her hand and stood, turning to stare out over the ocean. How much should he tell her? Seeing Oscar again made him want to spur into immediate action. He'd speak to Lance first thing tomorrow morning.

Deciding Claire had a right to know, he said, "I'd already decided to fight for him again once Mum…passed, but I need to take action now."

"What's wrong?" Claire coaxed, getting to her feet.

He sighed. "Claire, this may be difficult for you—"

She swallowed and straightened her spine, as though readying for what he had to say. "I can handle it." She took his hand. "I want to be here for you, Michael."

He smiled weakly then ran a hand down his face. "I suspect something is happening at home. He hasn't said much but the fear in his eyes, on his face." He shuddered at the memory. "He told me he doesn't want to live with Addison anymore, and he told Mum he's locked in his room when they have visitors." He balled his free hand into a fist. "My son isn't shy, Claire. He used to befriend everyone, but now…well, you saw how he reacted to you."

She winced and nodded.

"It's not like him, and I think it's connected. If he's not used to being around strangers, he's going to be like this. The problem is I can't prove anything. I'm terrified if they do that to him, what else are they doing?"

Claire released a breath and asked, "Have you asked him?"

"How do I ask a five-year-old if his mother is hurting him?" He shook his head. "If my suspicions are true, he would've been told not to say anything."

"Yes but this is where you need to know how to question him without asking outright."

He raised an eyebrow. "How exactly?"

Claire cleared her throat. "Asking 'are you happy at home' could be an excellent way to get him talking. Even if he says yes, if something *is* happening, he's bound to hesitate first. Kids can't pretend as well as adults."

He nodded in understanding and stroked his chin thoughtfully. It made perfect sense. "Yes, I suppose so." He shook his head. "I'll have a think, but for now I'm glad he's here away from his mother and…the other woman."

He couldn't bring himself to say her name. She'd destroyed his family. Sure, he was no saint and he admitted partial fault to their marriage breaking down, but *he* hadn't been the one who cheated.

For a few moments, neither he nor Claire spoke. The silence was a comfortable one, and he was so relieved to have confessed his past to her. Maybe now they could move forward, see where this relationship went.

Turning to Claire, he held her at arms' length, his eyes searching her face. Oh, how he wished they'd met sooner. Oscar could be *their* son.

A jolt shot right to his heart, and it burst with love for this woman. Yes, he might've only known her for a couple of weeks, but he was head over heels in love with Claire Stone. It was too early to declare such feelings, but the realisation shifted his thinking. The bitterness that'd surrounded him like an aura for so long began to ebb away.

Why was he even harbouring bitterness toward Mikayla? Yes, she'd destroyed his marriage, but in hindsight, she'd done him a favour. He'd thought he and Addison were in love, but they hadn't ever been. He knew that now. He held onto the hurt because of what Addison had done, but if he wanted Claire to be his future, it was time to forgive and let go.

"Are you okay?" Claire asked.

Blinking a couple of times, he realised he'd been staring. He nodded and pulled her into his side once more, securing his arm around her shoulders. "I was thinking. Well, wishing, I suppose. Wishing we'd known each other all those years ago. Things could be so different right now."

Claire sighed and rested her head on his shoulder. He loved that she was so comfortable around him now. And he especially loved how she fit so perfectly in his arms.

"I couldn't agree more," she said, "but since we can't change a thing, do you know what I think?"

He kissed the top of her head. "Go on."

"I think that, as horrible as it was going through what we did, it's made us into who we are today. Admittedly it hasn't been a bed of roses. We've become bitter, broken and untrusting, but we *are* better people for it. We learn a lot from life lessons, and as much as I regret what happened, I became a survivor and learnt how to stand up for myself. From now on, I'll no longer let myself be trodden on. If my life hadn't taken this course, I don't think it would have happened."

Michael smiled in disbelief. "You're so much like my mother, it's unreal. You're positive despite what happened, and you're able to learn something from a terrible event."

"But unlike your mother, I'm not going to let the past control me."

Michael's smile slipped. "Ah. She told you about my father?"

"Yes, but only because she was afraid of what might happen to me if I didn't let go of my fear. She taught me something. She's a wise woman."

"She certainly is." He sighed and moved away, taking a step closer to the water. He looked up at the night sky. The clouds had gone, and stars twinkled brilliantly. Tears stung his eyes when he asked, "She hasn't got much longer, has she?"

He hadn't wanted to admit he'd noticed a change in her, but he couldn't hide from the truth. He had to prepare himself for her death even if he didn't want to, because there was no coming back from this.

"I'm afraid not," Claire said from behind him. "Oscar arrived at the right time."

He gave a single nod then turned away and folded his arms, his gaze fixed on the night sky. His chest tightened, tears threatening to fall.

"I must go check on her," Claire said, touching his arm lightly. "Will you be okay?"

He nodded and placed a hand over hers, giving it a squeeze. The truth was, he didn't know if he would be okay, but somehow he had to find a way to be.

Claire reached up and kissed his cheek. "Thank you for everything tonight."

He turned to her and caught her gaze, losing himself in her depths. "Thank you too."

He wanted to add *I love you,* but instead, he leaned in and kissed her softly, pouring his love into it. This woman was everything he needed, and when the time was right, he'd tell her his true feelings. Until then, he was content with her by his side. She made coping with his mother's death and Oscar's custody battle bearable.

Chapter 22

Michael couldn't sleep. Sharing a bed with Oscar, he watched his son's sleeping form. He still couldn't believe he was here. That wasn't the only thing keeping him awake, though. He couldn't stop thinking about what Oscar had told Mum. Locking a child in his room? Remembering Oscar's fear around Addison and Mikayla put him on edge.

He had to do something. If he questioned Addison, she'd deny it. He needed proof.

A sliver of light cut through the gap in the curtains, telling him it was morning. Oscar stirred at the same time, balling his hands into fists and rubbing his eyes. He moved them away and blinked at Michael, a quizzical look in his eyes.

"Daddy?"

"Good morning." Michael brushed his hair away from his forehead.

Oscar still looked confused. "Where's Mummy?"

Michael's stomach dropped. He wasn't pining for her, was he? He didn't think he could bear it, especially after the way she'd acted the night before.

He forced a smile. "She's not here. You're staying with me now, remember?"

Oscar sat up and looked around the room expectantly. "Mummy's not here?"

"No." He swallowed. "Do you want to see her? I can call and ask her to come around."

Oscar's face contorted in fear. "No." He scuttled back on the bed, resting his back against the headboard. "Please don't call her, I don't want her here. I want to be with you."

"Okay." Michael moved closer and lifted Oscar into his lap. "I won't call her."

"You promise?"

Michael held out his little finger. "Pinky promise."

Oscar looked from it to Michael warily. A slow smile spread across his face, and he looped his tiny finger with Michael's.

"You told me I'm not allowed to break pinky promises," Oscar pointed out matter-of-factly. "So you can't call Mummy now."

A bubble of pride rose in Michael's chest, a broad smile spreading across his face. *He* does *remember things I tell him.*

"That's right," Michael said. "I won't call her unless I have to."

Oscar's smile disappeared, and he shook his head. "No, Daddy, you can't call her ever. I'm staying with you forever and ever."

Michael's heart clenched. "I might have to call her from time to time. You don't have to see her if you don't want to, though, especially while you're with me. Okay?"

Oscar's eyes filled with tears, and he shook his head.

Taking this as the perfect opportunity to ask the question, Michael rubbed Oscar's arm soothingly. "Osc, what's wrong? Why don't you want to see Mummy anymore?"

Oscar crawled off Michael's lap and sat on the bed, pulling his knees up and burying his face in them. "I'm not allowed to say. Mummy said so."

"Why are you not allowed to say?"

Oscar's eyes, brimming with tears, peeped up over his knees. "Because I'll be locked in the naughty room," he whispered.

Michael closed his eyes for a second and breathed in deeply. *What the hell are they doing to him?*

"The same room you told Nanny about last night?" he asked tentatively.

Rather than saying anything, Oscar nodded then hid his face again.

"Is it only when people visit?" When Oscar didn't respond, Michael reached across and took his hand. "Oscar, you know you can talk to me, don't you?"

After a few moments, Oscar looked up and nodded. Then he straightened his neck and asked, "Do you have a naughty room, Daddy?"

"No but I have a naughty corner for when you're *really* naughty."

"You mean if I don't eat my dinner?"

Michael shuddered. Is that what they did? "No. I mean if you do something terribly naughty, like if you hurt someone on purpose, or if you lie to me."

"I haven't lied to you, Daddy." His eyes grew wide.

"Well, then no naughty corner for you then."

A small smile appeared on his lips, and he looked deep in thought. After a few moments, he crawled across to Michael and looked at him intently. "Can I tell you a secret, Daddy?"

"Of course you can."

"Do you promise not to tell Mummy?"

"I can't promise that, buddy." When Oscar shrunk back, Michael quickly added, "If I don't talk to her, I won't be able to help you. That's why I'll have to call her sometimes. If I don't, I could get into trouble then I won't be able to help you at all."

Oscar's eyes filled with hope. "If you help me, can I stay with you all the time?"

"Perhaps. I'd try and make it happen."

He shrieked then leapt up and flung his arms around Michael's neck. "You're the best Daddy ever."

Laughing, Michael gently pried Oscar's arms away so he could look at him. "I'm not promising anything, okay? I can only try, but I need to know everything so I can talk to some people. I can't get anywhere if I don't know."

"What if Mummy finds out?" Oscar asked.

"She will find out, but I'll look after you. Do you trust me?"

Oscar nodded.

"Then trust me now. Mummy will find out, but I'll protect you."

He looked away when he asked, "Will you protect me from Mikayla too?"

Michael's throat constricted, making it difficult to breathe. How could he have been so blind to this? Why did he never know what was going on? Every other time he saw Oscar, he never appeared any different. Was it because he was older and able to understand what was happening?

"Yes, Mikayla too," Michael said. Inside his heart was breaking. The thought of his flesh and blood being hurt by anyone devastated him.

Finally, Oscar nodded, then sat back and crossed his legs. His little face was etched with worry, and he said nothing.

Oscar seemed to have shied away from revealing his secret, so Michael had to ask the questions. Even though he was sure of the answers, he needed to hear it.

"Oscar, does Mummy or Mikayla hurt you?"

Oscar froze, fear crossing his face.

"You know you can tell me," Michael coaxed. "I'm not going to hurt you. Remember what I told you before. This is important so I can help you."

Oscar looked at the quilt cover and used his finger to trace along an invisible line. After what felt like hours, he nodded. Anger gripped Michael's heart. He closed his eyes and breathed slowly. His worst nightmare had come true. First, Claire and her monster, and now his son had one too. How could such people exist in the world? How could one of them be his ex-wife?

Once his anger had subsided, Michael opened his eyes again and asked, "How do they hurt you?"

Oscar didn't remove his gaze from the quilt. He was now tugging on a loose thread. "They use a big stick."

"A big stick? Like a cane?"

He shrugged. "It hurts a lot."

"When do they do that?"

"When I'm naughty."

"How are you naughty?"

He shrugged again and dropped his head. "If I don't eat my dinner, or if I don't clean my room, or if I make too much noise."

Since when is that considered naughty enough to be hit with a cane?

Michael ran a hand down his face and released a heavy sigh. How was he supposed to deal with this?

"Are you angry, Daddy?"

"Not at you, Osc. I'm angry at Mummy and Mikayla but not you. Have they hurt you in any other way?"

"Sometimes they smack me and pull my hair and push me over."

Michael gripped the covers to stop himself from losing his cool. It was hard work keeping control. Having Oscar in front of him was the only thing making it possible.

"Come here." Michael held out his arms, and Oscar crawled into them. "I promise I'm never going to hurt you, okay?" He stroked

Oscar's hair away from his forehead. "I'm going to make some phone calls soon and see what I can do."

Oscar pulled away, and he grinned, any remnant of fear gone. "Can we still build a sandcastle later?"

Michael laughed. He wished he was a kid again. They got over things so quickly. "Yes, of course, we can. Perhaps Juanita would like to come around too."

Catching up with Norman and Jo while Oscar was visiting would give him an opportunity to offload and figure out what to do.

"Juanita?" Oscar shrieked. "I want to see Juanita."

"Well then, why don't we shower and have breakfast then see if she wants to visit?"

Oscar nodded then slid off the bed and ran around the room excitedly. Michael picked up his phone and checked the time. It was only six-thirty, but he knew they were early risers. He sent a text to Norman, asking if he was free. It was possible Juanita was as excited as Oscar, and if Michael didn't text, Norman and Joanna would show up anyway.

***

"You need to get straight onto Lance," Norman said after Michael had explained everything. "You may not have physical proof, but Oscar's word should amount to something. He's old enough to speak for himself now."

Nodding, Michael raked a hand through his hair and glanced around. He used his hand as a visor to block out the sun shimmering brightly on the ocean. When his vision cleared, he saw the two kids playing in the sand. Oscar looked back and waved a wet, sandy hand at him then returned to the sandcastle he and Juanita were building.

"I know, but..." He considered the fears he'd been ignoring. "What if they still don't look on me as a suitable parent? I'm not in a relationship, and I'm still caring for Mum."

"I hate to bring this up, man, but we both know by the time it comes for you to go to court she won't be here."

Michael's back stiffened, and he folded his arms. "Thanks for the reminder, mate," he said bitterly.

Norman held his hands up. "You can't bury your head in the sand, Micky. I hate the idea as much as you, but we both know it's the truth. Unfortunately, right now, you can't afford to mess about. This is Oscar's life at stake. God knows what else Addison is capable of if you don't do anything."

Michael sighed and shook the tension out of his shoulders. Norman was right. He couldn't delay it. As much as it hurt to admit it, Mum wouldn't be around long enough to affect the court case. In regard to the relationship aspect, Michael could only hope the evidence he had was enough to prove he was capable.

He opened his mouth to respond when Oscar yelled for help. His head whipped around in time to see Addison grab his arm. She held a *Thomas the Tank Engine* backpack in her other hand. When she turned to walk away, Oscar dug his feet in the sand, but she pulled on his arm and dragged him behind her.

Juanita was desperately calling for Norman, who was running toward her. Michael jerked into action and ran to Oscar. He didn't even think. The moment he reached them, he grabbed Addison's wrist to stop her from going any further.

"What the hell do you think you're doing?" he growled. "Let go of my son."

Addison's angry eyes bore holes into him. "Let go of me."

Realising what he'd done, he quickly released her and took a step back. *I should know better than to touch her. Next thing I know she'll be accusing me of abuse.*

"Let go of Oscar, you're scaring him," he said, keeping his voice even.

Michael looked across at Oscar who had tears running down his cheeks while he tried fervently to break free from Addison's grip. Rather than letting him go, she yanked him closer to her, her fingers tightening around his wrist. Oscar whimpered.

"He's fine," she said flippantly. "He's only upset because he wants to be with me."

"Daddy," Oscar cried, "Daddy, please don't make me go. Please, Daddy."

Michael raised an eyebrow. "Doesn't sound like it."

She waved a dismissive hand. "Whatever. He's *my* son, and he's coming with me. Bringing him here was a bad idea."

"Then why did you bring his clothes?" He gestured to the bag.

Addison stuck her nose up in the air. "I told you I'd bring them around. But when he wouldn't acknowledge me, I realised you'd corrupted him. He's coming home with me."

Michael took a step closer. "No, Addison. It's my turn to have him stay with me." He'd had enough of her controlling. It was time to do what was right for his son. "If you take him back you'll be breaking our custody arrangements."

"Daddy," Oscar sobbed, "please don't make me go back. I want to stay with you."

"Shut up, you little brat," Addison yelled back at him. Turning to Michael, she said, "You've had him one night and look what you've turned him into. You're telling him things about me that aren't true."

"No, you're wrong. The only thing I'm guilty of doing is letting our son talk and listening to him. When was the last time you did that? Or are you too busy locking him in his room to care?"

She gasped and dropped the bag she was holding. Michael's cheek stung when her hand connected with it. He groaned and rubbed it to ease the stinging. They stared each other down for a long moment. Addison's green eyes were stormy. She appeared out of control, which was out of character for her. As a woman who commanded and oozed control, something had to be terribly wrong to unravel her so much. It only strengthened Michael's resolve to protect Oscar. His son wasn't safe.

"How dare you," Addison said between clenched teeth. "Is he lying again? I haven't laid a finger on him, and if you dare tell—"

"Oh, I'm going to tell anyone I can," Michael threatened. "I'll do everything in my power to get Oscar in my care."

When Addison's arm swung back, ready to slap him again, he grabbed her wrist in time to stop it.

"I'll get you done for abuse if you keep this up," he said in a low voice.

For a moment, Addison looked worried, but then she began to laugh. "Are you freaking serious? *You'd* claim *I* abused you? How absurd. The courts would never believe it. However, they *will* believe me if I tell them you abused me, and you're a risk to Oscar."

A wicked grin crossed her face and Michael let go of her wrist, cold fear clawing through his veins.

"No, they won't," a voice said.

Norman stopped at Michael's side, arms folded across his chest threateningly. Michael sighed from relief, a small glimmer of hope flickering to life deep within him. If he could prove what she was like, he might have a chance to get custody of Oscar.

"I'm a witness," Norman said. "I heard everything you said."

She flung her raven-black hair over her shoulder. "So what? It's your word against mine. I've got the power. I always have had."

Norman reached into his pocket for his iPhone and held it up. "You know what I learnt the other day? Smartphones have a voice recorder on them. Go figure. My wife was telling me about it. Never thought I'd use it though...'til now."

Michael threw a grin Norman's way, who winked in response.

"It's over, Addison," Michael said. "I'd suggest you go home. You'll be hearing from my lawyer very soon."

Addison's eyes flashed, her cheeks reddening as her deafening squeal of anger pierced the air. She let go of Oscar's arm, pushing him back as he did so. He fell onto his bottom, but he quickly jumped up again then ran over and stomped on her foot.

"Oh my god." She lifted her foot and hopped on the spot. She glared at Oscar and let go of her foot. "You little bastard." Her face darkened as she swung her arm back.

It all happened so quickly. Michael couldn't react in time. In slow motion, Addison's hand connected with Oscar's cheek and his little body went flying into the sand. The sound of his sobs sped up time again, and anger gripped Michael in its talons.

Michael ran over to Oscar and knelt beside him, picking him up and cradling him in his arms. He looked up at Addison whose face had paled, regret oozing from her eyes. She opened her mouth to speak, but Michael didn't want to hear what she had to say. He pointed in the opposite direction and demanded, "Get away from my son. If you dare come here again, I'll call the police."

Pushing his anger aside for the time being, he gently wiped the sand off Oscar's face, away from his eyes, nose and mouth.

"Daddy," Oscar whimpered, burying himself deeper into the crook of Michael's arm.

"It's okay," Michael soothed, gently rocking him back and forth. "I'm not going anywhere."

Michael looked up to see Addison walking back down the beach, away from them. Norman watched her like a hawk, and it was only knowing he wouldn't let her come back that Michael could let his guard down. He couldn't be angry right now.

That scene would torment him forever. He had to get on to Lance straight away. There was no way he was letting Oscar go back to New Zealand.

"You okay, mate?"

Michael looked up into Norman's concerned eyes. He nodded, even though he felt far from okay. Juanita clung to Norman protectively, her eyes wide with fear.

"You?" Michael asked.

"Apart from wanting to murder her, I'm fine," he muttered. "Look I've got to take Juanita home, she's a little scared. Will you be okay?"

Looking down at Oscar who was staring at nothing, tears glistening his cheeks, Michael sighed and nodded. "I'll be fine. Thanks, mate, for everything."

Norman placed a hand on Michael's shoulder and smiled. "Anything for a mate. Let's try this again soon."

Norman took Juanita's hand then turned and walked away.

Michael looked back at Oscar then placed a kiss on the top of his head. *Children should never have to experience this sort of thing. What if this scars him for life? I could never forgive myself.*

They were more worries to add to his existing ones.

Chapter 23

Even though Claire was up every four hours to check on Daphne, in between she slept blissfully. Speaking to Michael and opening up about her past had lifted such a weight off her shoulders. She felt like a brand-new woman, ready to take on the world and explore her new future. She couldn't wait to spend more time with him.

While she was getting ready for the new day, she hummed to herself, happiness surrounding her like an aura. She heard Michael and Oscar head downstairs early, and her heart leapt. Her new future would involve Oscar too. It was a scary prospect, having never dealt much with kids before, but one she wanted to embrace.

Heading downstairs, she spotted Michael and Norman standing on the beach talking. Oscar and Juanita sat by the water's edge, building a sandcastle. She smiled and made her way inside to check on Daphne. Joanna was there, helping Von prepare breakfast.

"Good morning." Claire called cheerily.

Joanna spun around and grinned. "Well, good morning to you. Someone's extra chirpy today."

Claire's cheeks burned, but a wide grin spread across her face. "I had a good sleep, that's all."

Never one to do things quietly, Joanna gasped. "Oh. My. God. Don't tell me you two finally kissed."

Claire's cheeks were about ready to combust. She hadn't intended to announce it so publicly, but she should've known Joanna wouldn't be able to hold her tongue. Still, rather than being embarrassed, a giddy excitement overwhelmed her. She shrugged and managed a little nod.

Joanna squealed loudly and ran over to Claire, embracing her tightly. "Claire, oh my god, I can't believe it." She pulled away and grew serious. "You're happy, aren't you? I mean, this is what you want?"

"Of course, Jo." Claire couldn't help but laugh. "This is all a little new for me, that's all."

Joanna grinned again. "Well, that's understandable."

"Coffee, Jo?" Von called.

"Oh, yes please." Joanna broke away and made her way back to Von, who held out a mug of steaming coffee. She took a sip and groaned in pleasure. "Von, you make the best coffee ever."

Claire caught Von's gaze, and she winked at Claire but said nothing. Claire's cheek flush lessened as she went to check on Daphne. "What are you doing here so early anyway, Jo?" she asked.

Joanna stifled a yawn and took another sip of coffee. "Someone, not mentioning any names, decided to text Norman at six-thirty to say 'hey, why doesn't Juanita come over and play with Oscar'? So, no Saturday lay-in for me."

Claire laughed. "Fair enough. Well, I'd better get to work." One last glance out of the front windows and she saw Oscar look back at Michael and wave a wet, sandy hand at him.

Her smile remained when she went to check on Daphne. Yes, life was great right now.

Entering Daphne's room, Claire's smile slipped when she noticed she was still asleep. Even on her bad days, she'd usually wake around the same time. Frowning, Claire went about her morning checks. Daphne's blood pressure was low, her breathing shallow and irregular. All this had occurred in the last four hours. It wasn't looking good. Since Daphne would probably be too weak to swallow the tablets normally, Claire resorted to delivering her medicine intravenously.

Her happiness gone, Claire felt a heaviness settle in her chest when she stepped out of the room nearly an hour later.

"Will Daphne be joining us this morning?" Von asked.

Taking a deep breath, Claire shook her head. "She's still sleeping. Maybe keep some aside, and I'll check on her again soon. She might want something later."

She doubted that would be the case, but she didn't want to say anything to Von yet. Although the way her face had fallen, she'd already assumed the worst. Claire was no doctor and couldn't make that determination herself. It was the first time she'd noticed a change in Daphne, so she could only monitor it and alert Doctor Charlton if she didn't improve.

"Would you like some breakfast?" Von asked in a shaky voice.

Claire's heart constricted. This wasn't an easy time for anyone. "Yes, please. Will anyone else be joining us?" She sat at the table as Von brought plates across.

"Jo and Norm have taken Juanita home. Michael's upstairs with Oscar. They'll have something to eat later."

Claire's brow furrowed. They seemed fine an hour ago. Had something happened while she'd been in with Daphne?

After eating, Claire went back in to Daphne again and sat by her side. She didn't once wake. The dread settling in Claire's gut told her she didn't have long left. Von came in with a cup of tea at one point, but it still sat untouched on the cupboard.

After a couple of hours, Claire exited the room. Michael hadn't been in, and she wanted to check if everything was okay. When she came out, she found him sitting on the sofa with his head rested back, eyes closed. Dark bags settled underneath them, indicating he'd had very little sleep. She recalled their conversation the night before and his concerns about Oscar. Maybe that's what had kept him awake?

Oscar seemed lively enough. He had his back to her, sitting in front of the TV watching some children's program. He bounced up and down in time to the loud, happy music. She looked across at Von, who also looked at Michael and Oscar with a frown.

Making her way over, Claire stopped beside Von and asked in a whisper, "Is he okay?"

Von shook her head and handed Claire a cup of coffee. "Can you give this to him? I think he needs it." She smiled warmly and patted Claire's arm. "I think he might also need someone to talk to."

Something was *definitely* off. Nodding, Claire made her way over and stopped beside the sofa. Michael rubbed his eyes and sighed.

"You look like you could do with this," she said.

Michael's eyes snapped open and stared into hers. The whites were bloodshot, but he broke out into a grin and sat up. Butterflies came to life in her stomach, knowing he was pleased to see her. He reached for the mug and took it from her, their fingers brushing. She shivered from the contact, a silly smile breaking out on her face.

He took a sip of his coffee and sighed. "Thanks for this. You make good coffee."

She laughed and sat beside him. "No I don't, trust me. Von made it."

"Oh." Michael turned to Von and called, "Thanks, Von."

She smiled and nodded but said nothing as she continued working.

"So you don't make good coffee then?" he asked, turning back to Claire.

Claire shook her head and pulled a face. "Don't ever ask me to make you one. I promise it'll be like drinking dirty water."

He laughed then took another sip. "Duly noted." He wrapped his hands around the mug and sat back, his smile disappearing.

"Everything okay?" she asked.

Michael winced and turned to Oscar. She followed his gaze. He didn't say anything at first, but she didn't push, waiting for him to speak.

He downed the rest of his coffee and placed the empty mug on the floor. "Addison turned up this morning," was his reply as he ran his hands down his face.

Claire bit her lip. What happened? She didn't get to ask before Oscar turned slightly, and she caught a glimpse of a blue bruise forming on his face. She drew in a sharp intake of breath. What the hell?

Her hands balled into fists on her lap, fingernails digging into her palm. She turned to Michael in silent question—*did Addison do this*? They seemed to be so in tune—sadness filled Michael's eyes, and he nodded.

He leaned in and whispered, "She tried to take him away, and Oscar didn't want to go. She slapped him."

Claire gasped, her hand flying up to her mouth. Fury bubbled in her veins.

She reached across for Michael's hand and squeezed. "That wretched woman. Michael, I'm so sorry. What are you going to do?"

He opened his mouth to respond, but Oscar's excited shriek cut him off—"Claire!" He ran up to the sofa and jumped onto it, sitting in between her and the armrest. She drew in a deep breath to calm her fury and smiled at the little boy. He'd warmed to her quickly, and that spoke volumes. Oscar might not understand what instincts were, but if he didn't trust her, he'd steer clear.

"Hi Oscar," she said. "How are you?"

"Do you want to build a sandcastle with me?" His eyes were hopeful.

She turned to Michael to seek his permission, but Norman, Joanna and Juanita returned at the same moment. Oscar jumped off the sofa and ran to Juanita's side. He grabbed her hand and dragged her to the TV, the sandcastle request forgotten.

Claire stood and joined Joanna at the front of the door. "I was wondering where you'd disappeared to."

Joanna frowned and looked across at Oscar and Juanita playing. "Sorry, we had to take Juanita home. She was distraught after what happened on the beach." She looked back at Claire. "Did Michael tell you what happened?"

She nodded. Anger thrummed through her veins, and she linked her fingers in front of her to hide the tremble in her hands. She had to keep control for Oscar. Instead, she and Joanna turned to generalities while the kids played and Michael and Norman spoke in hushed tones.

After a few minutes, Michael stood and approached Oscar, crouching in front of him.

"Has he been to the police?" Claire whispered to Joanna.

"Not yet, but that's why we're here. Michael's in a bit of a state, understandably, so Norman has offered to go with him for moral support. Besides, he and Juanita saw it happen, so they need to give their statement of events."

Claire nodded and looked back at Michael. Her heart went out to him. It wasn't right for anyone to be abused, but somehow it seemed even worse when a child was involved. She silently prayed that something good could come out of this. Oscar needed safety, and this was the best place for him.

The men and the kids left five minutes later, leaving Claire to let go of her pent-up emotions. "How the hell does someone get away with that?" she yelled, throwing her hands up in the air. "Who gets away with hurting a child?"

"No one," Joanna said. "No one does, Claire. That's why they're going to the police."

Pacing the floor, Claire ran a hand through her hair then stopped again and turned to Joanna. "I hope she rots in jail. How...I don't..." She groaned in frustration, hot tears running down her cheeks. "I don't understand, Jo. How can anyone do it? He's an innocent child, for god's sake. It's not fair."

Joanna approached her and held her at arm's length. "I know, Claire." Her eyes glistened with tears. She pulled her into a hug, and they cried into each other's shoulders.

It was too close to home. Too many of her memories ran through her mind. At least she was able to defend herself. Oscar couldn't because he was too young.

Claire pulled away and wiped away her tears with the back of her hand. "I don't mean to get so emotional," she said with a sniffle. "It's so hard, Jo. It brings back all those memories I've tried not to think about."

"You of all people are allowed to get emotional, Claire. It's completely normal to feel this way. The thought of anyone abusing someone, especially a child, hurts the best of us. I can only imagine how much worse it would be for you."

Claire wrung her hands together. "But it shouldn't have anything to do with me. A poor little boy has been hurt, and I'm reminded of my past. How can I be so selfish?"

"Claire"—Joanna took Claire's hands—"you need to stop being so hard on yourself. You can't expect to overcome your past in a few months. It's going to take time. Even when you're recovered, there'll always be reminders."

Claire's shoulders slumped forward, and she shook her head. "I don't want to be reminded anymore. I want it to go away. I wish I could face this situation confidently and *not* be reminded of what I went through."

"It'll get easier in time," Joanna said with a smile. "You'll always have the memory, but one day it won't hurt so much."

Smiling, Claire shook her head and laughed softly. "How have I survived these last few years without you in my life?"

Joanna laughed. "Beats me. I'm too wonderful for words."

They shared a laugh, and the mood lightened.

"How about a cuppa?" Claire asked, walking to the kettle and switching it on. *Please don't ask for a coffee. I can't make a decent cup to save my life.*

"I'd love a tea, thanks."

Nodding, Claire smiled to herself and sighed from relief. She removed two mugs from the cupboard then went to ask Von if she wanted one. Von wasn't in the laundry room, so Claire stuck her head out the back door. She found the housekeeper standing in the driveway, arms wrapped around herself as her shoulders shook.

Claire furrowed her brow in worry. "Von?" She descended the stairs. "Are you okay?"

Von gasped and spun around, wiping tears away from her cheeks. "You gave me a fright." She forced a smile. "Are you okay?"

Claire stopped beside her. "I asked you first, Von."

"Oh, I'm fine." She dabbed at her eyes and sniffled. "It's a little dusty today. I must have got some in my eye."

Claire looked around. There was no dust. It was a still day and the warm sun beat down on them. Beads of sweat had already formed on her brow.

"Dust?" she questioned. "Yep, there's a ton of that around right now."

Von laughed weakly and turned to look out onto the street. "Fine, you caught me."

Claire stood next to her but said nothing.

"I'm not an eavesdropper, Claire," Von said. "But I happened to overhear your conversation with Jo."

Claire's stomach dropped when Von looked up at her with tears in her tired eyes. Of course, she didn't know about her past yet. They'd both been busy and she hadn't had a chance to talk to her.

"Yes, I was abused," Claire said, surprised how easily the words came each time she spoke about it. "Please don't think I kept it from you on purpose."

"Don't be silly. I never thought that. It pains me to know you suffered. You mean a lot to me, Claire, and hearing what you went through—" She held a hand to her mouth and released a shuddering breath but said nothing more.

Claire's cheeks burned. She was still struggling to grasp that people cared enough...so much so they even cried for her. She looped her arm through Von's. "It's no wonder you and Daphne are such close friends. You're both such wonderful women."

Von chuckled and wiped the fresh tears away from her cheeks. "So are you, my dear. The fact you survived something so horrible makes you amazing, like Daphne."

Claire shrugged awkwardly. "I knew deep down there was more to live for."

Von nodded then smiled, brighter this time. "Well, despite what happened, we're very blessed to have you in our lives."

Claire's cheeks only burned hotter. "Thanks, Von." Remembering why she'd searched for her in the first place, she added, "If you're feeling better, would you like a cuppa? I was about to make tea for Jo and myself."

"I would, but I'll make them." Von turned back to the house.

Claire sighed and followed. "But the whole point of me offering was to save you a job."

Von stopped at the top of the stairs and smiled down at Claire. "Yes, but I heard you tell Michael that you make bad coffee. I could do with a good one right now, so I feel it's in my best interests to take over."

Claire laughed and shrugged. "Touché, Von. Tell you what, I'll check on Daphne then I'll join you."

Chapter 24

Stopping at the door leading into Daphne's room, Claire breathed in deeply and released it slowly. She'd grown close to Daphne, and the idea of losing her weighed heavily on her heart. A small, irrational part of her held onto the slightest hope that her patient might've improved over the last half hour.

The rational, experienced nurse side knew it was futile. Once a cancer patient stopped eating and drinking, the other signs of death closely followed.

Taking one more deep breath, Claire turned the handle and entered the room. She'd barely reached the bed when Daphne's loud breathing halted her in her tracks. Forcing her legs to move, she made it to bed and stared down at Daphne's fragile form. Tears pooled in her eyes, and a sob rose in her chest. *Keep it together.*

It was nearly time.

She turned to leave when she heard Daphne mutter something. Walking back to the bed, Claire sat on the chair and waited. After a few moments, Daphne's head shook back and forth slowly, her cracked lips moving as she muttered under her breath. *What's bothering her?*

Daphne started speaking again, clearer this time. "Tom?" Her eyes remained closed, and her brow furrowed. "Are you here? I need to talk to you."

Claire reached across and took Daphne's hand. "Tom's not here."

Shaking her head impatiently, Daphne turned to Claire and opened her eyes. They were distant and confused. "Von? I'm so glad you're here. Can you get Tom for me? He's in the kitchen. I need to talk to him."

This was the part Claire hated most—the confusion and disorientation. It wasn't always possible to know what her patients were talking about. Claire found the best way to deal with it was to agree since they usually forgot what they'd asked for moments later anyway.

"I'll see if I can find him," Claire said. "For now, you should go back to sleep."

A small smile graced Daphne's lips as she closed her eyes and settled back on the pillow. Standing, Claire shook her head in defeat. For the first time since becoming a nurse, she questioned how much longer she could do it. Once upon a time she'd truly enjoyed her job. Now, it caused her nothing but pain. There was too much death.

With my new life, maybe it's time to get a new job?

Since starting this job, she hadn't adequately considered what she'd do once it ended. Yes, she'd thought about it fleetingly, and discussed her plans with Daphne and Joanna, but she'd never got around to taking action.

With a sigh, she pushed the thoughts aside for the time being and walked away. When she passed the window Daphne clearly said, "Claire, can you open the window, please? I wish to see the ocean one last time."

With a heavy heart, Claire did so then left the room.

It was time to call the doctor and get the family together.

***

Once Doctor Charlton arrived and went to see Daphne, Claire took a break. When she entered the kitchen, she found Von and Joanna at the table. Their hot drinks were long gone but they seemed content chatting. She held off saying anything yet. Perhaps her estimations weren't reliable.

Forcing a smile, she took a seat next to Joanna. The two women stopped talking and looked at her expectantly. Neither asked questions and Claire didn't reveal anything, but it was clear they suspected the worst.

Von was the first to speak. "How about that cuppa then?" she babbled, as though doing so would force the reality away.

Claire nodded. "Yes, please. Thanks, Von."

When Von walked away, Joanna moved her chair closer then asked in hushed a tone, "Claire, is Daphne okay?"

Should she say anything? Then again, Joanna *was* a nurse. If anyone could handle the situation calmly, she would.

Claire shrugged. "She's not good. I have a feeling she won't see the day out, but I can't be certain. That's why Doctor Charlton is here."

Joanna drew in a breath through her teeth and sat back in her chair. "What's her breathing like?"

"Laboured, loud. She's struggling."

"And she's sleeping a lot?"

"All the time."

"Disorientation?"

Claire nodded. She reflected on the times at university when she and Joanna would bounce thoughts and ideas off each other. They'd study together and quiz each other before exams.

"She was asking for Tom before," Claire said softly.

Joanna's eyes widened. "Does he know how sick she is?"

"I don't know. I can only presume Michael's told him. She keeps saying she wants to see him again. What do you think I should do?"

Before Joanna could respond, Von returned with a mug of steaming coffee. Placing it on the table, Claire looked up and smiled her thanks, and was met with watery eyes. She opened her mouth to ask once again if she was okay. Von shook her head and bustled off to recommence her chores.

Claire sighed. "She suspects what's wrong, but I don't want to confirm anything until I know for sure. I would hate to cause undue stress if I was wrong. She's already in a state."

Joanna nodded. "I understand. I'm certain you're *not* wrong, but I also agree it's better to wait."

Claire looked back at Von, who was scrubbing at the stove, which was already pristine. "Will she be okay?" she asked Joanna.

Joanna shrugged but her brow creased in worry. It was clear they both shared the same concerns. After losing her husband to cancer, Claire couldn't imagine Von coping well.

For a few moments, Claire and Joanna chatted while Von worked, but the atmosphere was tense. The laughter was fake and the conversations only passed the time while they waited for Doctor Charlton to reappear. Claire glanced at her watch. He'd been in there for ten minutes. *He should be done soon, surely?*

Claire finished her coffee when the sliding door opened and Juanita and Oscar came running in. Norman and Michael followed a few seconds later, large smiles on their faces.

"How'd it go?" Joanna asked, standing.

Claire followed suit and turned to face them.

"They're going to question Addison today," Michael said, his smile widening. "They'll also get in touch with the police in New Zealand to question Mikayla. For now Oscar's staying with me until it goes to court and they make a decision."

Joanna gasped and her hand flew up to her mouth. "Mick. That's great news." She ran up and flung her arms around his neck.

This seemed to encourage the children who started jumping around and squealing in excitement. The noise was deafening, but no one seemed to care. It cut the tension, even if it was only for a short while, and the room buzzed with happiness.

Claire's cheeks hurt from smiling. She moved closer but stood back while Joanna and Norman chatted about the good news. Once they'd moved away, with Joanna giving Norman a not-so-subtle dig in the ribs with her elbow, Claire stepped forward.

"I'm happy for you, Michael."

"Thanks." His eyes lit up, and he held out his arms. With no embarrassment or awkwardness present, Claire stepped into them confidently.

When he wrapped them around her tightly, she sighed contentedly. This was home. Her security. Her ever after.

She stepped back, still grinning like mad. Her cheeks burned when she noticed Norman and Joanna looking at them with wide smiles.

"It's not permanent," Michael added, "but it's a step in the right direction."

Everyone chatted animatedly for a few moments before Doctor Charlton cleared his throat behind them. The room went quiet.

As one, the adults spun around and stared at him. Doctor Charlton wore a grave expression and the previous happy vibe dissipated in a puff of smoke. Claire's stomach dropped, knowing exactly what words were about to be spoken. She glanced at Michael, whose face was pale. She cursed under her breath, wishing she'd had a moment to tell him the doctor was in there with his mother, but they'd been too caught up in the good news about Oscar.

Clearing his throat again, Doctor Charlton ran a hand through his thinning hair. He glanced around at everyone then said, "I'm afraid Daphne doesn't have long left. The way her health is deteriorating, I'd be astonished if she sees the weekend out."

Claire hung her head. A sharp pain ripped through her chest, like someone piercing it with a dagger. This was why she didn't get close to her patients. It hurt too damn much.

A thick cloud of tension filled the room, suffocating Claire. No one spoke, still too shocked to say a word. No amount of preparation ever made dealing with death easier. A burst of laughter cut through the tension. Claire turned to see Oscar and Juanita sitting in front of the television, laughing at two puppet animals dancing stupidly on the screen, oblivious to Doctor Charlton's presence and announcement.

Everyone sprang into action. Michael stormed outside, Von following seconds later. Joanna said something in Norman's ear then disappeared into Daphne's room. Norman sat beside his daughter. All Claire could do was stand in numb shock, helpless, unable to do a damn thing. It was only when Doctor Charlton approached that her brain sparked into action. Now wasn't the time to lose focus. She still had a job to do.

"Claire," Doctor Charlton said, stopping in front of her, "she's been asking for Tom, her ex-husband."

"Yes, I heard her ask for him before, but she was disoriented. I wasn't sure if it was a request or not."

"It may not have been before, but when I was in there, she recognised me and asked to see him. I've been their family doctor for years. I'll get in contact with him as soon as I leave. I think he needs to come today."

"Is he close by?" Daphne hadn't mentioned where he lived.

"He's in Perth. I'm pretty sure he'll come down immediately, so he should be here in about three hours. I think she's holding on for him."

Claire's heart leapt. "I understand."

It occurred to her that this was why Daphne had deteriorated so quickly. Now that she'd seen Oscar, she only had one more person to say goodbye to before she could stop fighting.

"I'd suggest staying by her side." Doctor Charlton's soft green eyes were full of emotion. "I've increased her pain medication, so keep her comfortable. Her family are going to want to be with her but no more than two visitors at once, okay?"

Nodding, Claire squared her shoulders and lifted her chin. Perhaps if she put on a brave exterior, it would make fighting the internal battles easier. She'd get through this. Somehow.

"Of course, doctor. You're leaving her in capable hands."

He smiled warmly and rested a hand on her shoulder, squeezing it. "I know I am. You're doing a great job, Claire. As soon as your job's over here, get in contact with me. I'll be able to line you up a position either at my surgery or the hospital."

Was it wrong to speak about her future when a woman was dying in the next room? Yet at the same time, she couldn't put it off any longer. His offer was tempting.

"Thank you, I appreciate it."

With a nod, Doctor Charlton walked away.

Uncertainty settled in her gut, unanswered questions flooding her brain. What would happen after Daphne died? Would Claire need to leave immediately? Where would she stay?

She'd hoped to discuss it with Michael once they'd settled into their new relationship. Bringing it up now was not only inappropriate but too soon. Her contract stated this was her residence only for the duration of the position. Daphne's death was the end. Claire had no choice but to make her own plans. She couldn't assume she could stay. She'd have to discuss it with Michael when the time was right.

Drawing in a breath, she pushed her worries aside and made her way to Daphne's room. When she entered, Joanna stood, wiping her eyes. She came up to Claire, hugged her then left the room. Neither of them spoke.

Stopping by the bed, tears filled Claire's eyes. Daphne lay on her back. Her chest rose and fell in quick succession, her breathing shallow. Her eyes were half-closed and she muttered quietly to herself. Most things were indecipherable, but occasionally a term or phrase would sound as clear as day.

After conducting her duties, Claire sat by the bed and took Daphne's hand. Her bottom lip quivered so she bit it to keep her emotions at bay. *I can't cry. I can't let this affect me. I'm the nurse. I must be in control.*

Daphne moved her head and opened her eyes, looking directly at Claire. "Claire?" Her voice was weak. "Is that you?"

"Yes, it's me."

A small smile graced Daphne's lips, and she moved her head back to the centre of the pillow. "Good, I'm glad you're here. Will you stay with me?"

"Of course I will."

"Until the very end?" A lone tear trickled down the side of Daphne's face.

Claire swallowed hard and took a deep breath. Her throat and chest hurt from holding back tears. "Yes, until the very end," she whispered.

Until that moment, Claire had been strong enough emotionally to handle death. It wasn't something she liked but she accepted it came with her job. After her parents' death, she'd hardened herself to it. Losing Daphne, though, it was like losing a mother all over again. Claire didn't think she could handle it a second time around.

"Thank you." Daphne closed her eyes. "Will Tom be here soon? I must see him."

"Yes, he will. Don't worry about a thing."

Daphne's breathing grew louder as she went into an instant deep sleep. Claire sighed and dropped her head into her hands. Why was life so unfair?

Chapter 25

Michael stood on the beach overlooking the ocean, trying to psyche himself up to go back inside. Von had supported and consoled him, but she was too upset to help. In the end, he'd insisted she go home. Now he was left to wallow in his self-pity.

He'd been so happy that life was looking up. Claire finally trusted him. Oscar was safely in his care. But hearing Mum might not make it through the weekend? That was the real kicker. Now nothing could quell the emptiness consuming him. His mother, the one and only person who truly knew him, would soon be dead. How on earth could he accept this?

He had to be in there with her, *wanted* to be with her, but it was so hard. He didn't know how to act, what to say, what to do. He felt so bloody helpless.

He kicked at the sand in frustration, but a gust of wind picked up at that exact moment and blew it into his face, some of it getting into his eyes. He cursed and dabbed at his eyes until they were clear again.

A moment later Norman appeared beside him. "You okay, mate?"

"I'm bloody fantastic," Michael muttered. He swallowed over and over, anything to stop the threatening tears. His mind wouldn't stop going over everything. When it got too much, he blurted, "What am I supposed to do, Norm? How can I sit by her side and watch her die? I don't want to remember her like this."

Despite the cool breeze, the atmosphere was thick. "Geez, Micky," Norman sighed, "I don't bloody know. I've never had to deal with this before either. If I know anything, though, she'd want you there. As hard as it is, she wouldn't want to be alone."

Michael's shoulders dropped as he hung his head and nodded his agreement. "I know, man, but it hurts even more when I see her."

He looked up into Norman's concerned eyes when he placed a hand on his shoulder. "Why don't I come in with you?" his friend suggested gently. "I'd like to see her myself." He shrugged and looked away when he added, "I suppose I could do with some moral support too."

Michael responded with a small smile. "Thanks. I'd like that."

Together they walked back to the house. When they stepped inside, they were greeted with overexcited laughter from Oscar and Juanita. They were still watching TV. Michael turned cold when he realised he had to tell Oscar the news. How could he tell him he'd never see his Nanny again?

"Daddy, Daddy look," Oscar shrieked, pointing at the television.

Michael looked at the screen but couldn't see what was on it, his eyes clouded with tears. He wouldn't tell him immediately. He'd rather wait and tell him on the quiet. He forced a smile, which appeared to be enough as Oscar grinned and turned back to the TV.

"You ready?" Norman asked.

Michael nodded. He didn't feel ready, but he never would. Fear clutched his heart and spread through his veins like ice. Legs trembling and heart pounding against his chest, he followed Norman to Mum's room. He vowed to spend every last moment with Mum, and if that was up to her last dying breath, then so be it.

***

After Norman and Joanna left, taking Oscar with them, Michael sat by his mum's side and held her hand. He was grateful to his friends for looking after Oscar since he wanted to be with Mum for as long as he could. Being with her wasn't as bad as he'd feared and now he couldn't bear to leave. He watched Claire wipe his mum's brow with a wet cloth.

"Can I do anything?" he asked.

Claire looked across at him and shook her head. "There's nothing you can do. All I'm doing is keeping her comfortable. She's sleeping on and off, make sure you talk to her."

He nodded and looked at his mother again. Her eyes fluttered open, and she turned to Michael.

"Tom?" she whispered. "Is that you?"

Michael's heart stopped, and he looked back at Claire in desperation. What was he supposed to do? Why didn't she recognise him?

"Tom's not here yet," Claire said softly. "Michael's here though."

Daphne stared at him, her eyes full of confusion then shut them again. She muttered something then drifted off to sleep.

"What did she say?" Michael's heart raced.

"I'm not sure. She doesn't always make a lot of sense. She's been asking for your father for a while though."

"I promised her I'd get him to visit and he said he'd be here next weekend. No one was expecting her to go downhill so fast." His heart leapt, panic rising in his chest. "I need to tell him how bad she is." He removed his phone from his pocket and searched for his father's number.

Claire's hand on his shoulder stopped him in his tracks, and he looked up at her in confusion.

"It's okay. Doctor Charlton said he'd call. He's probably already on his way."

He sighed from relief and ran a hand down his face. "Thank god. I should've called him the moment we found out how bad she was. How could I have forgotten? I haven't even told Oscar yet. I know Norm or Jo won't tell him, but was it the right thing to do? I keep thinking it'll be better holding off, but maybe it's not? He needs to know."

"You've got a lot on your mind." Claire squeezed his shoulder consolingly. "All you need to worry about at the moment is yourself, your mother and Oscar. Everything else is under control. Tell him when *you're* ready."

As Michael was about to nod in agreement, something occurred to him. He buried his face in his hands and shook his head. "What about the funeral? Is her will up to date? Oh, god, I should've—"

"Michael," Claire said, "please look at me."

He dropped his hands and found her crouching beside him. He met her gaze, her stunning blue-green eyes full of compassion and warmth. How did she keep it together? This couldn't be easy for her either.

"Don't do this to yourself." She reached out for his hand and held it. Her warmth radiated through his body, calming him. "You don't need to be concerned about any of that right now. Your mum's a smart woman. I'm sure the will is sorted. As for the funeral, those plans can wait. There's no rush. You don't need this stress right now."

"I'm sorry." He sighed. "You're right. There's so much to think about."

"I know, but now isn't the time to think about them. Your mum needs you more than you realise. I know it's difficult but being here will do wonders." She squeezed his hand then let it go. Standing, she moved past him to the other side of the bed.

He stood and stretched his arms above his head. He'd been sitting too long. Mulling over Claire's words, he remembered what'd happened earlier. His heart broke a little when he asked, "Does she remember me? I mean before—"

"Of course she remembers you. She's disorientated and she's been asking for your father, so she's probably confused. But she's aware you're here, I promise."

Michael walked across to her and took her hands, holding onto them tightly. He needed some semblance of happiness, and being near Claire, touching her in any way, provided it. He gazed into her eyes. How had he gone through life for so long without her? Despite the turmoil around him, one thing was certain. He couldn't lose her.

"You're wonderful, Claire." He let go of her hands and ran his hands up and down her arms. "I don't know how I'd get through this without you."

Her cheeks tinged with pink and she averted her gaze. "I'm doing my job. You'd still cope even if I wasn't here."

Shaking his head, he tilted her chin so he could look into her eyes again. "Don't say that. I'd still be a broken man if it weren't for you. I'm only coping because of you." He took in her beautiful features and cupped her face with his hands, running his thumbs along her silky, smooth skin.

She blinked a couple of times then smiled up at him. "That's where you're wrong. You're the one who helped me, Michael. I think you were always able to cope, but you didn't realise it. It was *you* who fixed *me*."

His heart fluttered and overwhelming love for her washed over him. If he hadn't already realised he'd fallen for her, there'd be no doubting it now. After Addison, it seemed impossible to fall in love again, but he had. It was all because Claire was so different. She saw him for who he truly was, flaws and all.

He pulled her against him, wrapping his arms securely around her. Somehow, she made everything okay. Facing a future without Mum was unbearable before Claire came along. Now, with her by his side, he could achieve anything.

When they pulled apart, he held her arms and whispered, "Thank you, Claire."

He tucked her hair behind her ear then leaned forward and placed a soft kiss on her forehead. When he pulled back, her eyes were closed, and she had a gentle smile on her face. Needing to feel her soft lips on his, he moved to kiss her mouth.

When his lips touched hers, his body burst to life. She gave him the strength to survive. He gently held her face with his hands as he deepened the kiss, pouring love, passion and promise into it. Claire returned the sentiments with confidence and surety, making his heart beat faster and harder.

Aware of where they were, he kept the kiss short, but when he pulled away, he craved more of her. He broke away and left feather kisses across her face, ending with one on the tip of her nose. He stepped back, smiling at her dazed expression.

Her eyes fluttered open and she returned his smile.

I love you. The words sat on the tip of his tongue, begging to be spoken. He held them back. There was a time and a place to speak them, and it wasn't here.

A knock sounded at the door and reality crashed around his feet. He sighed and dropped his shoulders.

Claire gave him a consoling smile. "You'll get through this, Michael, I promise." She turned to answer the door.

I hope she's right.

He went back to sit by his mother's side and took her hand, holding it against his cheek. She gently squeezed and he sat back, looking at her with wide eyes. She gave him a small, weak smile. "About time," she said between ragged breaths.

Realising she'd seen the kiss, a proud yet embarrassed smile crossed his face. He squeezed her hand again and placed a kiss on top of it. A small part of him felt guilty for kissing Claire when things were so dire, but according to Mum's reaction, it was exactly what she wanted to see.

"I love you, Mum," he whispered, hot tears dripping down his cheeks and onto the bedcovers. "Please don't go."

"I love you too, Michael, and I'm so proud of you," she whispered. "You're everything to me, and I know you're going to be so happy with Claire. I couldn't be happier."

Through tear-filled eyes, he looked at her, holding on to her hand for dear life. Life was so, so cruel.

Mum gasped softly and croaked out, "Tom."

Jerking around, Michael saw his father standing at the foot of the bed. "Dad."

"Hello, son," he said, his voice breaking.

A mixture of relief and fear ran through him. Relief that he was there, as Mum wanted, and fear because she wouldn't be alive for much longer.

Chapter 26

While Michael and Tom talked quietly next to the bed, Claire busied herself with other things. Every now and then she'd glance at them from the corner of her eye and marvel at the likenesses they shared. Tom was visibly older, evidenced by the wrinkles on his face and the streaks of grey in his hair, but she could imagine them being mistaken for brothers at some point in their lives. It was no surprise Daphne, in a dazed state, had thought Michael was Tom.

They were both tall, broad and handsome, but Tom was slightly taller than Michael. He also had a fierce look about him with a naturally downturned mouth, making it appear he was scowling. It could've been purely because of the situation.

Picking up the clipboard on the dresser, Claire's hands trembled. Attempting to write notes was impossible. Her throat closed and a sharp pain pierced her chest. This was so goddamn unfair.

Her lip quivered and she drew in a shuddering breath. Knees wobbling, she grabbed hold of the dresser and focused on breathing so she wouldn't collapse to the floor in a sobbing mess. She held a hand against her stomach, nausea swirling around like a whirlpool. Nothing worked. One treacherous tear escaped.

She needed air, and fast.

Thankfully Michael and Tom were too preoccupied with Daphne to notice her absence so she was able to slip out quietly. She'd keep it quick.

Letting the door click shut behind her, she stumbled to the kitchen sink and stood in front of the open window. The warm, spring breeze blew on her face and caught strands of her hair. Grabbing a clean glass from the draining board, she filled it with water and took a large sip. Closing her eyes, she breathed slowly in through her nose and out through her mouth.

Come on, Claire, hold it together a little while longer. You can't let them see you're struggling, you're the professional remember? This is about them, not you.

The little pep talk combined with the water and fresh air helped to calm her down. Downing the last of the water, she placed the glass in the sink and jumped in fright when someone cleared their throat behind her. Spinning around, a woman she didn't recognise stood inside the French doors. Her slender arms were folded, and she impatiently tapped her long, fake fingernails on her forearm.

She eyed Claire critically from head to toe. Rather than feeling inferior, which was clearly the other woman's intent, it had the opposite effect. Claire pulled her shoulders back and stepped closer. "Can I help you?"

"Who are you?" the woman asked snobbishly.

Something about her tone put Claire on edge. Her defences rose. "I think I should be asking who *you* are and what are you doing in this house?"

The woman tutted. "That's not important. I must speak to Michael. Is he here?"

This has to be Addison.

"He's busy." Knowing she'd be the last person he'd want to see after the latest drama, she added, "Can I get him to call you?"

She pursed her lips and shook her head, her long black hair swishing with it. "No, he probably won't call." She jutted her chin toward Daphne's door. "How's the old bag doing? She still kicking?"

Claire folded her arms and raised a single eyebrow. *The nerve of the woman.* "That 'old bag'," she said, using her fingers as quotation marks, "is extremely ill, if you must know. Now if you don't mind, I think you should leave. I'll tell Michael you popped over. What's your name?"

By this point, she was certain it was Addison, but she didn't let that on. All she wanted was her gone.

"Addison," she responded, "but I need to see him *now.*" She stepped closer, so she was only a few feet away from Claire, a smirk forming on her lips. "I presume he's in there?" She inclined her head toward Daphne's room. "Perhaps you can get him for me. I'd appreciate it very much."

If she doesn't leave soon, I'm going to slap that smirk right off her pretty face.

"Now's not a good time," Claire said firmly.

When Addison took one more step forward, she and Claire were only a foot apart at most. Addison's heels made her a couple of inches taller than Claire, and she had to step back so she wouldn't have to crane her neck.

"Who are you exactly?" Addison looked down her nose. "Are you Michael's new whore or something?"

Whore? Did she truly say that?

It took a couple of seconds for Claire to get over the shock. Her jaw dropped but she quickly composed herself and straightened her shoulders. "I'm Daphne's nurse," she said calmly. "And I'm telling you, now's not a good time to see him."

The smirk reappeared on Addison's perfectly made-up face and she chuckled nastily. "A nurse? You can't tell me what I can and can't do."

"I'm qualified enough to tell you now isn't a good time." She was beginning to sound like a broken record, but Addison didn't seem to get the hint. "I suggest you leave before I call the police and report you for trespassing."

Addison's face contorted in shock and she stumbled back. "You don't have any authority."

"I'm a live-in nurse," Claire corrected with a triumphant smile. "This is my place of residence at the moment, so I have the right to call the police. I'll tell Michael you popped in, now I suggest you leave."

The glare Addison gave her sent a chill down her spine but she kept her stand firm and held her gaze. Finally, Addison cursed then turned and walked toward the door. To Claire's horror, Daphne's door opened, and Michael stepped out. He was pale, a look of terror in his eyes.

Claire swallowed. *Oh no. This is it, isn't it?*

"Claire, something's wrong," he said desperately.

She rushed over to him, but his gaze had drifted to the doors where Addison now stood with a triumphant smile.

Michael's expression changed. His pale face turned red and his eyes hardened. "Addison." His tone was icy. "What are you doing here?"

Claire rushed to explain, "I told her you weren't available. I didn't want to—"

Michael's hard eyes turned to her, and he frowned. Hurt, confusion and anger washed over his features. "I think I'm capable of handling my personal affairs, Claire. I'd rather you focus on my mother like you were employed to do."

He stormed past her, his shoulder unintentionally brushing hers. Shock, hurt and panic swept over her like a tidal wave. Her legs grew weak and she stumbled, grabbing the wall for support. Her gaze followed him as he stormed outside, Addison following. Seconds later she heard raised voices.

Bile rose in her throat, her pounding heart making her head spin. *Now isn't the time, Claire. You have to see Daphne.*

Gasping for air, Claire fumbled for the doorknob. She turned it and went into the room. She tried not to let Michael's words affect her—he was under a lot of pressure after all—but it still hurt. A hell of a lot. Less than an hour earlier, they were sharing the most amazing, mind-blowing kiss. Now he acted as if he hated her. Had she overstepped the mark in keeping Addison away? She was sure she'd done him a favour.

When she reached the bed, nurse mode kicked in and her worries disappeared. Michael was right about one thing. She *was* here to help Daphne.

"It's okay," Claire soothed. "I'm here as promised." Daphne's breathing was laboured. She'd stop for a short time then she'd gasp but it seemed not much air was going in. Gently, Claire helped her onto her side to clear her airways. It wouldn't do a lot apart from making it a little easier to breathe.

While Claire rubbed Daphne's back, she looked over to the end of the bed where Tom stood rooted to the spot, his face pale.

"Is she okay?" he asked.

Looking down at Daphne's sleeping form, she shook her head. Glancing back at him, she said, "She hasn't got long. Her lungs are collapsing."

His brow furrowed, and he shook his head. "Is it normal for this to happen? How can someone go downhill so quickly?"

"Everyone's different." Claire approached him. "Some people stop eating and become nonresponsive for a few days before they go. Others can die very quickly. Daphne only started refusing food and drink today. She's been holding on for a long time to see Oscar and you. Having seen both of you, she knows she doesn't have to hold on anymore."

Tom nodded and glanced over to Daphne. "Is she in pain?"

What was going through his mind? Did he have feelings for her anymore? Even if he'd moved on, did he still love her? It wasn't uncommon.

"No," Claire answered. "She's comfortable. Why don't you sit next to her so she can see you? She's been asking for you for a while."

When Tom looked back at her, his eyes were wide and clouded with tears. "Will she know I'm here?" He cleared his throat to hide the waver in his voice.

"She may not respond, but she knows, trust me."

Nodding, he walked over to her and sat on the chair. "It's me," he said softly, taking her hand. "It's Tom. I'm here."

Claire didn't want to watch. They needed space, but she was struck by the scene before her. Tom looked at Daphne with such love and affection. It answered Claire's question. Despite moving on, he still loved her.

Daphne's mouth opened and closed as though trying to say something.

"You don't have to speak," Tom said, placing a tender kiss on her hand.

"I'm...sorry," Daphne whispered. It was taking all of Daphne's energy to say anything, proving she was a determined woman down to the very end. "I still...love you."

Eyes filling with tears, Claire turned away and picked up the trusty clipboard from the dresser, needing to do something with her hands. A long, deep breath in helped her control her tears. That was the sort of love she wanted to experience, the type that never died despite what happened in life.

"You don't have to be sorry," Tom said. "I know I moved on but—"

Claire glanced over her shoulder. Tom was now sitting on the side of the bed, one hand holding Daphne's, the other around her back. He leaned forward and placed a kiss on her cheek.

"—I never stopped loving you, either." Tom's words were barely a whisper, but the room was so quiet, Claire heard it.

Unable to stop the tears, Claire turned back and let them roll down her cheeks. How could they have gone so long without speaking those words to each other?

"I was devastated after we separated," Tom continued. "I thought moving on would be the right thing to do, so I did. Then when we finally allowed ourselves to talk openly, I knew I'd made the wrong decision, and I've regretted it ever since. I shouldn't have moved on so quickly. I should've fought harder for you. I love my children and I love my wife but…she's not you, Daphne. I can't turn back time, but I want you to know my feelings have never changed."

Claire angrily wiped her tears away. *I'm a professional. I don't cry on the job.* She placed the clipboard down again. Once she had herself under control, she left the room. It was more important Daphne spent her final moments with Tom, her one true love. Claire was confident she'd kept her promise.

Closing the door behind her, she heard raised voices again. Walking to the kitchen, she passed the window and spotted Michael and Addison standing in the back driveway.

"—you had no right to go to the police," Addison yelled, her fists clenched tightly by her sides.

"You abused my son," Michael yelled back. "What else was I supposed to do? Ignore it? I'm never letting him in your care again, Addison."

Moving away from the window, Claire tried not to listen, but it was impossible. Their voices were loud enough for the neighbours to hear.

"I'm a capable mother, Michael," Addison retorted. "Oscar's making up stories."

Michael's laughter was venomous. "Stories? What about what you did earlier, huh? I saw it with my own eyes."

"It was a reaction. I've never done that before. You have to believe—"

"Believe you? Not going to happen, Addison. I believe my son, not you. Now I'd appreciate it if you'd get off my property. I don't want to see you until the court case."

"You'll see me in two weeks, Michael. I'm taking my son home with me."

"Oh no, you're bloody not. He's in *my* care now, as you're fully aware. If you dare try to take him, you'll be done for kidnapping too. Now leave before I call the police."

"This isn't over," Addison threatened. "I'll drag your arse through the mud, Michael. I promise you'll never get custody of Oscar."

"Don't make promises you can't keep. I'm the one with the evidence, remember?"

Addison squealed like an angry child. A few seconds later, a car door slammed, and Addison shouted, "Wait until this goes to court. I'll bring you down."

Not wanting to get caught eavesdropping, Claire dashed back to Daphne's room. She reached for the handle as the door swung open. Tom's pale, distraught face told her all she needed to know. A single nod of his head was the only confirmation she needed. Her stomach dropped when she walked into the room and approached Daphne's bed.

Daphne lay on her side, unmoving, a content smile on her face. A couple of stray tears lingered on her cheeks. Claire checked for a pulse on her neck and when she felt nothing, checked her wrist. When she was sure, she turned and found Tom and Michael standing at the foot of the bed. They were both pale and looked like lost children. When they looked at her expectantly, and she nodded, they broke down and fell into each other's arms.

Turning away, Claire took her phone out and dialled Doctor Charlton's number. Her heart broke in two, but she hid her emotions. It was hard work, and her chest hurt so much she was certain it would burst. *Stay strong. Do your job. It's almost over.*

Chapter 27

Claire wasn't sure what to expect, but she wasn't surprised the tears didn't last long. She'd seen the same reaction so many times before.

Michael and his father stood next to the bed, their hands clasped, heads bowed in respect. As tragic as death was, there was always a sense of relief. After death, the cancer sufferer wasn't in pain anymore.

Yet for Claire, she felt a numbing emptiness. Perhaps it was because she'd gotten so close to Daphne even though she hadn't known her for long. Or perhaps it was because she was emotional in general. Whatever the case, she was on the verge of a breakdown and she didn't want anyone to know.

Claire glanced at her watch, her stomach knotted in agitation. Where was Doctor Charlton? After her call ten minutes ago, he said he was on his way. She was eager to get away for a few moments alone, needing to plan what to do. Would it be rude if she left before nightfall? Technically she was unemployed the moment Daphne died, and she didn't think it was appropriate to stay another night.

The knots tightened in her stomach. She should've taken it more seriously. Should've planned what she'd do after Daphne's death.

Should I speak to Michael?

Looking at him, she decided to wait. It wasn't because of how he reacted toward her earlier. The timing was all off. Perhaps staying in a motel would be better until everything settled.

It was the only plausible option, even if it only ended up being for a few days. It would give her time to sort something else out, including finding a job.

A knock sounded at the door, interrupting her thoughts. Claire was standing next to it and opened it, breathing a sigh of relief when she saw Doctor Charlton. His face was sad and her relief was short-lived when reality once again came crashing down.

Daphne was dead.

It was like a penny dropping. She looked over to the bed at Daphne's pale, lifeless form, and the tears she'd been trying so hard to contain dripped down her cheeks treacherously. Doctor Charlton nodded in understanding. Pushing past him, she ran out the main doors, desperate to get out of the house.

Once she was standing on the sand, she took large gulps of air and wiped her tears away. *Why am I like this? This isn't normal.*

Shaking her head in despair, she placed her hands on her hips as she stared out over the ocean. Perhaps giving up nursing was for the best. The emotions connected to it were too much to deal with. Was it time for a career change?

These thoughts ran around her mind for a little while, and thankfully having her mind preoccupied helped calm her down. A few moments later though, she was interrupted by Doctor Charlton. Her cheeks were still wet, and she wiped the tears away before turning to face him.

"I'm sorry." Fresh tears slid down her cheeks. She was like a leaky tap. "I was trying to get myself under control but—"

He approached her and rested a hand on her shoulder. She looked up into his sad eyes, glimmering with tears, and suddenly didn't feel so silly for crying on the job.

"You're allowed to grieve, Claire. Daphne was a remarkable woman. She'll be missed by many, myself included."

Claire chided herself for being so selfish. "Forgive me, of course you will miss her. How are you holding up then? I wouldn't expect this to be easy for you."

He laughed bitterly. "It's far from easy, but it's my job." He shrugged. "What can I do about it? I've lost many people I care about."

"How do you do it? I've found myself thinking that perhaps I can't continue. I've always hardened myself to death, but Daphne...I can't seem to cope this time." She looked down and traced a pattern in the sand with the toe of her shoe.

It was a relief to talk to someone who understood. Yes, it was tempting to give up nursing without giving it a second thought, but she'd probably regret it. Perhaps Doctor Charlton could give her some advice. He was a wise man and had been doing his job for a long time.

"You'll always have moments like this," Doctor Charlton said. "Some moments will be harder than others. You'll get times when you question if you can do it. Hell, I've lost count how many times *I've* questioned it. Now being one of them."

Claire looked up in surprise. He laughed a little more heartily this time. "Yes, I understand how you feel, Claire. But what it comes down to is how much you love the job. Personally, I love doctoring and the love of it keeps me going. I know this feeling will pass in a few days. You need to think about how much *you* love nursing."

Do I love it like I used to? I don't know anymore.

"Thanks," Claire said. "I hadn't thought of it like that before. I admire you, though. You do an amazing job."

"So do you," he said. "You may not have my qualifications, but to be able to tend to someone twenty-four-seven is a real accomplishment." Glancing at his watch, he added, "Anyhow, I must get back to the surgery. You know how to contact me. Remember to call me if you need a job."

Claire nodded. "I will, thanks, Doc."

When he left, she turned to go inside when her phone rang. Removing it from her pocket, she smiled when she saw Laura's name.

Swiping the screen, she held the phone to her ear. "Laura, hi. How are you?"

"I'm good. How are you? I haven't heard from you for a while so I thought I'd check in. I'm hoping this is good news."

Claire chuckled lightly. She considered the last two weeks, unable to believe how much had happened in such a short time. How much *she'd* changed. There was so much to tell Laura but where did she start?

"Overall, I've been good." She paused, then added with a smile, "Really good, actually." Despite the events of the day, she couldn't ignore the wonderful events that'd changed her life so much.

"Claire, that's wonderful." She could practically hear Laura's smile on the other end. "How about the job? That's going well too?"

Emotions of the day weighed heavily on her shoulders, and she sighed. "Daphne passed away today. It's funny, she was supposed to be a patient, but she was an amazing woman who I got close to. It's hit me a lot harder than I expected."

"I'm so sorry, Claire. You know firsthand how difficult it is deal with the loss of someone you care about. Remember to take time to grieve, okay?"

Claire nodded, even though Laura couldn't see her. "I will, but it feels wrong in a way. I mean, I only knew her for a couple of weeks. Her family and friends have lost someone who's been a part of their lives for years and years. How do I have the right to grieve someone who I barely knew?"

"They're your emotions talking, Claire. Some people we click with and they influence our lives in a big way, even after a short time. There's no rule to say you can only grieve for someone you've known for X amount of years."

Claire laughed weakly and looked up at the sky. A flock of seagulls flew overhead. "When you put it that way, it does sound kind of silly."

"It's not silly at all. If you can learn to quiet your emotions and let your logic speak, it'll help a lot."

Nodding, Claire averted her gaze to the house. "Oh, the doctor said to call him if I need a job, he said he'd be able to line me up with something."

"That's great, isn't it? You wanted to settle somewhere after the job ended. This could be fate paving the way."

Claire winced and her heart leapt when the door opened. Michael stepped out and looked at her briefly before sitting on the step and hanging his head.

"Perhaps." She turned away and lowered her tone before adding, "I don't know if I'm cut out for this anymore. I always try not to draw close to patients, but Daphne was different. She was so likeable, and she became like a mother to me. The pain of seeing her die was too much."

"I understand, Claire. This has to be your choice, but don't make any rash decisions, okay?"

"I won't. Look, I need to go." She looked back at Michael, wondering how she'd approach him. "Can I call you later to talk more?"

"Of course, whenever you're free."

They hung up. Before approaching Michael, Claire turned back to the ocean. She needed a confidence boost before speaking to him. In a few short hours, everything was different.

She mulled over what to do about a job when something occurred to her. Her indecisiveness wasn't only because she didn't feel she could deal with death. It was the fact that Ryan had taken away her freedom of choice and getting it back was hard. Her old self *did* love nursing and would've asked Doctor Charlton right away to line her up for a job.

Perhaps Laura's right. Fate is paving a new road for me. Rather than running, I should embrace it.

Her stomach quivered, and she decided to think about it a little more first. Perhaps she'd get Joanna's opinion too. Before she did either, though, it was time to talk to Michael. He hadn't moved from the step. A tiny part of her wondered why he hadn't approached her, but she pushed the selfish voice aside. His mother *had* died.

Approaching the house, she stopped in front of the steps. Michael looked up and their gazes locked. His eyes were dark and empty. Now what should she say? There'd never be enough words. Nothing would take away his pain or bring Daphne back. In the end, she sat beside him and said nothing. When he shuffled away, her chest tightened, and tears stung her eyes. She blinked them away. *Don't be offended. He's suffering right now.*

She wracked her brain for the right thing to say. Her mind went over the events of the day. So much had happened. Then she remembered Addison's visit, and she went cold. *Of course.*

"I'm sorry about earlier," she blurted. "I was—"

Michael jerked around to face her, his eyes dark and angry. "You were what? I can handle my own affairs, Claire. The last thing I need is *you* butting in and making everything worse."

Her breath caught in her throat, and she leaned back, his words hitting her like daggers. "I…I was trying to help." She looked away and clasped her hands in front of her. "You were with your mother. I didn't want you to leave her side. I was only thinking of you."

"That doesn't change anything." She flinched at his harsh, loud tone. "Because of you, I wasn't there when my mother died."

Oh, god. Is that what he thinks?

A treacherous tear dripped down her cheek. She wiped it away then whipped her head around to stare at him, eyes wide. "It wasn't my fault." A sob rose and lodged in her throat.

Michael stared at her, his eyes stormy. "You called Addison, didn't you? You both planned this as some sick joke to get back at me. How long have you two been scheming behind my back? Were you trying to prove I'm an unfit father?" He shook his head and raked a hand through his hair. "It explains everything. Her timing was spot on."

What the hell was he going on about? He knew she'd never met Addison before and had no way of contacting her. Claire stood abruptly and stumbled down the stairs. *I can't believe he thinks that low of me.* There was no controlling the flood of tears. She had to leave. Immediately.

His bitter laugh caught on the breeze, stopping her in her tracks. His words stung when he said, "I thought I could trust you of all people. It seems I was wrong."

She blinked away tears, but this only made way for more. Looking up at the sky, she silently asked for strength. Wiping her tears away, she turned. Anger replaced the sorrow as she balled her hands into fists. It bubbled low in her belly, slowly rising. Facing Michael, she lifted her gaze to meet his. A shiver ran along the length of her spine. His eyes were cold and dark, much like when she first met him.

Her heart tore in two and when she spoke, her words were venomous. "No, *I* was wrong about you, *Mr Karalis.*" She spat the words out like poison. Michael even jerked back, but she wasn't done yet. "All I did was tell Addison I'd get you to contact her. If I'm guilty of anything, it's caring about you enough to stop your ex from interrupting your final moments with your mother. Now suddenly *I'm* to blame for something I tried to stop?"

Michael stared at her for a long moment. His eyes were wide, full of disbelief and confusion. His mouth opened and closed a couple of times, but he didn't speak. Claire's chest heaved up and down, her breathing coming out in short, angry bursts. Michael was suffering. She understood that. Claire also understood that not being there when Daphne died was hard on him. Addison turning up when she did had been bad timing, not to mention downright cruel.

What she *didn't* understand was how he could believe she'd side with his ex or why she'd intentionally jeopardise his last moments with Daphne.

"You expect me to believe that?" Michael's words were as cutting.

"Yes." Claire gritted her teeth and ground them back and forth. "I don't understand why you won't believe me."

Michael stood and strode to Claire, looming over her. "How can I believe a woman?" His voice came out in a low growl.

The words crushed her heart, sending searing pain through her chest. She sighed, her shoulders slumping. "Are you serious right now? I thought we'd moved past this."

His eyes flashed. "We had until you betrayed me."

This last comment was her undoing. Rage bubbled over and she didn't even think when she reacted. She swung her arm and her hand connected with Michael's cheek with a resounding *slap*. His head snapped to the left.

Her hand stung, and that was when reality sunk in. She gasped and stumbled back, breathing heavily. *Oh my god.* Guilt weighed heavily on her shoulders, and she opened her mouth to apologise but the words lodged in her throat.

Michael slowly moved his head back to look at her. He blinked a couple of times as though breaking out of a trance. Shock, guilt and remorse clouded his features. He reached out for her, "Claire, I'm—"

She jumped back, chest heaving, tears hovering beneath her eyelids. "It's time I leave. My job here is done."

Michael visibly paled and he shook his head. "Claire, please, let's—"

She refused to listen. Instead, she shook her head and spun on her heel as the tears came cascading down her cheeks. Pain ripped through her heart and anger surged through her veins like a raging river.

When she reached her room, she slammed the door then dug her case out from under the bed. Hauling it on to the mattress, she unzipped it and rushed about the room like a tornado, removing everything from the dresser and wardrobe before throwing them into the case haphazardly.

A few moments later, she came out of the bathroom with the last of her items and threw them on top. Zipping the case shut, she slid it off the bed and set it on its wheels. She sat on the side of the bed, the case next to her, shoulders slumping forward. Wiping her tears away with the back of her hand, she breathed slowly and deeply.

Had she done the right thing? Michael had hurt her deeply, but she hadn't been a ray of sunshine herself. He *had* tried to talk to her, maybe even apologise, but she'd metaphorically given him the middle finger and stormed off. She rapped her knuckles on her forehead. *Idiot, idiot, idiot.*

She snapped her head up when voices drifted in from the open balcony doors. Standing, she quietly walked out onto the balcony and looked down. Tom and Michael stood on the sand next to each other.

"Someone will be here soon to take her away," Tom said, his voice wavering.

Michael nodded but continued to stare out over the ocean, saying nothing.

"I've called Von too, she's on her way," Tom added. "You want to call your mate? Norman, is it? I don't have his number."

"I've already done it." Michael's tone was flat.

"Oh…good."

Claire watched with bated breath as the two men stood awkwardly next to each other, neither of them knowing how to express themselves. Eventually, Tom placed a hand on Michael's shoulder. "We're all going to miss her, son. Don't feel you can't grieve."

Michael's head fell forward. His sobs carried on the wind and echoed in her ears, crushing her heart once more.

Stumbling back into the room, Claire closed and locked the doors after her, fresh tears sliding down her cheeks. Turning back to the bed, she grabbed the handle of her suitcase and wheeled it toward the bedroom door. She stumbled to a stop in front of it, doubts running around her mind, questioning every decision she'd made.

Michael had lost his mother…now she was leaving him too. What the hell was she doing? Trying to destroy the poor guy?

Okay, so he still had trust issues. He'd accused her of siding with Addison when he should've known she wouldn't do such a thing. But truth be told, didn't Claire still have trust issues too? The fact she'd stormed away from the best thing that'd ever happened to her, without hearing him out, was proof of that. Now, what did she do?

Drawing in a breath, she took a step closer and grabbed hold of the doorknob. She tried to turn it but had no strength. Leaving Michael was like leaving her heart behind. She thought selling her house, the only remaining connection to her parents, had been hard. But, hell, this was harder. She'd fallen in love with Michael Karalis, the man he truly was inside, but how could she stay if they didn't trust each other?

Maybe she wasn't ready for this big step. It had been a glorious two weeks, despite everything, and she'd learnt a lot. But she still had more to learn.

Her hand slipped away from the doorknob, her arm falling to her side. Shaking her head in despair, Claire's knees gave way and she collapsed in a heap on the floor. Hot tears ran down her cheeks for what felt like the millionth time that day.

How the hell am I supposed to do this?

Chapter 28

Claire's head snapped up when someone knocked at her door. How long had she been stuck in her position? Her knees were aching, indicating some time had passed. It took a while for her fuzzy mind to catch up, but when it did, the ache spread throughout her entire body, settling in her chest.

Another knock sounded.

I hope it's not Michael.

Heart racing, she scrambled to her feet, wiped her cheeks dry and smoothed down her dress. Drawing in a calming breath, she opened the door.

"Von." She sighed from relief and greeted the older woman with a hug. When they pulled away, Claire looked at her closely. Von was still dressed in the work clothes from earlier, her eyes red and puffy. "How are you doing?" Claire asked.

Von's eyes filled with tears, and she shook her head. "I've lost a dear friend. I'm not too sure how to feel right now."

When she broke down, Claire embraced her again and patted her back soothingly. *How can I leave when she's like this?*

"I'm sorry," Von said when she pulled away, wiping her eyes with a tissue. "I didn't even come up here to break down. I came to see how *you* were."

Claire smiled encouragingly. "Oh, I'm fine…" She trailed off when she realised her words sounded fake. Von's raised eyebrow indicated she didn't believe her anyway.

Von looked over Claire's shoulder, brow furrowing. She looked back at Claire with confusion in her eyes. "Are you going somewhere?"

What am I supposed to tell her?

Deciding to go with the semi truth, she said, "It's time for me to move on. My job is done. I can't stay here anymore. This was only my home while Daphne was…" she shrugged. Speaking of Daphne's death was difficult for everyone, it seemed.

Von gave a single nod of understanding but Claire didn't miss the unaccepting look in her eyes. "Michael didn't ask you to stay?" She sounded surprised.

Claire winced and averted her gaze, wishing she and Michael hadn't made it so obvious what was going on between them. In the end, she gathered up enough courage to look Von in the eye and say, "No, he didn't, and he has no reason to." Before Von had a chance to argue, Claire added, "I think I'll find a motel to stay at while I get myself sorted."

"Oh no, you don't." Von huffed and folded her arms. "I respect you don't want to talk about whatever's going on between you and Michael, but there's no way I'm going to let you leave here without a place to stay. You'll stay with me." She gave a firm nod.

"Von, I couldn't—"

"I'm not taking no for an answer." She pursed her lips. "Besides, I daresay I'd quite enjoy the company. It can get awfully lonely sometimes. I'm going to speak to Michael and take a few days off. It'll be wonderful to spend them with you."

Claire sighed and shrugged. "I don't have much choice, do I?"

Von chuckled and stepped back. "No, you don't, and you're welcome to stay for as long as you need."

Realising how rude and ungrateful her comment sounded, Claire said, "I do appreciate the offer, Von. It's very kind of you. I didn't want to intrude, that's all."

"It's no intrusion." She glanced at her watch. "I should be ready to leave in about ten minutes. I only came by to say my final goodbyes." She choked up and cleared her throat. "I need to see Michael briefly. Is your case heavy? I walked—"

"It's on wheels. It won't be a problem. I'd be happy to walk back with you. Shall I meet you out the back then?"

Von nodded then turned and walked away.

It was very kind of Von to offer, and Claire couldn't deny the sense of relief washing over her. She'd been worried about Von dealing with this alone but now she didn't need to. They could both support each other. All Claire had to do now was decide what to do for work.

In light of a new life before her, the decision was easy. She *would* call Doctor Charlton and see what he could line up for her. He was right. It came down to how much you loved the work, and she loved nursing. She'd regret it if she gave it up on a whim.

With her mind made up about a job and where she'd live, she left it at that. That was enough decision making for one day.

A small smile formed on her lips as she reached out and gripped the handle of her case. She didn't know what her future would bring, but finally, *she* had control of it, and that was exhilarating.

Glancing around the room one last time, she drew in a deep breath then walked out, dragging her case behind her. When she shut the door, she froze. It felt so wrong to leave. This house had become her home in such a short time. Not only was she leaving behind her heart, but her soul would be left here too.

When tears threatened to fall once more, she sniffed them back and jutted her chin out.

No more tears. I've cried enough for one day.

It's time to forget about Michael, forget about what they had, and embrace what her new life threw at her.

Her mother used to tell her that things had a way of sorting themselves out, and Claire believed it. So, with or without Michael, her life would go down whichever road she was destined to travel.

***

With a heavy heart, Michael stood in the doorway, staring into Mum's room. Her body had been taken away, the bed remade with fresh sheets. Everything else was the same—the medical equipment was still in place. It would be taken away at a later date.

His head still spun at how quickly everything had happened. When he'd first learnt she was terminal, he was devastated but thankful to have that six months with her. Then out of nowhere, it'd changed. Then, in a flash, she was gone.

Tears blurred his vision, and he stumbled over to the bed, lying on top to be close to her. Pulling the quilt over his form, he held onto it and squeezed his eyes shut, tears dripping onto the pillow. Apart from the sounds of the ocean outside, the house was in complete silence. He had no clue where everyone was, but he didn't care. He needed time alone.

How did anyone recover from grief? The pain was like no other. It tore his insides apart, leaving him with nothing but emptiness. How was it possible he'd never see her again? Hear her voice, her laugh? More than anything, he wanted to hold her hand, tell her he loved her one last time, apologise for all the times he'd upset or disappointed her.

But he'd never get that opportunity again.

Gripping the quilt tighter around his shoulders, he let the tears go, sobs echoing throughout the quiet house.

He stayed like this for an indeterminate amount of time. It was only when he became aware of the room growing dark that he stirred. A tiny light flickered to life deep within him, enough to get him moving. Pushing the covers back, he dragged his lethargic legs to the side of the bed and sat up straight. When he forced himself into a standing position, he felt like an old man.

Rubbing his eyes, he finally managed to find the strength to move. When he exited the room, he glanced back once more. The bed was mussed up now but everything else was the same. Soon it would be unrecognisable with the medical equipment gone. Maybe this wasn't a bad thing though. The heartbreaking reminders of Mum needed to go. He only wanted to remember her as the warm, honest and loving person she was before cancer stole her away.

His chest tightened and he turned away, closing the door behind him. Walking into the kitchen, he stared toward the fridge for a long moment, contemplating food. His stomach let out a loud growl, reminding him he hadn't eaten in hours. Dragging his feet to the fridge, he opened it and inspected the contents.

His stomach growled again but this time it turned over and he shut the door. He couldn't stomach anything. Not yet. So, ignoring his hunger pangs, he made his way to his room. Taking the stairs to the second level felt like a marathon. When he reached the top, he shook his head in an attempt to snap out of the darkness but failed. Instead, he made a beeline for his bedroom and collapsed on his bed. With the room now in darkness, sleep overcame him, taking away the pain for a short while.

***

The next morning when his eyes opened, he was flooded with memories of yesterday. Mum's death. Addison. The argument with Claire.

Claire.

He sat bolt upright, his stomach lurching when he recalled the words he'd spoken. *Bloody hell. What have I done?* It was instinctive to blame grief but even he wasn't fooled by that. He'd screwed up good and proper. He'd been angry because he missed saying goodbye to Mum, but he should've taken it out on Addison, *not* Claire.

What the hell had he been thinking, accusing Claire of being in cahoots with Addison? It was completely absurd. Hell, Claire had never met Addison before. The fact he'd even spoken the words made him cringe. He needed to apologise to Claire and make it up to her. But how? He'd hurt her in the worst possible way. It was likely she'd never want anything to do with him again.

Not wanting to think about the mess he'd made, he pushed the thoughts to the back of his mind. Flopping back onto his pillow, he pulled the covers over his head and willed sleep to claim him once more. Norman and Joanna wouldn't mind looking after Oscar for a while longer.

Sadness, emptiness and guilt ate away at him. There was nothing he could do to ease any of it without making it worse. Sleep was the only reprieve he had. It was better than turning to drink, right? Although he'd kill for a bottle of scotch right now…

Forcing the thoughts aside, he closed his eyes but had barely done so when his phone rang. Not in the mood to speak to anyone, he ignored it.

It rang again.

Gritting his teeth, he covered his ears with his hands, but he could still hear it. When it stopped, he removed his hands, but it only rang again.

Clearly, the caller wasn't giving up.

Kicking off the covers, Michael sat up and snatched his phone from the bedside cupboard. Glaring at the number, he frowned when he didn't recognise it. *Even more reason to ignore it.* He denied the call but of course, it rang again while it was still in his hand.

What the hell?

Growling, he swiped the screen and held the phone against his ear. "Who is it?"

"Michael? It's Addison."

His blood turned cold, and he gripped the phone tightly. "Why are you calling me? I thought I made it clear I wanted nothing—"

"You won, Michael."

Michael's jaw dropped. "What?"

"I said you won. I'm probably going to jail, thanks to you. You'll have full custody of Oscar. Congratulations, I hope you're happy." Her voice was bitter, venomous. "Our lawyers will speak to each other, and you'll need to sign some paperwork, but otherwise it's a done deal."

Michael's heart skipped. He wanted to shout for joy, cry from relief, find Oscar and tell him the news. But. This was Addison. He didn't know how long she was going away for, but in time she'd be released, and the battle would start all over again.

She's going to have a criminal record. That'll go against her.

He breathed a little easier and pushed the thoughts from his head. Addison's release was the last thing he should be worrying about. Oscar was safe, that was the most important thing right now.

Michael tried to speak but the words in his head tumbled into each other. Finally, he said, "I did what was best for our son, Addison. He deserves to feel safe. Besides, you obviously agreed with the accusations, you could've denied it if you were that desperate."

There was a long pause on the other end. "Yes, well, I had no choice."

"What does that mean?"

Addison's sigh was audible. "Mikayla broke up with me. She was sick of the drama around Oscar's custody. I think she was sick of Oscar, to be honest. Why do you think I turned up out of the blue on Friday?"

This was unexpected but not surprising. Michael had noticed something different about Addison when he saw her on Friday and Saturday. Now it made sense.

"I'm sorry to hear it," Michael said. "But what's that got to do with admitting to the abuse?"

Addison laughed but it held no humour. "We had a huge argument, it turned nasty. We'd been drinking and Mikayla threatened to report me to the police for child abuse. Before she could, I grabbed Oscar and got the next flight to Perth. I'd intended to lay low until it blew over, but things got out of control the other day. I messed up, there was no getting away with it, so I figured if I was going down for something Mikayla was also part of, she'd go down with me." Her tone oozed malevolence. "When I was being questioned, I told the police she was as bad, worse even. Let the bitch fight her way out of that one."

"Revenge is all you two could think about?" Michael asked in disbelief.

"Seems that way."

Michael laid back on the bed, staring up at the ceiling. There was one question he had to ask. "Why'd you do it, Addison? Oscar's an innocent child for heavens' sake."

"I don't know." Addison's voice was bitter. "He was the one thing keeping Mikayla and I together, I suppose. For the first couple of years it was great. We had a baby, the one thing we both wanted. Nothing prepared us for toddler life and that's when the problems started. Oscar can be a handful and I guess we realised we weren't cut out to be parents, neither of us had the patience."

"That's no excuse to hit an innocent child and lock him up." Michael sat up again, gripping the phone tightly.

"What else were we supposed to do? He disrupted our lives."

"That's something you should've thought of before you stole him from me," Michael growled. Breathing in deeply, he released it slowly then calmly added, "You could've talked to me, Addison. Rather than fighting and threatening, we could've come up with a better solution. Released some of the pressure. I would've loved to have had Oscar more."

Addison huffed. "Oh let it go, Michael. What's done is done. Why does it even matter?"

"It matters because Oscar is going to have to live with this for the rest of his life. He's going to be scarred by what you two did to him."

Another silence. "Well," Addison said tersely, "let's hope he forgets it then. Take good care of our son, okay?"

Michael ran a hand down his face and shook his head. "I will, I promise."

The line went dead.

Michael moved the phone away from his ear and stared at the blank screen for a long moment. Addison's callous words cut deep, but there was no stopping his heart from swelling with happiness. Oscar was all his now. At last.

He breathed a sigh of relief, overwhelming happiness washing over him. He raised his eyes heavenward and said a silent prayer of thanks.

The happiness was short-lived though, as reality came crashing down. How could he be happy when his mother had died, and he'd scared off the only woman he'd ever truly loved? Gritting his teeth, Michael stood and changed. Perhaps a long walk would help him make sense of everything. Too much had happened in such a short time.

Chapter 29

Six days later, on Friday evening, Claire waved goodbye to her colleagues then left. The automatic door closed behind her and she slid the handles of her handbag onto her shoulder.

After contacting Doctor Charlton about work, he'd offered her a job at his surgery. It was five days a week, seven and a half hours a day, and one Saturday a month for four hours. She experienced the usual weariness any job had, but she didn't go home and collapse in exhaustion like she used to at the hospital. This new venture was less taxing, and she still experienced the joy of nursing. It was absolute bliss.

When she arrived back at Von's, she put her things down, changed into something comfortable and started on dinner. As usual, Von wouldn't be joining her. Even though she probably didn't need to anymore, she still had dinner at Michael's and probably wouldn't be home for a couple of hours.

Claire tried not to think much about it, but occasionally she wondered if Von stayed to give Michael some company. He had no one else now.

A pain shot through her heart and Claire rubbed her chest. Pushing thoughts of Michael aside, she strode over to the stove. Turning the dial to medium-high, she placed a frying pan on the preheating element with a drizzle of oil. She then retrieved the chopping board and an onion from the pantry and began chopping.

One thing was certain. Giving in and agreeing to stay with Von had been a godsend. During the three days before they returned to work, they spent every moment together. They chatted, baked, laughed and had a wonderful time. It'd made recovering from Daphne's death easier than it would've been otherwise. Claire still missed her, and so did Von, but they could function. That was often the hardest part after losing someone close to you.

There'd been no funeral yet, which was a surprise, but Claire didn't question it. It was up to Michael, and probably Tom too, to organise. Claire would rely on Von to tell her when it'd been scheduled.

Michael.

His name invaded her consciousness once more. She cut down on the onion, but the knife slipped and nipped her finger. She hissed as it stung, blood pooling from the wound. Dropping the knife, she raced to the kitchen sink and held her finger under cold water. Thankfully it looked worse than it was and she was able to put a simple plaster around it.

Cursing her clumsiness, she got back to chopping, taking more care this time. She had a habit of hurting herself when it came to Michael. She sighed and shook her head, letting the thoughts come. Pain seared her heart yet again. Oh, how she ached for him.

Never a night went by when he didn't invade her dreams. Never went a day when he wasn't in her thoughts. She wished so much she could redo their last day together. She regretted not giving him a chance to speak. It hurt that he partly blamed her for not being there when Daphne died, but she should've remembered that grief made people lash out. The way he'd snapped out of whatever trance had hold of him was proof he had no control over what he was doing.

He probably regretted everything too. Yet neither of them did anything about it. It was like they were back to where they were three weeks earlier.

She huffed and took the chopped onion to the heated frying pan, scraping it in. The onion spat and jumped about in the hot oil. Placing the chopping board to the side, she sautéed the onions until soft then added garlic, some herbs and beef mince.

She'd hoped after a week away from Michael it'd get easier. It didn't. If anything, it got harder. What was that saying? 'Distance makes the heart grow fonder.' Was this proof of it? Did they have a genuine, *true* love? The type Norman and Joanna had?

Claire foolishly believed she'd had that with Ryan. When they were dating in school, he was much like Michael was now. Attentive, loving, loyal. But then, it all changed.

Why didn't I listen to Dad?

She shivered, the thoughts coming out of nowhere. Neither of her parents had liked Ryan. They'd said there was something 'not right' about him. Claire, being an immature sixteen-year-old, had laughed it off and told them they were ridiculous. They never mentioned it again, proving they trusted her judgement.

If only they knew.

Her bottom lip trembled. Placing the wooden spoon aside, she stepped back from the stove. For the first time *ever*, she was happy her parents weren't alive to see how badly she'd screwed up her life. They would've been so heartbroken to know she'd suffered.

They would've loved Michael, I know it.

The tears came freely now. She held a hand over her heart and leaned against the wall with her eyes closed. How could she fix this? It seemed like such an impossible task. Like a huge wall stopped her from moving forwards. It needed to be demolished. But how? She didn't have the tools to do so.

Perhaps Laura would know?

Her eyes flew open and she wiped away her tears. Yes, Laura would know exactly what to do. After adding the final ingredients and giving the bubbling mixture another stir, she reduced the heat to low. Removing her phone, she found Laura's number but didn't get a chance to call before it rang, Joanna's name appearing on the screen.

Claire drew in a breath and answered with a chirpy, "Hi, Jo. How are you?"

"You need to speak to Michael," she blurted.

Ice flooded her veins, and her mouth turned dry, like sandpaper. "What?"

"Please, Claire." Joanna sounded desperate. "He's not coping. He won't admit it but he needs you. Would you consider visiting him? Perhaps if you two talked…"

Claire released a shaky breath and stumbled over to the four-seater table, pulling out a chair and collapsing into it. It was uncanny how in tune she and Joanna were. The fact she rang when Claire was considering how to fix things. But how could she talk to him when she couldn't get her own thoughts straight? She couldn't bear to have a repeat of their last day together.

"I…I don't know if I can." Claire's voice was hoarse. "We both said some terrible things. And I…I refused to talk to him when he tried to apologise." She winced at the memory. She blew out a breath and ran a hand through her hair.

Joanna sighed but said nothing.

After a lengthy silence, Claire asked, "What does Norman say about this?" The question came out of nowhere and Claire instantly regretted asking it.

"He's worried sick," Joanna replied. "Michael won't open up to him. About anything. They've barely spoken the past week. We're both worried about him getting custody of Oscar. Norm's worried if he doesn't snap out of it, he won't have a chance of winning. The courts could have a field day over this, claiming he's unfit to be a father."

A shudder ran the length of Claire's spine. Oscar couldn't go back to Addison.

"Claire," Joanna said urgently, "please will you consider seeing him?"

Tears brimmed Claire's eyes. Despite what Joanna said, she couldn't seem to budge. She knew she wanted to talk to him, *needed* to, yet that bloody stone wall stopped her.

"I…I want to," Claire whispered, her voice trembling. "But I can't. I can't explain it, Jo. It's like some invisible force is stopping me." Hot tears dripped down her cheeks when she added in a whisper, "I'm scared."

The words came out before she could stop them, and she realised that's what the barrier was. A representation of her fear.

"Because of Ryan?" Joanna's voice was soft, calming.

Claire sniffled and wiped her eyes on the back of her hand. "Yes."

"You know Michael's *not* Ryan, don't you?"

Before Daphne's death, she would've answered yes in a heartbeat, but now she hesitated and she didn't know why. Deep down, of *course* she knew, but saying it aloud was impossible.

"I thought I knew." The words were out before she could stop them. "God, Jo, I don't know what's wrong with me. I was fine before—"

She didn't even need to finish her sentence.

Joanna sighed then said in a resigned voice, "I think I know what you need to do."

Claire laughed bitterly. "I'm glad you do because I have no freaking clue."

"Really?"

Claire furrowed her brow. Was she missing something? "Uh, well I was going to call my therapist, Laura. She'll be able to help."

Joanna laughed softly. "Of course she will, and I won't discourage that, but I have a feeling she might tell you what I'm about to."

Claire's heart stilled. She didn't think she'd like this. "What is it, Jo?"

"I think you need to see Ryan."

"What?" Claire leapt up from her chair so fast, it tumbled to the floor with a loud *crash*. She fumbled to right it again, her heart pounding a hundred miles an hour. "Are you insane? Why the hell would I want to see him?"

"Closure perhaps? Yeah, he's in jail, and yes you've done so well in moving on, but he's still got a hold on you."

Her heart rate slowed, and Claire sat again, contemplating Joanna's words.

"Okay, so how Michael reacted last week was wrong," Joanna continued, "but you said yourself he tried to apologise, and you didn't let him. He was grief-stricken and had missed out on saying goodbye to his mother. I think if it was one of us in that situation, we probably would've reacted the same way. And let's face it, if the situation was any different, if Ryan had never been in your life, I think it would've had a different outcome."

Claire nodded, even though Joanna couldn't see her. It made sense, but the idea of seeing her ex again made her sick to the stomach. The smell of dinner cooking didn't help her nausea, and she suddenly lost her appetite.

"I'll think about it," she said in a whisper. "And I'll think about seeing Michael again too, I promise. But I think I need to get myself sorted first otherwise I'll only make it worse."

"I understand. You focus on that. Norm and I will keep an eye on Michael." There was a loud squeal in the background. Joanna sighed. "I better go. Juanita fell over and hit her head. Let me know what you decide to do, okay?"

Claire said she would then they hung up. Letting her phone drop to the table, she rested her head in her hands and rubbed her temples. Was Joanna right? Would visiting Ryan and getting closure help? She never *had* gotten closure and that'd hindered her a lot. She loved Michael—deep down she knew that without a doubt. Still holding onto anger, bitterness, and not being able to trust him fully wasn't doing her any good.

She stood and checked on the dinner. The sauce was reducing well, so she put the pasta on. While it cooked, she finally rang Laura.

She couldn't go back to being the old Claire again. It was time to act. Getting Laura's advice, along with Joanna's, was the best way of moving forward.

Chapter 30

Come on, Michael, it's time to snap out of this.

Reluctantly he opened his eyes but snapped them shut again when the bright sunlight blinded him. Rolling over, he shielded the light with his arm and gradually tried again. Someone jumped on the bed and he groaned.

"Daddy, Daddy," Oscar cried excitedly, bouncing up and down. "Let's build a sandcastle."

What is it with this kid and sandcastles? Seems it's all he wants to do nowadays.

When Oscar stopped jumping, Michael removed his arm and found his son on all fours staring at him with an excited smile. Despite the turmoils eating away at him for days, Michael couldn't help but smile in return.

"Please?" Oscar added as an afterthought, a hopeful look making its way onto his face.

It was nice to see Oscar smile. He'd taken his grandmother's death hard, and then with Claire leaving the poor kid didn't have a lot to be happy about.

It didn't help that he hadn't told anyone about the custody arrangement yet. Not even Oscar. He'd met with Lance yesterday and signed the papers, so everything was official, but since the trial still hadn't occurred, a small part of him still feared it was too good to be true.

"Daddy," Oscar whined, growing impatient.

Michael shook the thoughts out of his head and sat up. "All right, we'll build a sandcastle, but how about breakfast first?"

Oscar shook his head. "I'm not hungry."

Michael feigned shock. "Who are you and where's my son?" He grabbed Oscar and tickled his ribs, making him giggle and squirm. "The Oscar I know always wants to eat."

"Stop, Daddy." Oscar cried, squealing when Michael hit a particular ticklish spot under his arms. "Stop."

"What's the magic word?" Michael stopped tickling but held his fingers at the ready, taunting him.

"Please?" Oscar questioned, eyes bright from laughter.

Michael pretended to think about it then shook his head. Oscar squealed when Michael dug his fingers in again. "Sorry, wrong word," Michael said with a laugh. It felt good to laugh again. It'd been too long.

"Mercy." Oscar cried in between giggles. "Mercy, Daddy."

"So you *do* remember?" Michael stopped tickling.

Oscar scrambled off the bed and started jumping up and down. "Sandcastle, Daddy."

"Change out of your PJs first then we'll go, okay?"

Oscar nodded and sped to the tallboy, pulling open the bottom draw and withdrawing his clothes.

Michael's phone dinged from the bedside cupboard. He swung his legs around, sat on the side of the bed and reached for it. It was a text message from Lance. Even on a Sunday he never stopped working.

Mick, I have news. Full confessions from Addison and Mikayla and they're both in custody pending trial next week where formal sentencing will occur.

Breathing in sharply, Michael squeezed his eyes shut for a second. Had he misread it? He opened his eyes and reread it. Nope, it was still the same.

He held his breath in anticipation as he read the last part of the message.

You may need to testify but it'll be done over video link. Nothing to worry about, they have all they need, we're following protocol. So, relax and enjoy being with your son. I'll be in touch.

Lance

He released the breath in a whoosh, tears pooling in his eyes. This was exactly the news he needed to silence his fears. The trial didn't faze him. He trusted Lance, and if he wasn't worried, Michael wouldn't worry either.

A smile spread across his face as he typed back a response. Once he'd sent it, he stood to get ready when Oscar halted in front of him, grinning. Dressed in a blue Lycra top, green Lycra undies, and a hat, he was set for a solid few hours on the beach.

"Can we go now?" He bounced up and down on the spot.

Michael chuckled and gave him a brief once over. "In a minute. You forgot something important."

Oscar was practically jumping out of his skin, so eager to get on to the sand. A frown pulled on his lips and he shook his head to say he didn't know.

Michael reached back to his bedside cupboard and grabbed a tube. "Sunscreen," he announced, screwing open the lid and squirting a good amount on to his hand. It was still early, but he wasn't taking any chances.

"Now can I go?" Oscar asked excitedly after Michael had lathered him up.

Michael wasn't ready yet, but he hated making Oscar wait. He stared at him for a long moment, a smile tugging at his lips. It was as though Oscar had changed overnight. He looked older somehow, like the events of the last few days had matured him. It was hard to believe he'd be six in a few months' time. He'd lost the little boy look he'd kept for so long.

"Okay," Michael said, deciding Oscar was old enough to stay on the sand alone. He knew the safe distance away from the water and Michael could see him from the balcony anyway.

Oscar whooped loudly. Michael added, "But first, I have a surprise for you."

After Lance's text, he couldn't put off the news any longer. God alone knew they needed some happiness in their day.

Oscar's eyes grew wide. "Is it a new toy?"

"No, it's better than a toy."

Oscar practically vibrated with excitement as he awaited the surprise. Crouching, Michael leaned in and whispered the news in Oscar's ear. When he moved back, Oscar's eyes had widened even more.

A small smile appeared on his face, then he squealed and threw his arms around Michael's neck in a death grip. "I'm staying with you forever, and ever, and ever."

With his arms still locked tightly, Michael stood and hugged his son to him.

"That's right, buddy," he said in his ear. "You're with me forever."

Oscar pulled back and grinned, his hazel eyes shining brilliantly with unshed tears. "I love you, Daddy."

A lump formed in Michael's throat and tears threatened to spill when he said, "I love you too, Osc."

The moment didn't last long before Oscar began wriggling and begging to go to the beach. Michael set him on the ground. "Don't get too close to the water's edge, okay? Stay on the sand and I'll help you with the water when I get there. I'll be out in a few minutes."

Oscar nodded erratically then whooped and sped out the room. Michael could hear him yelling in glee even after the screen door shut. He walked to the balcony in time to see Oscar stop on the wet sand, a couple of metres from the water. Once satisfied he was okay, Michael went into his ensuite to shower.

His smile wouldn't leave his face knowing Oscar was finally his. Now he only had one issue to deal with.

Claire.

His smile slipped, memories of how horribly he'd acted filling his mind. He'd been a different person that day, grief and anger controlling every fibre of him. It was like he couldn't do anything to stop the train wreck occurring right in front of him.

It was only when Claire had slapped him that he'd been able to snap out of it. Bloody hell, he'd never been so mortified in his life. He'd tried to apologise but Claire had brushed him off. Not that he blamed her. Now, he didn't even know if she'd want him back.

Wouldn't she be better off without him? Maybe he should let her go.

This thought had plagued him on and off over the last week but the stab in his heart told him not to give up. He wanted to spend his life making it up to her and showing her how much he loved her. The only way to do that was to give her the choice.

He had no idea if she wanted to be with him but he had to try. If he didn't, he'd regret not knowing for the rest of his life.

Now he had to plan *how* to see her, and when. He knew where she was. Von hadn't kept it a secret. Many times before now he'd wanted to visit but never had enough courage, cold fear always stilling his heart. What if she rejected him? He couldn't live in fear though. It was time to swallow his pride and be the bigger man.

Turning the taps off in the shower, he wrapped a towel around himself and stepped into his room. A quick glance outside told him Oscar was okay, happily playing in the sand and working methodically on his sandcastle.

He changed quickly and before going downstairs, stopped in front of a mirror and took a long, hard look at himself. His face, which had been pale for the past week, had gained some colour, but he still had bags under his eyes, a result of too many sleepless nights.

The slump he'd been in since Mum's death hadn't lifted until today. He'd been a robot the last week, going about life on autopilot and only because he had to. There was no effort put into it, at work *or* at home. He did what he had to do but kept to himself. It was too much hassle to do anything else. Even eating had become a chore.

Today would be different. He'd make it so.

He went downstairs and entered the house. His father, who was still visiting and staying in Claire's old room, sat at the table with a coffee while chatting to Von. They both looked up when he entered, looking at him warily. He winced. He'd been such an ogre.

"Morning," Michael greeted, reaching for the plastic bucket Oscar used for carting water.

"Coffee, love?" Von asked.

"No, thanks." He smiled and turned to exit the house but then stopped and turned back. "Oh, and Oscar's going to be living with me for good from now on. I signed the papers yesterday, and today Lance said Addison and Mikayla will be sentenced in a couple of weeks."

Von gasped and rushed up to him, embracing him tightly. "Oh, Michael, that's such wonderful news."

When she moved away, he looked across at Tom who was nodding, a proud smile on his face. He wasn't one to show much emotion, but there was no doubt he was happy.

"I better get back out to Oscar. We'll come in for breakfast in about half an hour."

Von nodded and, with a wide grin, started preparing breakfast.

He joined his son outside and helped him with the sandcastle. Half an hour later, it was nearly complete with an impressive moat leading back to the ocean.

"Looking good." Michael sat back on the sand and ruffled Oscar's hair. "We'll work on it more later, but for now I think it's time for breakfast."

Oscar nodded without argument and scrambled to his feet, dashing inside.

Michael stood and called after him, "Don't forget to wash your hands."

Tom exited the house and came to join Michael, standing in front of him. "It's good to see you in a better mood, Mick."

Michael winced but offered a weak smile. He might've improved, but he wouldn't be one hundred per cent until he had Claire back...if he ever did.

"Good news about Oscar, eh?" Tom added.

Michael nodded. "Very."

If only I had more good news to tell.

Tom eyed him for a long moment. "It's the nurse, isn't it?"

Michael's heart leapt but he played ignorant. "I don't know what you're talking about."

He hadn't let on about Claire, too ashamed of his behaviour to confess their attraction. He should've known his father would've caught on to it though.

Tom chuckled and shook his head. "Could've fooled me. I can't believe I never thought of it before now. You two had a thing, didn't you? I saw the way you looked at each other when I first arrived. She seemed like a nice girl but I never got to know her. She left fairly quickly."

Michael dropped his gaze to the sand, observing a shell. He didn't like where this was heading.

"Did you do something to scare her off?"

Michael looked up, his gaze clashing with his father's. His light brown eyes were a mixture of confusion and disbelief.

"Dad, it's—"

"Don't go changing he subject, son. I want to get to the bottom of whatever's made you so grouchy this past week. It can't be your mother, bless her soul. Speaking of which, are we having a service or something for her? If so we must get it organised, I need to return home soon. How about next Saturday?"

Relieved for the change in conversation, Michael nodded. "Mum didn't want a service," he explained. "I found a letter from her. She asked to be cremated and have her ashes scattered over the ocean. I thought we could hire a yacht and invite close friends along."

Michael had this thought after reading the letter but never acted on it. At first, he wasn't sure why he'd delayed but it finally came to him. He wanted Claire to be there.

"Sounds reasonable," Tom said. "I know someone who we might be able to hire a yacht off. I'll get onto it. Now back to the other issue."

Rubbing his forehead, Michael sighed in frustration. Why wouldn't he leave it alone? "Please leave it. I've got to make sure Oscar's okay."

"He's with Von. He'll be fine." Tom waved a dismissive hand. "So? Are you going to tell me what's wrong?"

Michael looked away but kept his lips pursed, his thoughts running rampant in his mind. There was no point in hiding the truth. Perhaps his father could help somehow, offer some advice even. He sighed. "All right, you win. Yes, it's the nurse…" He shook his head, hating how degrading it sounded for someone who was so much more. "Claire," he corrected.

"Hmmm." Tom stroked his chin thoughtfully. "So you did have a thing?"

"It was more than a thing." He shrugged. "I fell in love with her, Dad."

Tom's jaw dropped, and his hand fell to his side. "By golly." He shook his head in disbelief. "I don't believe it. You mean it? You actually went and fell in love, even after what Addison did?"

"Afraid so, but…" Michael sighed and ran a hand through his hair. "I said some pretty terrible things to her, scared her off. Now"—he shrugged again—"she won't speak to me."

"Have you tried?"

Michael shook his head. "How can I? She wouldn't want a bar of me."

"You don't know that." Tom took a step forward and rested his hand on Michael's shoulder. "Take it from me, son, if you truly love someone they're worth fighting for. I learnt the hard way. Does she feel the same?"

Michael nodded but then stopped and said, "Well I'm certain she did but—"

"No, no buts. If she loves you, it won't change overnight. I don't know the full story, but whatever happened can be fixed. Both of you have to be willing to fix it. If she loves you, she'll come back. You need to make the first move, though. When it came to your mother, I didn't. I regret leaving her. I should've helped her more, proved to her over and over again I wasn't like her father. Sadly I didn't, and it's my life's biggest regret. Prove to this girl you're sorry. If, after you've spoken, she needs time to think, give it to her, but whatever you do, don't give up."

Michael smiled a proper smile for what felt like the first time in days. Tom patted his shoulder. Now all Michael had to do was plan how to go about it. He turned to go back inside.

Apparently, Tom had other ideas. "Where do you think you're going, son?"

Michael stopped and turned, looking at his father in confusion. "I was going to have some breakfast. Last time I checked that wasn't a crime."

Tom walked over to him. "But aren't you going to do something?"

"Yes but I can't go begging for her forgiveness on an empty stomach."

Tom laughed loudly. "Righty-o, I can't argue that one, but why not take advantage of it? Ask her out for breakfast. Take her somewhere you can talk."

This wasn't a half-bad idea. There were some charming cafés around. "What about Oscar?"

"I'll look after him. I won't get to see him much once I go home so might as well make the most of it."

Looking back at the house, in particular Claire's old room, Michael's stomach fluttered with nerves. He missed her so much. His father was right. It was time to fix things.

"Go," Tom coaxed. "Bring the girl back before the weekend. I'd like to get to know her properly before I leave."

Michael looked to his father and blinked a couple of times in confusion. Suddenly his heart lurched. *What if she doesn't want me?*

The fear almost paralysed him, but he couldn't let it win. His father was right. Something had to be done.

He rushed back inside and searched for Von. She wasn't in the kitchen. The food was already on the table, Oscar the only one eating. After a quick search of the house, he found her in Mum's old room dusting a dresser. He froze outside the door. He hadn't been inside since Mum's death.

He missed her like damn crazy, but he'd survived the last few days even though he was once convinced he wouldn't. Knowing she wasn't suffering anymore made it easier, and if he was honest, Mum wouldn't want him to mourn her forever. She'd want him to move on, so that's exactly what he'd do.

With a deep breath, he forced his feet to move and entered the room.

Von looked up and gave him a warm smile. "Breakfast is on the table."

"Yes I saw, thank you, but I won't be able to stay." He rubbed the back of his neck. "Look, Von, I owe you an apology. I know I've been difficult to get on with lately."

She put the duster down and turned to him, placing her hands on her hips. "That's an understatement, young man. You've had us all worried sick."

He hung his head in shame. He owed Norman and Joanna an apology too. They'd also suffered the brunt of his breakdown.

"I know, and I'm sorry, really I am."

"We all miss your mother, Michael. I know this is hard for you—"

Realising Von didn't know the details, he interrupted her, "It's not Mum. I mean I miss her, and I'd do anything to have her here now, but it's not her. It's…it's Claire."

Von's face flooded with realisation. "Of course. Claire didn't say anything, but I knew you two had fallen out over something." She came up to him and embraced him tightly. When she pulled away, she said, "Claire's a wonderful woman, and I know you'll be good for each other. Something tells me you two need each other."

Michael's heart swelled with love. It was true. They did need each other. They were two halves of the same whole, incomplete without the other.

"I was going to take her out to breakfast so we could talk," Michael explained. "Is she home today?"

"No, she's flown to Adelaide. Something to do with her ex?" She turned back to her dusting.

Michael froze. Ryan? *Oh, god. Is she okay?*

Without turning, Von added, "A little birdie told me her flight arrives in Adelaide around two this afternoon then she's driving to Port Augusta. She's staying at a motel there tonight then will be visiting her ex tomorrow morning before driving back to Adelaide and flying back to Perth."

A slow smile spread across Michael's face. He strode over to Von and kissed her cheek, "Von, I love you. I think I'd better eat on the run. I'm not sure when I'll be back, but I'll keep you updated."

Von chuckled as he left the room. After confirming with his father that he was okay to look after Oscar for a night or two, he went upstairs to pack a few essentials. Before leaving, he texted Norman to apologise for his behaviour over the last week then asked if he could manage the garage for a couple of days.

Once everything was sorted, he hopped in his car and sped off for the two-hour journey to Perth. For the first time in days, some of his bitterness dissipated. Finally, he knew what he wanted and what he had to do, but there was no time to mess about.

Chapter 31

Claire spilt her heart out to Laura, telling her everything, including falling in love with Michael down to their breakup. And while Laura had been apprehensive about Claire seeing Ryan again, she also agreed with Joanna. Closure would make a world of difference.

This was how, early Monday morning, Claire found herself sitting in the reception area of the Port Augusta prison waiting to see Ryan. Situated in the far north of South Australia, it was too far to do the trip in one day, so it was easier to spread it over two days. She hadn't wanted to take time off work, but she only needed a day off in the end. As always, Doctor Charlton was ever accommodating.

Picking up a magazine from the small table next to her, she fanned herself. Despite being ten in the morning, it was already hot. The air conditioner was cranked to full, but it struggled in the heat. Sweat dripped down her back and she shifted uncomfortably. The heat in country South Australia was stifling. Having never come this far north before, she underestimated how hot it could get, even in late spring.

Claire stared at the door, waiting to be called. Laura had asked whether she wanted a companion, but Claire refused. She needed to do this alone, even if she *was* petrified. She was stronger now, but she didn't know what she'd be like in front of Ryan. He had a way about him that made her wilt in his company.

Stay strong. He has no hold over you anymore.

She sat up straight and pulled her shoulders back. She could do this.

"Claire Stone?"

Wincing, she stood and placed the magazine on her chair. Striding over to the guard at the door, she made a mental note to change her surname back to her maiden name—Jackson. Sharing Ryan's name was the last thing connecting her to him. If—big *if*—

she and Michael sorted things out and if—an even bigger *if*—they ever got married, she wanted to sign the marriage certificate as Claire Jackson, not Claire Stone.

She mentally shook her head and followed the guard through the door. After being checked through security, she found herself sitting in front of a pane of glass five minutes later. The chair in front of her was vacant for now. The other chairs on either side were taken up by other prisoners, and there were people either side of her talking to them.

Being separated by glass helped her breathe easier. Ryan couldn't get to her. This was a good start. Knowing she wasn't the only one who visited prisoners put her nerves at ease. Strangely, she'd never stopped to think that other people did this, sometimes regularly. Well, one thing was certain. This would be her first and last time. From now on, her life was hers to live however she wanted.

There was a loud clang followed by squeaking hinges. Claire held her breath in anticipation. Unable to see Ryan yet, she hung her head and focused on breathing. In. Out. In. Out.

"Hello Claire-Bear. They told me you wanted to see me." Ryan's gravelly voice scattered goosebumps along her skin. She was thankful the air conditioning in the visiting area was colder than in reception and she'd put a cardigan on before sitting down. Ryan wouldn't see how he affected her.

Gritting her teeth, she took a deep, calming breath before lifting her eyes. Her gaze clashed with his and a vicious shudder ran along the length of her spine. Those steel-grey eyes never changed. So hard. So evil.

"Hello, Ryan." Her voice came out strong despite the fact she was trembling.

She lifted her chin and held his gaze calmly. She wasn't sure where this strength was coming from, but somehow it was as though having this barrier between them lessened the impact of his presence. Her fear and nerves dissipated, calmness washing over her. He couldn't hurt her anymore. Not while he was here.

It was an epiphany. One she hadn't properly grasped before. Old Claire would've fretted over his twenty-five-year sentence, worrying about his release. New Claire wasn't going to let it bother her.

Twenty-five years was a bloody long time, and she wasn't going to waste those years worrying about the trash behind the barrier.

Ryan stared at her hard. "Couldn't keep away, eh? I knew you'd miss me." He smirked and stretched his legs out, the chains around his ankles jingling.

"No." Claire pulled her shoulders back. "I only came to remind myself of what I *wasn't* missing."

Ryan's smirk turned into a wicked grin. "Closure, huh? I did that much damage to ya, did I?"

She bit the inside of her cheek and silently counted to ten. *Don't let him get to you. You're the bigger person.* Laura's words, spoken the night before on the phone, calmed her.

She drew in a breath and managed a sweet smile. "I'm not going to deny it. You screwed me up big time."

Ryan's smile grew. It was as though it was the best news he'd had in a long time. It wouldn't last long though.

Claire leaned forward in her chair, resting her arms on the small ledge. "But with the help of a new man in my life, I'm moving on. Someone who respects me, *loves* me."

She paused and mulled over her words. The fact she could say them with such certainty cemented in her mind that had to speak to Michael. She couldn't lose him over a petty argument. The moment she returned to Busselton she'd fix things. She only hoped he'd be willing to take her back.

She shuffled forward a little more, her nose nearly touching the glass. "Unlike you," she added, spitting out the words like they were poison.

She raked her gaze over him, seeing him for who he truly was. Old Ryan had perfectly styled blonde hair and shaved daily. New Ryan had longer hair, in desperate need of a cut, and a messy beard. Add to it dressed in all orange with handcuffs around his wrists and chains around his ankles, he was nothing but a pathetic human being.

Meeting his gaze once more, she gasped when she saw sadness in his eyes.

"What?" he whispered. He moved forward too, their faces so close now. If it weren't for the glass, she'd be able to feel his breath on her face.

"You heard me," she said, not moving back even though it was instinct to do so. "I'm done with you, Ryan. I only came to say goodbye once and for all, so I can finally move on."

His lip quivered and his eyes moistened. "You're serious?" He sounded surprised, like it was the last thing he'd expected to hear.

She gave a single nod in response.

He sat back again, releasing a long, slow breath. "I loved you, Claire," he said, his sad gaze holding hers. "I loved you so much."

This change in him was unexpected, it threw her off kilter. She shook her head and drew in a breath, composing herself.

"You *abused* me, Ryan. You can't have loved me that much."

To her utmost surprise, Ryan dropped his head and began sobbing. Tears slid down his cheeks and landed on his orange shirt, leaving wet marks.

"I'm sorry," he whispered. "I'm so sorry."

She sat back, speechless. An apology? Now *that* was unexpected. Sitting before her was the man she fell in love with all those years ago. The *real* Ryan. Seeing him now made her remember *why* they were so compatible in the first place. When he actually *felt* emotion and cared for others. She loved him so much back then. Her heart ached at the memory and then it broke at what they'd lost. What'd changed him?

Tears threatened to fall but she blinked them away. "Sorry won't fix anything," Claire said. "What's done is done, Ryan. You ruined what we had and you ruined me." Realising her voice was rising, she clamped her lips together and closed her eyes. She wasn't here to lose control.

"I know," Ryan said softly.

Claire opened her eyes again and looked across at him. He stared at his hands.

Slowly he looked up, his face etched with sadness. "I know we can't get it back, but it doesn't stop me from wishing we could. Would you ever forgive me, Claire?" He leaned in again, his gaze capturing hers. "I can't cope knowing you think so badly of me."

Is he serious?

She sat back, staring at him in confusion. One moment he was happy he hurt her, the next he was apologetic. How genuine was he? Was it all an act to make her doubt herself?

Claire glared at him, not about to let him win again. "How can I forgive you? After what you've done, how the hell am I supposed to do that? What you did to me was unforgivable."

Ryan shook his head. "Please," he begged. "Please, Claire. How am I supposed to live like this? There's nothing for me to live for. If I had your forgiveness, I'd have the hope of starting a new life when I'm out of this hellhole. Please, Claire, give me some hope."

It was an act, it had to be. He did this so many times when they were together. He'd act all contrite and promise to do better but he never did. This was proof she'd grown stronger. This time she recognised it and knew she couldn't believe him. The old Ryan was still there but only as a puppet. That side of him only appeared when he wanted something. In this case, it was forgiveness.

"You've got to be freaking kidding me," she said with a disbelieving laugh. "I'm not the person I used to be, Ryan. You can't control me anymore."

"I don't want control, damn it." Ryan yelled, banging his cuffed hands on the ledge in front of him. Claire jumped. "All I want is a little goddamn compassion. Is that so hard?"

And there it was. The anger that always resulted in his loss of control.

"You're pathetic," Claire said, standing so she now stood over him. Now *she* was the one with the control and it felt damn good. "Do you think you of all people deserve compassion? Where was your compassion when you were beating me to death, huh?" She roughly pushed her fringe back so he could view a scar on her forehead. Then she pulled her shirt down, enough so he could see the scar above her breast. "Take a good look at what you did to me. I want this etched in your memory forever."

Ryan's tears had dried up and he sat back, staring at her in an odd way. Then a slow, cold smile spread across his face. He hadn't changed a single bit.

"I did a number on ya, didn't I?" he said with a low chuckle.

How could he change so quickly? What was going on in that head of his?

"Perhaps you did, but it's not enough to stop me living my life. I hope you rot in hell, Ryan, because I'm done with you. This will be the last time I'll ever think of you."

Ryan laughed loudly, gaining the attention of the other prisoners and visitors, all of whom hadn't paid any attention to them before now.

"Good luck with that," he said, laughing again.

A guard came up to Ryan and took his arm, hauling him to his feet. Another guard came up to Claire, telling her time was up.

She nodded, but before she left, she said, "I have one last question."

The guard nodded and Ryan stared at her, his eyes steely and hard once again.

"Why?" she asked simply. "Why'd you do it? What happened to you?"

Ryan shrugged and grinned. "Why not?"

Was it truly that simple? He did it because he could? Did he get some sick enjoyment out of it? She shook her head sadly. She'd probably never know. Maybe it wasn't worth trying to. She came here to get closure and got it. Now she was ready to see Michael, fix things and start their new life. *If he'll still have me.* And if not, well, she was strong enough to live her life alone now.

"I pity you, Ryan," she said. "I *am* going to forget all about you. I promise. The moment I walk out that door, my new life begins. The imprint you left on me can and will be overwritten. I'll go to my new home, sleep in the arms of the man who loves me and who'd never hurt me, and together we'll make new memories. Ones that will gradually erase all imprints of you until you're nothing more than a passing thought."

Ryan stared at her for a long, long moment before the guard yanked on his arm and pulled him away.

"Goodbye, Ryan," she said, then turned and followed the guard out of the visiting area.

When she left through the reception door and stepped out into the hot morning sun, she breathed a sigh of relief. It was over. She stopped and turned. Staring at the prison, she bid it a silent good riddance, a huge weight lifting from her shoulders. She had no reason ever to visit again. This part of her life was over.

Now all she had to do was see Michael.

Drawing in a deep breath, she turned and started toward the hire car then stopped when a figure emerged from another car. She stopped and held her hand over her eyes to shield the sun. Her heart skipped. Surely not? It had to be a mirage.

She took a step closer the same time the figure stepped around the car and came towards her. No, not a mirage. Sure enough there he was…Michael. He was in Port Augusta of all places. At the prison. Heading straight for her.

Chapter 32

Blood rushed in Claire's ears. Her heart thrashed against her chest. She swallowed hard, unable to believe he was here. It was as though he'd read her mind.

A smile threatened to bloom on her face, but she held it back. She didn't want to come across too eager. Pulling her shoulders back, she took a deep breath to calm her nerves and waited for him to approach. It took all her willpower not to run into his arms.

The moment he stopped in front of her, Claire was rendered speechless. All she could do was stare. Memories of their final day together threatened to overwhelm her with fear, but she pushed it aside. Michael wasn't Ryan, she knew that. Now it was time to talk…calmly. He'd followed her all the way here for a reason, even though he didn't have to. That itself spoke volumes.

She lifted her gaze to meet his. His eyes were so much more alive now. The pain of losing Daphne was still there, but the warmth had returned.

Clearing her throat, she wiped her sweaty hands on her jeans. "Hi. How'd you know I was here?" It occurred to her before he could respond. She added, "Oh, of course, Von."

"She might've let it slip," he said with a small smile. "I wanted to see you." He opened his mouth to say something then stopped and shook his head. "I suppose I wanted to make sure you were okay."

There had to be more to it, but it must've his way of breaking the ice. "Thanks," she said with a smile. "I appreciate it, but you didn't have to come all the way here."

That's what didn't make any sense. Why couldn't he wait until she got home? It was an expensive trip.

"Yes, I did." He reached out and took her hands.

Oh, how she'd missed his touch. It was like being home again.

"You shouldn't have to do this sort of thing alone," he added.

Her heart stilled. Even when she was with Ryan, she always felt alone. Never had any sort of support, emotional or otherwise. To hear Michael wanting to offer this was a dream come true. Almost *too* good to be true.

"Why?" she blurted before she could think about what she was saying.

His brow furrowed. "What do you mean why?" His thumbs ran along the tops of her hands, sending her pulse racing. "You should never have to do anything like this alone, Claire. I only wish I could've been here sooner. I didn't realise your ex was sent to such a godforsaken place."

Claire chuckled and looked back at the prison once more. "Yeah I know, but it was worth it."

"Was it?"

She looked back at Michael, seeing a hopeful look on his face.

"Yes. I didn't realise I needed closure until Joanna mentioned it recently. Seeing Ryan again, it was…" She mulled over her words. "Unpleasant," she said with a wry smile. "But it finally put that part of my life to rest." With no reason to doubt her feelings anymore, she reached up and caressed Michael's cheek. "I'm so sorry for everything, Michael."

"I'm sorry too." He rested his hand on hers, then moved his head around to kiss her palm before linking his fingers through hers and holding her hand tightly. "I should never have blamed you for siding with Addison, especially since you didn't even know her. Her sudden visit, along with her threat to take Oscar away, and missing out on saying goodbye to Mum, got to me. I couldn't seem to see past the fog, couldn't think rationally." He furrowed his brow and stared at something over her shoulder. After a pause, he looked back at her and added, "My excuses don't make my behaviour right, so please know I'm *truly* sorry for everything. I appreciate what you did to keep Addison away."

He was genuine, no doubt about it, and it was why Claire could confidently say, "It's okay."

And it was. Joanna was right. If Ryan had never been a part of her life, she wouldn't have reacted the way she did. She would've given him some space and not taken it so personally.

Michael's contrite gaze held hers. "Do you forgive me?"

"On one condition," she said.

His eyebrows drew together and he nodded for her to continue. "You have to forgive me too."

Relief flooded his face, and he gave her a small quizzical smile. "Why? What have you done?"

"I acted pretty horribly." She cringed at the memory. "So if you can forgive me then you have my forgiveness also."

Michael's smile spread across his face, lighting it up like a beacon. "Oh, Claire." He pulled her closer, wrapping his arms around her waist. "I'd forgive you a million times over if it meant having you in my life forever." He paused, his eyes searching her face. "Can we move past this?"

"I'd like to." She placed her arms around his neck. "After all, you followed me all the way here. That's pretty impressive, Mr Karalis."

He grimaced. "We're not going back to that, are we?"

Claire smirked and looked up at him through her eyelashes. "Maybe in private."

Michael's eyes widened before he pulled her flush against him. "Well then, that I could get used to."

She'd surprised herself at her boldness, but it was like breaking free from Ryan had given her the ability to accept *everything* a relationship with Michael would offer. It was time to open her heart fully, let him in and stop being afraid.

Holding him tight, she melted into his body and breathed in his masculine scent. She pulled away and looked up, their faces only inches apart. His warm breath fanned her face, sending shivers down her spine. Smiling up at him, she stood on her tiptoes and kissed him softly on the lips.

"Thank you for following me here," she whispered, running her free hand through his hair then lowering it to his neck and pulling him in for another kiss. She closed her eyes and devoured every delicious emotion.

"I'd do anything for you, Claire," Michael said when they pulled away, placing a feather kiss on the tip of her nose.

She smiled up at him, her heart swelling with love and happiness. "I love you, Michael." The words slipped out without her even thinking, but she meant them wholeheartedly. The love for Michael was so different than what she thought she'd experienced with Ryan. This new love was *real*.

Hope filled Michael's eyes, a smile spreading across his face. "Do you mean that?"

She nodded. "I do. I love you so much, Michael Karalis. I can't imagine my life without you."

Michael's eyes grew dark and he looked at her with such lustful hunger it sent a shudder through her body. "You're an exceptional woman, Claire Stone." His voice grew husky. "I love you so damn much." He pulled her against him again and crashed his lips to hers.

Fireworks exploded and energy pulsed through her, awakening desires she'd been so afraid of experiencing for so long. Ryan was nowhere in her thoughts, and she knew her promise to him only a little while ago would come true. She was already starting to overwrite the memories he'd left.

When they pulled apart, Claire kept her eyes closed to savour the moment. She was vaguely aware of where she was but was too caught up in the moment to care. All she could think about was how different the kiss was to all the others they'd shared.

After a few moments, Michael said, "There's something I need to tell you."

Claire pulled back and gave him a questioning look.

A beaming smile lit up his face. "I have full custody of Oscar now."

"Oh my god." Claire lunged at him and wrapped her arms around him in a tight embrace. "That's so amazing."

"He's over the moon," Michael said when they pulled apart, a grin fixed on his face.

"And you're not?" Claire teased.

Michael smiled sheepishly. "Well, I might be. Can you blame me, though? I've got my son and the woman of my dreams in my life. What else could a man want?"

For the first time in a long time, Claire was at peace. There was still a lot she had to work through. She wasn't entirely recovered, but with the help of Michael and her other friends, she'd be back to her old self in no time. One thing *was* certain, though—Michael *wasn't* Ryan. She trusted him implicitly.

Even though she didn't speak the words aloud, the look in Michael's eyes told her he knew what she'd been thinking. This newfound knowledge had their lips colliding again. His hands gently held her face while his thumbs stroked her cheeks lovingly. As they breathed each other in, Claire sensed the light salty smell of the ocean that clung to his cotton shirt. It was so intoxicating it had her knees weakening, and if it wasn't for Michael's arm wrapped tightly around her, she would've fallen.

When they pulled away, their breathing was heavier than before. Michael was the first to speak. "You're an amazing woman, Claire. I meant what I said. I love you with every fibre of my being." He stepped back but kept her at arms' length. "I know our lives won't always be easy, but I promise I'll look after you and always put you first."

Claire wanted to speak but she had no words. When their eyes met, she knew he understood.

Becoming aware of her surrounds, she looked around and smiled. It wasn't a dream…she *was* free. She touched her throbbing lips and smiled.

"Oh." Michael removed an envelope from the back of his jeans pocket and handed it to her. "I wanted to give you this."

Looking at him quizzically, she took it hesitantly then looked inside. Seeing a wad of cash, she looked up at him in confusion. "What's this for?"

"The money you loaned me when I wanted to bring Oscar over. I had insurance, and the airline refunded me when I told them the situation. Consider me repaid in full."

Claire shook her head and smiled up at him. She'd forgotten all about it. "I honestly didn't expect repayment but thank you."

Michael took her hand and inclined his head to the car park. "Now, how about we go home? I've organised for someone to pick up the car I hired so we can drive back together."

"Home." She smiled at the word. Yes, Busselton *was* home now. "Yes, let's go home."

When they reached the car, she found herself wondering how much longer she'd stay at Von's. What if 'home' meant staying with Michael? He hadn't spoken the words, but she had to admit, she quite liked the idea of living with him in the beach house.

Chapter 33

The hired yacht sat anchored in the ocean, gently rocking with the small waves. Claire stood at the stern, looking out over the water. The sun shimmered on the dark blue water and in the distance, she could make out land.

It'd only taken them forty-five minutes to get to where they were but to Claire it felt as though they were miles out. Everything looked so far away.

Well, this is it. Not only the day we say goodbye, but the day we also start afresh.

Claire stood next to Michael with Joanna, Norman and Juanita next to her. On Michael's left stood Tom, Oscar and Von.

Michael removed the lid from the urn then stood staring at it for a long moment. When he finally looked up, tears shimmered in his eyes.

He took a deep breath. "Goodbye, Mum." Stepping closer to the rail, he scattered the ashes out over the ocean.

Bits of it caught on the breeze and drifted away while the rest settled on the water. Everyone bowed their heads in respect and stood silently as they said their final goodbyes.

Claire expected to break down, to feel empty and lifeless, but she didn't. Instead, a feeling of calm descended over her. She and Daphne were so similar, which was why they'd grown so close. They'd both been through so much, but their suffering had ended. They were free of their turmoils once and for all. They'd let go of what'd controlled them for so long.

After the moment passed, the atmosphere settled with a happy vibe. It appeared everyone had grieved enough and had no reason to anymore. At least not today.

When everyone stepped away from the rail, Claire stayed put and watched the goings on around her. Tom and Michael chatted animatedly and laughed together. Juanita and Oscar chased each other around the boat, after being warned not to get too close to the rail. Then there was Joanna, Von and Norman who talked quietly, occasionally sneaking glances at Claire and giving her knowing looks. Of course, she knew exactly what they were talking about. Her relationship with Michael was no secret. She shook her head good-naturedly then turned away.

A few moments later a voice interrupted her thoughts. "Claire?"

Looking around, she found Norman standing beside her.

"I haven't had a chance to thank you," he said. "You brought Michael back to life again. I was worried about him, but I see he's in good hands now. I never thought I'd see him so happy again."

When she turned and saw Michael still talking to Tom, a smile tugged at her lips. Norman was right. He *was* happy. Her cheeks warmed from the compliment. Hadn't Daphne said something similar a few weeks ago? At the time she hadn't felt she'd done anything but she now realised she had. He'd done the same for her. *Who would've thought it was possible after how we started off?*

She'd never been so happy to have misjudged someone before.

Claire turned back to Norman. "Thank you, although I think it's safe to say he did the same for me."

Norman smiled and walked away. The next moment Oscar and Juanita started arguing and hitting each other.

Claire was about to join Michael when Von approached with a beaming smile. Rather than saying anything, Von embraced Claire in a big bear hug.

"My dear girl," Von said when she pulled away, her eyes shining brightly, "I'm so happy today. This is exactly what Daphne would've wanted. Look at everyone." She waved her arm around the boat. "They're so happy. Isn't it wonderful?"

"Yes, it is," Claire answered with a smile. "And I want to thank you again, Von, for putting me up these last two weeks."

"Oh, don't be silly. It's been wonderful having your company. I'll miss you terribly though."

After Claire and Michael had returned to Busselton a week earlier and announced to everyone they were back together, Michael asked Claire if she'd live at the beach house with him. Of course, she said yes, but not wanting to leave Von's so quickly, she agreed to move in after the service.

"You won't get a chance to miss me," Claire said. "I'll see you every day."

"Perhaps, but I'll certainly miss the company at home."

Von squeezed Claire's hand then joined Joanna, who was scolding the two children. Juanita sat on top of Oscar. Tears streamed down her cheeks while she pinned his arms above his head. Claire had to look away to hide her smile. *How the hell do they get themselves into these situations?*

Claire heard Norman say, "I'll start the engine. I think it's time to head back."

Turning to find a seat, Claire found Michael sitting on one of the benches next to Tom, so she joined them. For a few moments, the three of them chatted generalities before Tom excused himself and joined Norman at the wheel. Over the last week, she'd got to know Tom well and liked him a lot. She could see why Daphne loved him so much. He and Michael were very similar.

Michael placed his arm across Claire's shoulders and pulled her close. "You okay?"

She looked up at him and smiled. "Couldn't be better." She looked around and frowned when she realised something. "Where's Doctor Charlton? I only noticed he's not here. I thought he was coming."

"He had an emergency at the last minute so couldn't make it."

"Oh." She made a mental note to ring him later to ask if everything was okay. Looking at Michael to say something, she noticed his brow furrowed in worry. It'd come on so suddenly she glanced around, wondering what was wrong. "Are you okay?"

He turned to her. Removing his arm from around her shoulders, he took both of her hands in his.

His gaze captured hers, full of worry. "Are you sure you're okay with this?"

"Okay with what?" Her eyebrows drew together.

"Us." He shook his head and looked away. "I was so happy to finally be together but..." He looked back again and sighed. "I'm worried about Addison, Claire. She's capable of anything, and despite having a criminal record, she might still try and stir up trouble once she's released. If she does, I don't want her to scare you away."

Is that all?

Claire offered him a consoling smile and squeezed his hands. In the last week, Addison and Mikayla had been sentenced to five years in jail. Ever since they'd received the news, she'd sensed something bothering Michael, but he hadn't spoken about it. Until now.

"She won't scare me away," she said. "For all we know, she may not do anything. Jail time might change her. If not, then we'll face it together."

Relief flooded his face. He let go of Claire's hands then pulled her close to his chest and cocooned her in his arms. "Are you sure? Because if you're not, I'd understand. I don't expect you to deal with my baggage. If you feel you can't be with me then—"

Claire pulled away from the embrace and turned so she could press her lips against his. She poured as much passion as she could into the kiss, proving to him she wasn't going anywhere. His kiss was as passionate and she knew nothing would break them apart. Their future was bright, and as long as it didn't include Ryan, Claire could handle anything.

When they pulled away, she looked him in the eye and said, "I'm not going anywhere, Michael. I love you and I want to be with you forever."

Michael smiled as the worry left his eyes. "I'd like that. I think, when we're both ready, we should start over again." His eyes gained an intense look. "Get married, be our own little family. You, me and Oscar."

Her heart skipped at his words and she bravely added, "And perhaps a sibling for him too?" Ever since the miscarriage, she'd yearned to be a parent, and she loved that it could become a reality in the future. With Michael.

Michael's eyes lit up. "Definitely," he whispered. "Maybe two or three."

She sighed contentedly and rested her head on Michael's chest. "Yes, I'd like that very much."

"Me too." He wrapped his arms around her and placed a loving kiss on top of her head. "And you know what else?"

"Hmm?" She closed her eyes, enjoying the balmy breeze on her skin.

"I've been putting off renovating the house for too long. How'd you like to help me? It can be our project. Make it into a family home."

Her eyes snapped open again, and she grinned up at him, nodding excitedly. "Oh, yes, I'd like that very much. No more outside staircase?"

He laughed and tightened his hold around her. "Definitely not. I want it to be the finest house on the beachfront. It's what Mum would've wanted."

Claire sighed contentedly. "I think that sounds wonderful."

As water splashed against the boat, Claire listened to Michael's heartbeat. The combined sounds were soothing, and she closed her eyes again to enjoy it. Her past didn't have to dictate her future anymore, and a small smile curved her lips. She'd finally let go.

Now she was free.

ABOUT THE AUTHOR

Ever since she could string sentences together, Lisa has been writing. As a child, it started off with princesses in castles being rescued by Prince Charming. As a teenager she moved on to angsty teens struggling through life with raging hormones. Now, as a semi-mature adult, she writes contemporary romances about real people going through real struggles that want their HEA.

When she's not writing, Lisa reads anything she can sink her teeth into, and occasionally binges on the latest Netflix series. She loves lazy days at the beach, reading or writing, but rarely swimming, and loves spending time with her husband and her friends.

Say G'Day to Lisa:

• website: lisastanbridge.wixsite.com/lisastanbridgeauthor
• instagram: @lisa_stanbridge
• facebook: LisaStanbridgeAuthor
• twitter: @LisaStanbridge
• linkedin: lisa-stanbridge

www.BOROUGHSPUBLISHINGGROUP.com

If you enjoyed this book, please write a review. Our authors appreciate the feedback, and it helps future readers find books they love. We welcome your comments and invite you to send them to info@boroughspublishinggroup.com. Follow us on Facebook, Twitter and Instagram, and be sure to sign up for our newsletter for surprises and new releases from your favorite authors.

Are you an aspiring writer? Check out www.boroughspublishinggroup.com/submit and see if we can help you make your dreams come true.

Printed in Great Britain
by Amazon

80868261R00140